"You can't just g...
strangers," Kate...

Jack held out his hands. "You said you weren't married."

"What if I were engaged? Or a nun? Or what if I didn't like men?"

"Engaged isn't married, so I'd say tough luck to the guy." Grinning, he continued. "You as a nun would be a crime against nature, definitely worth ignoring." He glanced down at her, his stare taking in her hardened nipples and her trembling legs. The musky scent of aroused woman teased his nostrils. "And not liking men isn't in the realm of possibility," Jack finally said smoothly. "You want me pretty badly."

Her jaw dropped and he tipped it back up with the tip of his finger. "Now, for introductions. I'm Jack. It's very nice to meet you. And you are...?"

She ignored his question. "You followed me."

He didn't try to deny it. "Guilty as charged."

That stopped her. "Why?"

He shrugged. "Fate? Instinct?" Then he lowered his voice, whispering into her ear as he leaned in closer, aligning his body with hers. "Or maybe so I could see what color eyes my children are going to have."

Dear Reader,

When the new Blaze line launched last year, I knew I wanted to be a part of it. Anyone who's read the stories I write for Temptation know I have no problem turning up the heat. But whenever I sat down to work up a story, I had trouble coming up with the right premise. My critique partner, Jill Shalvis, was having the same problem. But with the encouragement of our wonderful editors at Harlequin, we put our heads together and came up with the outrageous stories of two cousins who want to wreak a little havoc by opening a sex shop in their old hometown. Throw in a little sexual revenge, and the BARE ESSENTIALS miniseries was born.

I loved working on this project with Jill. It challenged me as a writer to work with another author's characters and story line. I'd also like to say a special thank-you to Harlequin for allowing us to be a part of this trend of simultaneously released books in a miniseries. So look for Jill's book, *Naughty But Nice*, out right now.

I love to hear from my readers. Please write to me at P.O. Box 410787, Melborne, FL 32941-0787, or drop me an e-mail through my Web site www.lesliekelly.com. And don't forget to check out tryblaze.com.

Happy (and hot!) reading,

Leslie Kelly

Books by Leslie Kelly

HARLEQUIN TEMPTATION

NATURALLY NAUGHTY

Leslie Kelly

HARLEQUIN®

TORONTO • NEW YORK • LONDON
AMSTERDAM • PARIS • SYDNEY • HAMBURG
STOCKHOLM • ATHENS • TOKYO • MILAN • MADRID
PRAGUE • WARSAW • BUDAPEST • AUCKLAND

To Jill Shalvis—
a great critique partner, an even greater friend.
Thanks for always being there.

And, as always, to Bruce.
Thanks for the Christmas gifts/tax write-offs.
Research has never been more fun.

ISBN 0-373-79066-X

NATURALLY NAUGHTY

Copyright © 2002 by Leslie Kelly.

All rights reserved. Except for use in any review, the reproduction or
utilization of this work in whole or in part in any form by any electronic,
mechanical or other means, now known or hereafter invented, including
xerography, photocopying and recording, or in any information storage
or retrieval system, is forbidden without the written permission of the
publisher, Harlequin Enterprises Limited, 225 Duncan Mill Road,
Don Mills, Ontario, Canada M3B 3K9.

All characters in this book have no existence outside the imagination of
the author and have no relation whatsoever to anyone bearing the same
name or names. They are not even distantly inspired by any individual
known or unknown to the author, and all incidents are pure invention.

This edition published by arrangement with Harlequin Books S.A.

® and TM are trademarks of the publisher. Trademarks indicated with
® are registered in the United States Patent and Trademark Office, the
Canadian Trade Marks Office and in other countries.

Visit us at www.eHarlequin.com

Printed in U.S.A.

Prologue

Ten Years Ago

HOLDING HER PINK taffeta dress up to her knees, Kate Jones trudged toward home wishing the ground would open up and swallow her. Live burial seemed better than spending one more night in Pleasantville, Ohio. Her cousin's favorite expression came to mind—*This town's about as pleasant as a yeast infection.*

Without a doubt, this evening would have a place on Kate's list of all-time worst experiences. No, it wasn't nearly as bad as when her dad had died, or when her mom had brought her here to live, a town where their family was treated like dirt. In terms of teenage experiences, however, tonight was bad. Kate had been resoundingly dumped. On prom night no less.

You should have stayed, a voice whispered in her brain.

Kate snorted. "Stayed? After being jilted by Darren McIntyre for Angela Winfield, wickedest witch on earth? Right!"

Cassie wouldn't have run away. No, her cousin would have popped Angela one, kicked Darren where it counted, and told them to stick it where the sun didn't shine. Too bad she'd left early.

She passed another dark house. Its inhabitants were probably cozy in their beds, reflecting on their *pleasant* days. They wouldn't think twice about her trudging in the street.

Who'd expect anything else from a trashy Tremaine? Her last name might be Jones, but no one let her forget her mother's maiden name. In spite of being a straight-A student who'd never gotten into any real trouble, people here believed Kate must have hit every no-good branch on her way down the Tremaine family tree.

Turning off Petunia onto Pansy Lane, Kate grimaced for the half-millionth time at the dumb street names. *I'd love a giant bottle of Weed-B-Gone.* She could think of a creeping pest she'd like to zap. Darren.

"Darren's a conceited jerk." Kate knew she shouldn't have gone with him, especially since his mother hated her. But just for one night she'd wanted to be part of the in crowd. She'd wanted to be cool and popular, instead of the nice, quiet girl who tried to disguise her family's poverty by getting good grades and working harder than anyone ever expected.

Tonight at the prom Angela had pawed all over Darren, urging him to ditch Kate and leave with her instead. The whole school knew Angela put out. And despite being a trashy Tremaine, Kate did not. Hmm, such a tough choice for Darren—Angela the tramp from the most respected family in town? Or Kate the pure, from the trashiest one? What was a horny eighteen-year-old boy to do?

He'd left so fast Kate's head had spun.

Kate was nearly home when the rain started. "What did I do to deserve this?" she said as drops hit her face. She was long past the point of caring about her panty hose. Nor did she worry about her makeup smearing—her tears had accomplished that.

The rain was just one more insult in a rotten night.

Spying her family's duplex, she prayed her mother was asleep, and Cassie home in the adjoining unit where she and Aunt Flo lived. If Cassie was home, Kate would knock on her bedroom wall, which butted right against Cassie's in the next unit. They'd communicated by knocking on it since they were little girls. She'd signal her to sneak out back for one of their late-night gab sessions and fill her in about her lousy prom night.

Then she noticed a parked car out front. When her mother emerged from it, Kate wondered who Edie could have been out with so late. As a man exited she said, "Mayor Winfield?"

Yes, Angela's father. Rich, jolly John Winfield who kept her mother busy cleaning his fancy house on Lilac Hill. Once again the mayor thought nothing of working Edie late in the night, as if she didn't already spend forty hours a week scrubbing other people's toilets. Kate raised a brow as the mayor played gentleman and walked her mother to the door.

Walk away, her inner voice said. But she couldn't. Moving closer, she'd reached the steps when they began to kiss.

Kate moaned. Her gentle mother was having an affair with the very *married* mayor? John Winfield was the patriarch of the town, a family man, father of Angela and of town golden boy, J.J., who'd gone away to college years ago and hadn't returned.

After their kiss Winfield said, "I don't know what I'd do without you. You've made life bearable for me all these years."

Years? Mr. Mayor, the pure saintly leader of Pleasantville, has been having an affair with his cleaning woman for years?

"Here," Winfield continued, reaching into his pocket. "Your paycheck. I'm sorry it's so late, sugar, you know how she is."

A sweet smile softened her mother's face. "I'm okay,

John. If she's overspent again and you're in need, I can wait
a bit.''

Kate shook her head in shock. The phone bill hadn't been
paid. They'd had canned soup and tuna sandwiches for dinner all week. And her mother was giving back her paycheck
to the richest man in town? Worse...the son of a bitch took
it.

Blinking away tears as she acknowledged her respectable,
much-loved mother was the willing mistress of a married
man, she darted around back. Kate instinctively headed toward the ramshackle tree house where she and Cassie had
played as kids, seeking comfort like a child would seek her
mother's arms. Kate whimpered as she realized she no
longer had that option. Her mother wasn't the person she'd
always thought she was.

Looking up as she approached, she saw a glow of light
from within and the burning red tip of a cigarette.

Cassie. Kate paused. She simply could not tell her cousin
what she'd witnessed in front of the house. Cassie and Kate
had long ago accepted the truth about their mothers. Cassie's mom, Flo, was the wild charmer who'd let them have
makeup parties at age seven, and bought them their first six-
pack. They loved her, no matter what the town thought of
her outrageous clothes and numerous affairs. But Edie had
been the real nurturing mother figure, the kind one who'd
dried their tears and encouraged their dreams.

For Kate, Edie would never be the same. How could she
destroy Cassie's image of Edie, too? In spite of her outward
toughness, Kate knew Cassie would be very hurt by this.
As hurt as Kate had been. So no, she couldn't tell her. Not
now. Maybe not ever.

"Kitty Kate, you down there?"

Wiping away her tears, she climbed the rope ladder. Inside the tree house, Cassie's golden hair was haloed by candlelight. "Hi."

"Hey." Cassie took another long drag of her cigarette.

"Got another one?" Kate sat next to her cousin, noting the way their dresses filled up nearly every inch of floor space in the tiny house. Hers a boring pink. Cassie's a sultry black that screamed seduction and showcased her curvy figure.

"Last time you smoked you ralphed all over the bathroom."

Feeling sick enough already, Kate didn't risk smoking. "You okay? You skipped out on prom pretty early."

"Yeah. I'm sure the gold-plated set missed me real bad."

Kate ignored the sarcasm. "I missed you. What happened?"

Cassie gave a bitter laugh. "Biff said we were going to a party. Turns out he had a two-person, naked party in mind."

"Perv."

"Total perv. Then he gets pulled over for drunk driving."

"You were drinking?" Kate raised a surprised brow, knowing Cassie thought alcohol made guys stupid and mean.

"No. He wanted to get beer, so we stopped at the store before the prom. He said I should buy it since I look older. Friggin' moron. Like the clerk wouldn't notice I was wearing a prom dress."

"What'd you do?"

"I pretended I couldn't. He found somebody else at the prom who gave him some." Cassie squashed out her cigarette and leaned her head against the wall. "Look, Katey, I don't want to talk about this. Why are you here? Shouldn't you and Darling Darren be celebrating as king and queen of Pea-Ville High right now?"

Kate told her everything, leaving out what had happened when she got home. "Guess we both had disastrous prom nights."

Cassie took Kate's hand. "Did I say Darling Darren? I meant Dickless Darren. I hope you told him to eat shit and die."

"I told him he deserved a girl like Angela, and took off." Frankly, she liked Cassie's comeback better. If she'd thought about it long enough, maybe she could have come up with it. But Kate was so used to being the sweeter of the Tremaine cousins, she generally refrained from mouthing off out loud, as she often did in her brain, or when alone with Cassie.

"Good for you."

Cassie opened an old, dusty Arturo Fuente cigar box in which they hid the stashes of stuff they didn't want the moms to find. It held candles, diaries, even a *Playgirl* they'd dug out of Flo's trash can a few years ago. "I hate this stinking town."

Remembering the way she'd felt as she watched Mayor Winfield and her mother, Kate completely understood. "Ditto."

"I'd give anything to get outta here. Make it big, make lots of money, then come back and tell them all to stuff it."

Kate had the same fantasy. Hours spent in the old Rialto Theater had introduced her to places she wanted to go, people she wanted to meet. Women she wanted to become. Far away from here. "Wouldn't that be something? The trashy Tremaine cousins coming back and stirring up some serious trouble," Kate said. "You know what I'd do? I'd open up a shop right next door to Mrs. McIntyre's Tea Room. And I'd sell...dirty movies!"

Cassie snickered. "Go all out, triple-X porn, baby."

"And sex toys. Darren's mom could really use a vibrator."

"You wouldn't know a vibrator if it fell in your lap. *Turned on.* So, first stop in the big city, we buy sex toys."

Kate giggled. "And when we're rich and famous, we come back here and shove 'em right up certain people's noses."

Cassie reached into the box, grabbing Kate's diary. "I've been sitting here listing all the things I'd do to get even with some people in this town. Why don't you make one, too?"

"A list?"

"Yep. We each list the things we'll someday do to the cruddy populace of Pleasantville, if we ever get the chance."

The idea made perfect sense to Kate. "Publicly humiliate Darren McIntyre and Angela Winfield," she said as she wrote.

As they wrote Kate watched Cassie's smile fade as she thought of something else. Kate couldn't stop her own thoughts from returning to her mother. John Winfield.

She ached, deep within, at the loss of her own childhood beliefs.

Tears blurred her vision as she secretly added one more item to her list. *For Mom's sake, get even with the Winfield family...particularly John Winfield.* She didn't know how, but someday she would do to that family what they'd done to hers...

Cause some serious heartache.

1

AS SHE PULLED UP in front of the Rose Café on Magnolia Avenue, Kate Jones took a deep breath and looked around at the heart of Pleasantville. Heart. Probably the wrong word. The town hadn't possessed that particular organ when she'd left ten years ago. Judging by what her mother had told her in their last phone call, she feared it hadn't grown one in the intervening decade.

The street appeared the same on the surface, though was perhaps dirtier, its buildings grayer than she remembered. Warped, mildew-speckled boards covered some of the windows of the once-thriving storefronts. Very few people strolled along the brick sidewalks. The cheerful, emerald paint on the benches lining the fountain in the town square had faded to a faint pea-green. A reluctant grin crossed her lips as she heard Cassie's voice in her head. *Welcome back to Pea-Ville.*

Hers wouldn't be an extended stay. She had a job to do, then she'd drive away forever. Reaching for the door handle of her SUV, she paused when she heard her cell phone ring. "Yes?"

"Kate, I'm going crazy. Tell me you're on your way home."

"Armand, I've only been gone one day," Kate said with a laugh, recognizing the voice of her high-strung, creative business partner. "Besides, you were crazy before you met me."

"Crazy and poor. Now I'm crazy and rich and I can't take this kind of pressure. You are going to pay for leaving me in charge. Nothing that happens at Bare Essentials while you're gone is my fault. Understood?"

"Nothing's going to go wrong in two or three days. Tell me what happened so we can fix it."

"The shipment didn't arrive from California. We're down to *one* Bucky Beaver. And he was featured in the ad this weekend."

Oh, yes, the world would indeed stop revolving without their bestselling special toy. "I don't think it's a problem of catastrophic proportions. We sell lots of other products."

"None that were featured in the ad. I can see an entire girl's college softball team coming in to stock up for an out-of-town game, and finding the shelves bare." She heard Armand groan. "I see riots. Stampedes. Ten-inch rubber dildoes lobbed at my head until I am knocked unconscious. Imagine having to explain that to the handsome young police officer in his tight blue suit with his jaunty black cap when he comes in response to my frantic call." He paused. "Hmm…maybe this isn't such a crisis after all."

"Definitely not, but just call the supplier anyway."

"Maybe I should ask your cousin to use her connections…"

"Cassie's still in Europe. I think." Kate wasn't quite sure where her famous model cousin was working this week. She'd tried to track her down after getting her mother's news and had left messages with Cassie's agent and publicist. So far, no word. Cassie almost seemed to be in hiding. Another worry.

"So how's business today?" she asked.

"As thriving as ever," he replied. "Two different bridal

parties came in this morning, hence the shortage of Buckys.''

"I do love those wedding showers."

"Dewy brides and do-me bridesmaids. A delightful, money-spending combination.''

"Absolutely. Now, have there been any calls for me?" She wondered if Edie had tried to reach her again from her new home in Florida. Their last conversation had ended somewhat abruptly.

Edie hadn't told her all the details of what some people in this town had put her through during her last weeks of residence. What she did say had made Kate wince. She gave her full opinion on the matter, though never revealing she knew the truth of Edie's relationship with Mayor Winfield.

"None that matter. But I warn you, if Phillip Sayre calls again, I'm stealing him for myself. So you better hurry your pretty fanny back here to Chicago."

"You're welcome to him. One date was quite enough for me. The man has a huge ego.''

"You know what they say, big ego, big…''

"I think you mean big hands. Or big feet. In any case, I don't have any interest in finding out when it comes to Phillip. Who needs a big, sloppy real one attached to an arrogant, untrustworthy man, when a small, clean vibrating one with no strings attached is sufficient?''

Armand tsked, though she knew he wasn't shocked. After all, he was one of the few people with whom Kate felt comfortable enough to reveal her occasional less-than-nice-girl qualities.

"Playing with the merchandise?" he asked.

"Ah, you caught me. How can I sell it if I can't attest to its effectiveness?''

"As long as you paid for it first and weren't sampling the wares then putting them right back on the shelves.''

Yuck! Kate snorted a laugh. "Okay, you win, you nasty thing." Armand always won in games of sexual one-upmanship.

"Besides, small vibrating ones don't have hands or mouths."

"Some have tongues," Kate pointed out with a grin, remembering one of their more popular models of vibrator…a wagging tongue. Cassie had seen it during her last visit to the store in Chicago and had declared it the most disgusting thing she'd ever seen. When Kate had turned it on to show her what it could do, Cassie had bought two of them.

"I'm hanging up now. Be good," Kate said.

"Impossible. Don't you be good, either. It's bad for you."

Kate smiled at Armand's kissy sounds as she cut the connection. She remained in the driver's seat, missing Armand. He was the only man in her life she had ever completely trusted.

A shrink might surmise that it was because Armand was gay, and therefore not a romantic possibility, which allowed Kate to open up and trust him.

The shrink would probably be right. Trusting men had never been her strong suit. One more thing to thank Mayor Winfield for, she supposed. Not to mention the few men she'd dated over the years, who had never inspired thoughts of true love and Prince Charming. More like true greed and Sir Fast Track.

"So, do I get out or restart the car and drive away?" she asked herself, already missing more than just her friend and partner. She also missed her apartment overlooking the water. She really missed her beautiful, stylish shop with its brightly lit, tasteful decor, such a contrast to some of the more frankly startling products they sold.

Two stories high, with huge front glass windows, soft

lemony-yellow carpet and delicately intricate display cases, Bare Essentials had done what everyone had sworn couldn't be done. They'd taken sex and made it classy and elegant enough for Michigan Avenue.

Yes, she wanted to be home. Actually, she wanted to be *anywhere* but here.

Could she really go through with it? Could she walk along these streets, enter her mother's house and go through her childhood things so her mother could list the place for sale?

Well, that was the one good thing. At least Edie had finally gotten out, too. Though Edie had taken frequent trips to the city, she'd resisted moving away from Pleasantville for good. No, it had taken Mayor Winfield's death, his subsequent will and some vicious gossip to accomplish that feat.

Kate thought she'd outgrown the vulnerability this place created in her. She wasn't the same girl who used to hide in the tree house to cry after school when she'd been teased about her secondhand clothes. She was no longer a trashy Tremaine kid from the wrong side of town. She and her cousin had bolted from Pleasantville one week after high school graduation, moving to big cities—Kate to Chicago, Cassie to New York's modeling scene—and working to make something of themselves.

Kate had long ago learned the only way to get what you wanted was to work hard for it. Being smart helped, but she knew her limitations. She wasn't brilliant. And as much as she hated to admit it, she wasn't talented enough to pursue her teenage dream of a career in theater, though she'd probably always fantasize about it.

No, common sense and pure determination had been the keys to achieving her goals. So she'd worked retail jobs by day and gone to school by night, taking business and accounting courses, sneaking in a few acting or performing credits when she could.

Then the fates had been kind. She'd met Armand, a brilliantly creative lingerie designer, at exactly the time when Cassie's career had taken off and she'd had the means to loan Kate the start-up money for a business.

An outrageous, somewhat *dramatic* business.

Combining her need to succeed, her innate business sense and her secret love for the flamboyantly theatrical, she'd dreamed up Bare Essentials. Though originally just designed to be an upscale lingerie boutique to feature Armand's creations, bringing in other seductive items—sexy toys, games for couples, seductive videos and erotic literature—had really made Bare Essentials take off like a rocket when it opened.

The fabulously decorated, exotic shop had taken Chicago by storm. With the right props, location and set design, what could have been a seedy, backroom store was instead a hot, trendy spot for Chicago's well-to-do singles and adventurous couples.

Coming back to Pleasantville should have been absolutely no problem for the woman who'd been featured in Chicago's *Business Journal* last month as one of the most innovative businesswomen in the city. Still, sitting in the parked SUV, she felt oppression settle on her like two giant hands pushing down on her shoulders. The long-buried part of her that had once been so vulnerable, made to feel so small and helpless and sad, came roaring back to life with one realization.

She was really here.

Taking a deep breath, she opened the door. "Home lousy home," she whispered. Then she stepped into Pleasantville.

As HE SAT gingerly on the edge of a plastic-covered sofa in the parlor of his childhood home, Jack Winfield considered

committing hari-kari with the fireplace poker. Or at least
stuffing two of the cow-faced ceramic miniatures his mother
collected into his ears to block out the sound of her chewing
out the new housekeeper in the next room. *Sophie, the
luncheon salad was unacceptably warm and the pasta un-
forgivably cold.*

As if anyone cared about the food's temperature when its
texture was the equivalency of wet cardboard.

"She'd never forgive me if I got blood on the carpet."

He eyed the poker again. Maybe just a whack in the head
for a peaceful hour of unconsciousness? At least then he
could sleep, uninterrupted by the prancing snuffle of his
mother's perpetually horny bulldog, Leonardo, who seemed
to have mistaken Jack's pant leg for the hind end of a
shapely retriever.

"Sophie," he heard from the hall, "be sure Mr. Winfield's drink is freshened before you start clearing away the
dishes."

"Sophie, be sure to drop a tranquilizer in his glass, too,
so Mr. Winfield can get through another day in this bloody
mausoleum," he muttered.

He rubbed a weary hand over his brow and sank deeper
into the uncomfortable sofa. The plastic crinkled beneath
his ass. Sick of it, he finally slid off to sit on the plushly
carpeted floor. Grabbing a pillow, he put it behind his head
and leaned back, wondering how long it had been since he'd
relaxed.

"Three days. Five hours. Twenty-seven minutes." Not
since he'd returned home to Pleasantville for this long weekend.

Jack didn't like feeling so caged-in. He needed to be
home, in his own Chicago apartment, away from grief and

the smell of old dead roses and talcum powder. Away from his mother's tears and his sister's complaints.

Actually, when he thought about it, what he really needed to bring about sleep and a good mood was a seriously intense blow job. Followed by some equally intense reciprocal oral sex. And finally good old, blissful, hot, headboard-slamming copulation.

He hadn't been laid in four months and was feeling the stress. It almost seemed worth it to call his ex and ask her to meet him at his place the next day for some we're-not-getting-back-together-but-we-sure-had-fun-in-the-sack sex.

Home. Chicago. Late tonight. And not a moment too soon.

Jack supposed there were worse places to visit than his old hometown of Pleasantville, Ohio. Siberia came to mind. Or Afghanistan. The fiery pits of hell. Then again...

"You're sure you have to leave tonight?" his mother asked as she entered the room. "I thought you were going to stay longer than three days. There's so much to do."

"I'm sorry, Mother, you know I can't."

Tears came to her eyes. If he hadn't seen them every hour or so since his birth, they might have actually done what she wanted them to do—make him change his mind.

Sadly enough, his mother simply knew no other way to communicate. Honest conversation hadn't worked with Jack's father, so she'd relied on tears and emotional blackmail for as long as Jack could remember. His father had responded with prolonged absences from the house.

Dysfunctional did not begin to describe his parents' relationship. It—and his sister's three miserably failed walks down the aisle—had certainly been enough to sour Jack on the entire institution of marriage.

Relationships? Sure. He was all for romance. Dating. Companionship. From shared beer at a ball game, to can-

dlelight dinners or walks along the shores of Lake Michigan
on a windy afternoon, he thoroughly enjoyed spending time
with women.

Not to mention good, frantic sex with someone who blew
his mind but didn't expect to pick out curtains together the
next morning. Someone like his ex, or any number of other
females he knew who would happily satisfy any of those
requirements with a single phone call. Not calling any of
them lately had nothing to do with his certainty that he
wasn't cut out for commitment or happily-ever-after. It had
everything to do with his father's death. Work and his ob-
ligation to his family had been all he'd thought about for
several months.

"Why can't you?" his mother prodded.

"I've got to wrap up the mall project I'm working on.
You know I've planned some extended vacation time in
July. I'll come back and help you get things settled then."
*Unless I get hit by a train or kidnapped by aliens...one can
hope, after all.*

Nah. Trains were messy. And after watching the
"X-Files" for years, the alien thing didn't sound so great,
either. He really couldn't get into the whole probing of body
orifices gig.

So, a summer in Pleasantville it would be.

Thinking of how he'd originally intended to spend his
long summer vacation—on a photographic big-game safari
in Kenya—could almost make a grown man cry. Pampered
poodles instead of elephants. Square dances instead of native tribal rituals. The chatter of blue-haired ladies sitting
under hair-drying hoods instead of the roar of lions and the
crackle of a raging bonfire. Small town, pouting blond prin-
cesses with teased up hair instead of worldly beauties with
dark, mysterious eyes.

He sighed. "I think I'll take a walk downtown. To walk

off that great lunch.'' What he really needed was to escape the stifling, decades-old, musty-rose-tinged air in the house.

"Just be careful, J.J."

Jack cringed at the nickname that his mother refused to give up. No one but his parents had called him J.J.—or John Junior—in twenty years. Still, he supposed he could put up with it if it made her happy. She could probably use some happiness right about now; she'd taken his father's death very hard.

"And it looks like it's going to rain. Take your rubbers."

He almost snorted. If she knew how badly he wanted to use a few rubbers—though, not the kind she imagined—she'd faint.

Kissing her on the forehead, he shrugged away a pang of guilt. He needed a brief break from her sadness to deal with his own. Besides, he wanted to get out of the house before his sister got back. With the three of them together, the absence of the fourth became all the more obvious.

His mother would sob quietly. His sister would wail loudly. And Jack would remain strong and quiet. He grieved for his father, too. But always alone, always in silence.

No, they hadn't been on very good terms lately. His father had never forgiven Jack for accepting a scholarship and moving to California fifteen years before. Even after grad school, when he'd gotten a job with an architecture firm in Chicago, he'd managed to avoid all but a handful of visits. The most recent, four months before, had been to attend his father's funeral.

He'd always figured there would be time to mend that fence, to try to make his father understand why he couldn't stay here, couldn't continue the family tradition and become king of Nowhereville. He'd never said that, of course, knowing the old man would have been cut to the quick at an insult to his town. He'd reminded Jack at least once a week

growing up about his ancestors, who'd lived here since before the Civil War.

His mother's roots ran even deeper, a fact she enjoyed
bringing up whenever his father had started pontificating.

Funny. Walking past his father's study, eyeing the brandy
decanter and the old man's favorite glass, he realized he'd
have gladly listened to his father pontificate if it meant seeing him once more. Amazing how there always seemed to
be time for one more conversation right up until time ran
out. That realization had helped a lot lately in dealing with
his emotional mother.

He considered it a new life's lesson. Tomorrow might not
ever come, so don't put off what you want to do today.
Grab it now or risk losing the chance forever. John Winfield,
Junior...Jack to his friends...planned to stick to that mantra.

Starting today.

THE FIRST THING Kate noticed during her walk downtown
was the absence of the pungent odors of the Ohio General
Paper Mill. The unpleasant aroma used to hang over the
town, which had once seemed appropriate to Kate and Cassie. The mill had closed three years ago, according to her
mother. That had caused the town's bad economic situation.
Kate couldn't even conjure up any satisfaction about it. She
felt only a sharp tinge of sadness, particularly when she saw
the sorry condition of the town square and the courthouse.
Pleasantville might not have been pleasant for the Tremaines, but it had actually once been pretty.

As she walked, she got a couple of curious looks. No one
recognized her, not that she'd expected anyone to. She was
no longer the pretty-in-a-quiet-way, nice girl she'd once
been. That was one good thing about her move away from
Pleasantville. She no longer felt the need to always be the
good girl. Without Cassie around to be so flamboyantly bad,

Kate had become free to speak her mind. She sometimes went out of her way to shock people, even if it was really only a defense mechanism to keep others from trying to get too close, as Armand claimed.

There were one or two people she wouldn't mind seeing. Some of her mother's friends had been kind. And Kate's high school drama teacher, Mr. Otis, had been one of the smartest people she'd ever met. She imagined he was long retired by now.

Feeling hot, Kate went into the deli for a drink. She didn't know the couple who ran the place, and they were friendlier than she'd expected. She began to relax. Maybe ten years of dislike had created an unrealistic anxiety about her trip back here.

After the deli, she continued her stroll. Heavy gray clouds blocked all but a few watery rays of sunlight and kept the unusual spring heat close to the ground. The soda helped cool her off, but her sleeveless silk blouse still clung to her body, and her ivory linen skirt hung limply in the thick humidity.

A few buildings down, in what used to be a record shop, she noticed a new business. A nail salon, judging by the neon hand in the window, which beckoned customers inside. From an angle, the middle finger on the hand appeared abnormally long, almost as thought it was flipping the bird to everyone on the street. Then she saw the name—Nail Me. "Well, now I've got to go in."

"Pull up a chair, angel face," she heard. "You want your fingers, your toes or both? I'm runnin' a special."

Kate had to grin in response to the welcoming smile of a skinny girl, who looked no more than eighteen, sitting on a stool in the empty shop. "Uh, I don't actually need a manicure."

The young woman, who had bright orange hair and at

least a half-dozen pierced earrings in one ear, sighed. "You sure?"

Kate nodded and held out her hands, knowing her regular manicurist would throw a fit if she ever went to someone else.

The girl whistled. "Nice." She then pointed to some chairs in a makeshift waiting area. "Have a seat anyway. You're a stranger, I can give you directions to anyplace you need to go."

"I'm familiar with this town. I've been here before."

"And you came back voluntarily?"

Kate chuckled. "You're not a fan of Pleasantville?"

"It's all right," the girl said, shrugging. "Could be a decent place, if it would move out of the 1940s and into the new millennium. Just needs something to shake things up."

The return of a trashy Tremaine could do the trick...not that Kate would be here long enough to renew any acquaintances.

"I wanted to see how the place has changed. I really should go now, though." She'd seen enough of downtown. Time to stop putting off the inevitable and to go out to her mom's house.

Bidding the girl goodbye, she exited, crossing Magnolia Avenue to walk back to her parked SUV. She'd only gone a few yards when someone across the street caught her eye.

A man. Oh, without question, a man. A tiny wolf whistle escaped her lips before Kate could stop it. *Mister, you are definitely in the wrong place.*

No way did this blond god belong here. He should be in Hollywood among the beautiful people. Not in this Ohio town where some men considered changing from crap-covered work boots into non-crap-covered work boots dressing up for a night out.

She sighed as she realized even her thoughts had regressed. Kate Jones, successful business owner, did not generally think about crap-covered anything.

Unable to help herself, she looked across the street at the man again. He appeared tall. Of course, to Kate, most people appeared tall since she stood five foot four. The stranger's dark blond hair caught the few remnants of sunlight peeking through the gray clouds. It shone like twenty-four-carat gold. Though she wasn't close enough to determine the color of his eyes, she certainly noted the strength of his jawline, the curve of his lips. And a body that would moisten the underwear of any female under ninety.

Knock it off, Kate. He's going to catch you staring.

She couldn't stop herself. She had to look some more, noting the tightness of his navy shirt against those broad shoulders and thick arms. Not to mention the tailored khaki slacks hugging narrow hips and long legs.

They hadn't grown them like this when she'd lived here.

From behind her, she heard a man shout, "Hey, Jack!"

The blond man looked over, probably searching for the person who'd shouted. But his stare found Kate first.

She froze as he spotted her. So did he. Though several yards of black paved street separated them, she could see the expression on his face. Interest. Definite interest. A slow smile. A brief nod.

The person who'd called to him was a man, so she figured Mr. Gorgeous—Jack—was smiling and nodding at *her*. And staring just as she had at him. An appreciative stare. An I'd-really-like-to-meet-you stare. A totally unexpected stare, considering her frame of mind since she'd pulled into this place a half hour ago.

She smiled back, simply unable to help it. Damn, the man had dimples. Someone needed to come along with a big street sweeper and clean her up, because, unless she was mistaken, she was melting into a puddle of mush from one heartbreakingly sexy grin.

"Hi," he said, though she couldn't hear him. She could tell by the way his lips moved. Those lips... Lord save her, the man had to kiss like a sensual dream with a mouth like that. And those thick arms to wrap around her. The hard chest to explore.

An old, seldom-heard voice of doubt mentally intruded. *He must be talking to someone else. Why would he be talking to me?*

Once Kate had reached Chicago, it had taken her a while before she'd begun to accept that men might really want to look at *her*...even when her stunning blond cousin was in the room. She almost couldn't get used to it, even now. Sure, she knew she had always been pretty. Sweet Kate. Quiet Kate. Smart, dark-haired, petite Kate with the pale, delicate face and the boring chocolate-brown eyes who'd always been too easily wounded by the meanness of others. Nothing like show-stopping bombshell Cassie, who was every 36-24-36 inch a Tremaine, with a mile of attitude and a ton of confidence.

Yet this Mount Olympus-bound hunk had stopped to flirt with *her*? He tilted his head to the side and raised one eyebrow. When he pointed to her, then to the sidewalk on which he stood, she knew what he was asking. *Your side or mine?*

Remembering where they were, she stiffened and shook her head. *Forget it. No way are you going to even say hello. Do what you have to do and get outta Dodge, Katherine Jones. You've got no time to get all drooly over the local Don Juan.*

He stepped closer, toward the curb. By the time his feet hit the street, Kate realized he was coming over, though not to talk to the man who'd hailed him. No, his stare had never left Kate's face. She forced herself to move, hurrying down the sidewalk.

She peeked over her shoulder only once. A mixture of relief and disappointment flooded through her as she realized the man who'd hailed him had planted himself firmly in the path of the blond hunk. He couldn't follow her even if he wanted to.

Did he want to? *Doesn't matter.* She kept on walking.

A plop of rain landed on Kate's shoulder. She experienced an instant of déjà vu, remembering walking the streets of Pleasantville on a rainy night when the raindrops had warred with her tears to wash away her makeup.

Seeking shelter, she turned toward the nearest doorway. Somehow, without realizing where her steps had carried her, she found herself standing outside McIntyre's Tea Room. "Oh, no."

The Tea Room, owned by Darren McIntyre's mother, had been the worst spot for any Tremaine ten years ago. The old guard of Pleasantville—the Winfields and the other Lilac Hill set, considered this "their" territory. Kate's mom and her friends had been more comfortable at the beauty parlor in the basement of Eileen Saginaw's house, so it wasn't until Kate had gotten friendly with Darren that she'd ever even been in the Tea Room.

"Still the same," she mused, looking at the small, discreet sign in the window. Next door, though, Mr. McIntyre's menswear shop was gone, closed, dark and empty.

Don't, Kate. Just don't. Casting one more quick look up the street, she saw the handsome stranger watching her from over the shoulder of his companion. He wouldn't follow her, would he? Well, he certainly wouldn't follow her into the Tea Room, a notoriously female establishment.

Knowing she must have some liking for self-torture, she walked up the wood steps to the awning-covered porch and reached for the doorknob. Once inside, she had to pause for a moment as sense memory kicked in and her mind identified the smells of her youth. Yeasty bread. Raspberry jam. Spiced teas. Some old lady perfume…White Shoulders? Lots of hair spray. Dried flowers.

She had to stop in the foyer to take it all in.

This place, at least, was hopping, every table full. She recognized some faces, though they'd aged. Physically, nothing had altered. From the white-linen tablecloths to the lilac-tinted wallpaper, the room looked the same as the last time she'd been in it. All it needed was a glowering, frowning-faced Mrs. McIntyre to flare her nostrils as if she smelled something bad whenever Kate walked in, to make her trip down memory lane complete.

No one paid a bit of attention as she stood watching. They were all, it appeared, engaged in a room-wide debate over some poor soul they kept calling shameless and shocking.

Things hadn't changed here at all.

Knowing there was absolutely nothing in this place for her, Kate turned to leave. Before she could walk back out the door, however, she heard the only word that could have stopped her.

Tremaine.

2

___

As Harry Billingsley, the town's ancient barber, engaged him in conversation, Jack watched every step the brunette took. She walked quickly, almost tripping once on an uneven brick, as if she wanted to escape the rain. He knew better. She wasn't running from the rain. When she peeked over her shoulder at him, he knew she was avoiding *him*.

Something downright electric had happened a few moments ago when their stares had met across Magnolia Avenue. There'd been an instant connection, a shared intimacy though they were complete strangers. It was like nothing he'd ever experienced before.

Obviously she had been just as affected. Only instead of intriguing her, as it had him, their silent, thirty-second exchange had bothered her, scared her even. Her feet had turned cold and she'd run off.

No matter, he'd be able to find her again. The woman stood out here like a bloodred rose in a bouquet of daisies.

A few months ago he might not have let the charged stare across a deserted street affect him. His new attitude toward life, however, made finding the brunette and talking to her a must. No more letting opportunities slide. Now, when Jack Winfield saw a good thing, he was going to go after it. He somehow knew the stranger could be a very good thing indeed.

Jack tried to brush off Harry as politely as he could.

"Yes, but I really have to go now. Maybe we can talk in July when I come back for a longer stay."

Harry continued. "Your father made some mistakes. Stirred up a lot of gossip around here with his will and Edie Jones."

Gossip. His least favorite word, and it was used as currency in this town. Jack had never listened to it and never would. So his father had left his maid a small bequest. Only in a town like this could that be considered gossip-worthy.

Watching as the dark-haired stranger in the sexy green blouse went into the Tea Room, he cringed. Of all the places she could have picked, why did she have to go into that hen's nest?

"I'm sorry, I really have to go," Jack said, finally simply walking away in the middle of Harry's long-winded monologue. He didn't care to hear about any old town scandals, especially not if they involved his father, the former mayor.

Following a stranger down a public street wasn't Jack's M.O. In fact, he didn't think he'd ever done it. But something about this stranger...this perfectly delightful stranger...made him certain he could follow her anywhere. He simply had to see her, up close. To determine if her face was really as delicate and perfect as it had appeared from across the street. If her eyes were possibly the same dark, rich brown as her long hair.

Shrugging, he walked to the entrance of the Tea Room and stood outside the door. For a second he wondered if old lady McIntyre would come out and shoo him away. She used to shout at all the boys who'd plant themselves on the stoop, hoping a customer with a take-out bag would hand over some free sweets.

Never happened, as far as he recalled. The snob set of Pleasantville was notoriously tight-fisted with their sweets.

Crossing his arms in front of his chest, he proceeded to wait. "You've got to come out sooner or later."

It took less time than he expected. Before he even realized what was happening, the door to the Tea Room opened and she barreled out, crashing straight into his arms.

Just as if she belonged there.

"OH, I'M SO SORRY!" Before Kate could step away from the person she'd crashed into, she quickly reached up to dash away some angry tears blurring her vision.

That these people could make her cry infuriated her. Somehow, though, anger and sharp hurt for her mother had combined to bring moisture to her eyes while she stood in the Tea Room listening to her family being torn apart yet again by a bunch of small-minded, small-town witches. It was either turn and hurry out or throw a big screaming hissy fit telling them all to jump on their broomsticks and fly straight to the devil.

She couldn't have said which course of action her cousin Cassie would have chosen. But for Kate, who'd become quite adept at maintaining a cool and calm composure, it was think first, react second. Kate didn't believe in hysterical fits—particularly not when she had tears in her eyes. She did, however, believe in well-thought-out retaliation. *Someday.*

Finally turning her attention to the person she'd nailed, she sucked in a breath. "You."

Mr. Gorgeous. Jack. *This is* so *not my day.*

"Nice to meet you too," he said with a sexy grin, as if they were exchanging handshakes instead of being practically wrapped around one another on the steps of the Tea Room.

He made no effort to move away, seeming content that

her hand was on his shoulder, her belly pressed to his hip and her leg between both his thighs.

Of course, Kate didn't move, either. Funny thing the sudden lethargy in her limbs. Particularly considering the sharp heat shooting from the tips of her breasts—which brushed against his shirt—down to her stomach. Lower.

"Did I hurt you?" she whispered.

"Only my ego when you ran away from me a few minutes ago."

Kate blinked, but remained still, somehow unable, or perhaps unwilling, to break their intimate contact. Her breaths grew deeper as she watched him stare at her. His gaze studied her long, dark hair, her face, her mouth. His eyes glittered and a smile played about his sensual lips, as if he liked what he saw.

As did she. Up close, he was even more devastating than he'd been from across the street. Tanned skin, square jaw, beautiful green eyes with lashes a cover model would envy. Her fingers tightened slightly into his cotton shirt.

Move, Kate. Put your hands in the air and step away from the hunk.

"Are you married?" he asked.

She shook her head. But before she could ask him why he wanted to know, before she could do anything—including disengaging their much-too-close-together bodies—he moved closer. Kate thought she heard him whisper the word, "Good," just before he caught her mouth in a completely unexpected kiss.

Kiss? A gorgeous stranger was kissing her, in broad daylight, outside Mrs. McIntyre's Tea Room?

That was as far as her thoughts took her before she shooed them away and focused on what was happening.

Yes, the kiss was unexpected. And unbelievably pleasurable.

She didn't try to step back, didn't shove him away and slap his face as she probably should have. Instead she let him kiss her, let this incredible stranger gently take her lips with his own. Soft and tender at first, then more heated as he slipped his hands lower to encircle her waist and pull her even tighter against his body. As if they weren't already so close together a whisper couldn't have come between them.

As the kiss went on, she briefly wondered if she'd fallen asleep, if she was still at the motel where she'd spent the previous night. Maybe she'd popped one too many nickels into the Magic Fingers and they'd gotten her all worked up so she was having an amazingly intense, erotic dream.

Kissing had never been this good in real life. Besides, no man this perfect could exist in this nightmare of a town.

So she could be dreaming, couldn't she? And if it was merely a dream, couldn't she, uh, kiss him back?

She softened her mouth and tilted her head. Feeling the flick of his tongue against the seam of her lips, she whimpered, continuing to tell herself that this couldn't be happening. The beeping of a passing car horn and the musty damp-wood smell of the old porch on which they stood were merely realistic elements of her dream. These weren't real lips now tugging gently at hers, tasting her, exploring her. She hadn't fallen into the arms of a complete stranger…and stayed there quite happily.

Feeling a few drops of rain plop down from the striped awning over the Tea Room's porch onto her face, she focused on their descent down her cheek. Cold water. Warm kiss. Gentle tongue. His clean, male scent. Hard chest pressing against hers. A thrilling bulge in his pants pressing firmly against her lower belly, which made her rise up on her tiptoes to line things up a little better. The sudden hot flood of moisture between her thighs. Definite car horn beeping. Nosy-faced old lady stepping around them to go down the steps to the sidewalk.

The clarity of detail assured her she was not dreaming.

Insanity. She didn't care. His breath tasted minty as his mouth caressed hers, gently, then deeper. She moaned slightly, deep in her throat, no longer able to pretend this wasn't real, knowing she had to either just go for it, part her lips and let their tongues tangle and mate, or else shove him down the steps.

Kate's rational side said to shove. For once she told it to shut the hell up.

Her entire body hummed with energy. She lifted her leg, sliding it against his, delighting in the friction of her stocking against his trousers. As he moaned and pushed closer, she considered how simple a thing it would be to lift her leg to his hip, to let him pick her up until she encircled his waist with her thighs. To slide onto the wonderfully hard erection straining against the seam of his pants.

She wanted to. Desperately. If only there were no car engines, broad daylight…and the minor fact that he was a complete stranger.

He finally pulled away and smiled gently at her. She shook her head hard and gulped, noting the slowness of a passing car, the curious stare of a face in the window of the Rose Café across the street. Finally she took a wobbly step back. "You're insane."

He stepped forward. Following her. "No, I'm Jack."

Kate shook her head, still bemused. "You kissed me."

"I'm so glad you noticed."

"You can't go around kissing strangers on the street. How could you do that? Just…just…kiss me?"

He shrugged. "You said you weren't married."

"What if I were engaged? A novitiate? A lesbian?"

"Engaged isn't married, so I'd say tough luck to the

guy.'' Grinning, he continued, ''Novitiate would simply be a crime against mankind, definitely worth ignoring.'' He glanced down at her trembling body, his stare lingering on the hard tips of her breasts, scraping so sensitively against her blouse. Then at her legs, which she had to clench together to try to stop the trembling. Not to mention the hot, musky smell of aroused woman.

''Lesbian isn't even in the realm of possibility,'' he finally said, his voice nearly a purr. ''You want me pretty badly.''

Her jaw dropped. He tipped it up with the tip of his index finger. ''Now, introductions. Remember? I'm Jack. It's very nice to meet you. Who are you, and what in God's name are you doing in Pleasantville?''

She ignored the question. ''You followed me.''

He didn't try to deny it. ''Guilty.''

That stopped her. ''Why?''

He shrugged. ''Fate? Instinct?'' Then he lowered his voice, almost whispering as he leaned even closer until his body almost touched hers from shoulder to knee. ''Or maybe so I could see what color eyes my children are going to have?''

Kate opened her mouth, but couldn't make a sound come out.

The man was unbelievable. Outrageous. Sexy. Charming and heart-stoppingly handsome.

And still standing much too close. So close she could see his pulse beating in his neck and the cords of muscle on his shoulders. His upper arms were thick beneath the tight navy cotton of his shirt, so different from the Chicago health club addicts she sometimes dated. As if he didn't work out for his health, but because he was the kind of guy who just needed to pound something once in a while.

Her breath caught as she imagined his sweaty, hard body

pounding something. Pounding *into* something. Into someone.

Focus!

"How do you know I don't already have a live-in guy and three kids somewhere?" she finally asked, hearing the shakiness in her voice. She took another step back, needing air, needing space, needing control of her own mind, which seemed muddled and fuzzy as she examined the tanned V of skin revealed by his shirt. Had she really been kissed by him? Held in his arms? And, damn it, why hadn't she thought to move her fingers to that V to tangle in the light matting of chest hair just below his throat? *Cool it, Kate!*

"Do you?"

Yes. Tell him yes. Then run like hell. "No."

He smiled. "I didn't think so. So, tell me your name, tell me your phone number, and let's go to dinner."

Dinner. Only a few hours till dinnertime and she hadn't even made it to her mother's house yet.

"No. I can't."

"You take my breath away, run right into me, ruin my pants and you won't even tell me your name? Cruel."

"Cruel. Yeah. Welcome to Pleasantville," she muttered.

"Ah, I suspected you weren't a native."

Remembering his other comment she asked, "What's wrong with your pants?" She glanced down, noting the rigid bulge in his crotch, and had to gulp. Yeah, she guessed their embrace had ruined the *fit* of his pants, anyway.

He obviously saw her stare and lifted a brow. Then he turned, pointing ruefully at his taut backside hugged close in the expensive khaki trousers. Expensive, wet and *dirty* khaki trousers. Somehow, during their embrace, he must have leaned back against the soggy wood porch railing.

"You're making it worse," she noted, watching as he

tried to brush off the dirt, but only succeeded in smearing the stains around.

"You could offer to help."

Uh, right. Her hands. On his perfect male butt. Brushing against those lean hips. Trying not to squeeze his firm thighs. She swallowed hard. Glancing at him, she saw laughter in his eyes. Green eyes, dimples, thick blond hair, a body to stop traffic and what looked to be a good solid eight inches of hot and ready hard-on just waiting to be let loose.

On a public street. In broad daylight. In *Pleasantville*.

Sometimes life simply wasn't fair.

"Sure, take off your pants and I'll drop them off at Royal Dry Cleaners for you," she finally managed to say, striving for nonchalance.

"That'd cause some eyes to pop, wouldn't it?" he asked with a wicked grin. "You really want me to take them off now?"

She felt heat stain her cheeks. "I mean, you can…go somewhere and change."

He chuckled. "I was teasing you. It's not a problem. Besides, Royal closed several years ago. Pleasantville has no dry cleaner anymore."

"A shame, given this town's dirty laundry," she muttered.

He gave her a curious look, but she certainly wasn't going to elaborate.

"So, are you going to make it up to me?"

"I'm sorry if my running into you caused you to fall headfirst onto my lips and then back into the railing to ruin your pants," she said, crossing her arms in front of her chest.

"Apology accepted," he said succinctly, as if he'd had nothing to do with what had just happened.

She found herself almost grinning. Finally she admitted, "My name's Kate."

He brushed a strand of hair off her face, his fingers warm against her temple. Her heart skipped a beat.

"It's nice to meet you, Kate." He somehow made the simple words seem much more suggestive than they were. *It'd be nice to have you, Kate.* And, oh, it'd be nice to be had.

Before she could reply, Kate heard the Tea Room door open. Three women emerged, eyeing them curiously.

"I have to go," she whispered, feeling the blood drain from her face. How this stranger could have made her forget the things she'd heard in the Tea Room, she didn't know. The memory of the vicious gossip came back full force now, though.

Gossip about her mother. Her aunt. And the men in this town who apparently had left them each money or property.

According to the harpies, Edie had been left a fortune by Mayor John Winfield. Which, they believed, had to have been a payoff for a secret, torrid love affair.

Kate mentally snorted. The man had left Edie a measly thousand bucks. As far as Kate was concerned, that didn't even cover the interest on all the late paychecks over the years.

It was almost laughable, really. The town in a tizzy, rumors of a scandalous affair. It could have been downright hilarious…if only it hadn't been true. Kate suspected she was the single person who understood that, just this once, the vicious, mean-spirited Pleasantville grapevine was spreading a rumor actually based in truth.

The old saying about the truth hurting had never been more appropriate. In this particular case, the truth made her ache. She'd never completely gotten over the shock and hurt of that life-altering moment when her childhood illusions had shattered and her mother's saintly image had become all too human.

"Don't leave."

She turned her attention back to the amazing stranger. He didn't plead, didn't cajole or coerce. He simply stared at her, all gorgeous intensity, tempting her with his smile and the heat in his eyes.

"I have to go somewhere. I'm only in town for today." She wondered if he heard the anger and hurt in her voice. Did he see her hands shaking as she watched the audience inside the doorway of the Tea Room grow and expand?

Then, perhaps *because* the audience in the doorway was expanding, or perhaps because she simply wanted to know if he'd really kissed as well as she'd thought, she leaned up on her toes and slipped a hand behind the stranger's—Jack's—neck.

"Thanks, Jack, for giving me one pleasant thing to remember about my visit back to this mean little town." His lips parted as she pulled him down to press a hot, wet kiss to his mouth. She playfully moved her tongue against his lips, teasing and coaxing him to be naughty with her.

He complied instantly, lowering his hands to her hips, tugging her tightly against his body. The kiss deepened and somewhere Kate heard a shocked gasp.

As if she cared.

Finally, dizzy and breathless, she felt him let her go. Somehow, a simple "Up-yours" to the occupants of the Tea Room had turned into a conflagration of desire. She found it hard to stand. Her whole body ached and she wanted to cry at the thought of not finishing what she'd so recklessly restarted.

"I'll be seeing you, Kate," he promised in a husky whisper.

And somehow, not sure why, she felt sure he was right.

AFTER SHE GOT IN her SUV and drove away, Jack stood on the porch for several moments. He ignored the people exiting the Tea Room—his mother's cronies who'd probably already called her. And the men staring unabashedly from the barber shop—his late father's buddies who probably wanted to change places with him.

They'd all watched while he'd done something outrageous. He'd seen a chance, seen something he wanted, followed his instincts and kissed a beautiful stranger. In his years playing the male/female sex/love game, he'd never done something so impulsive. Yeah, he'd probably had a few more women in his life than the average guy. But he'd never been as deeply affected by one, just from a heated stare across a nearly deserted street.

Jack still had the shakes, remembering the feel of her in his arms, the way she'd tilted her supple, firm body to maximize the touch of chest to chest, hip to hip. Man to woman. Her dark eyes had shone with confusion, but had been unable to hide the unexpected flare of passion. "Kate," he whispered out loud.

He felt no sense of urgency to go after her since he knew who she was. As soon as she'd said her name, he'd remembered her face from the picture in the Chicago paper a few weeks ago.

He hadn't read the article, and couldn't remember much—only that she owned some trendy new women's store on the Magnificent Mile. But he definitely remembered her face, and her name—Katherine…Kate—because, with her thick, dark hair she'd reminded him of an actress of the same name. Kate Jackson? No…but something like that. He couldn't place the last name yet, but he felt sure he would.

What on earth she was doing in Pleasantville he couldn't fathom. But tracking her down really shouldn't pose much of a problem at all. A scan of the newspaper's Web site archives and he'd be able to find the article easily enough.

His return to Chicago tonight couldn't come soon enough.

KATE DIDN'T PLAN to spend much time in her mother's house. Edie had packed up everything she really wanted when she'd moved to Florida a few weeks back. The place was immaculate, the cabinets emptied and the furniture covered. All Kate had to do was go through her own personal belongings and load what she wanted to keep into her SUV for the drive back to Chicago.

There wasn't much. Edie was a practical person, not an overly sentimental one. So there weren't scads of toys or Kate's first-grade papers to sort through. Just some precious items. Family pictures. Her first doll. The stuffed bear her father had given her for her sixth birthday—that was a month before he'd been killed in an accident involving his truck.

She carefully packed a carton with those things, rubbing the worn fur of the bear, remembering how she'd once been unable to sleep through the night without it curled in her arms. Leaving it behind when she'd left town had been an emotional decision, not a logical one. She'd left to escape her childhood, to escape the burden of her family name and the sadness over her mother's situation. She'd left everything that might connect her to this place, telling her mother over the years to feel free to get rid of her old stuff. Thankfully, Edie never had. She'd known exactly what to keep. And, judging by the absence of most of her high school junk—with the exception of the programs from plays in which Kate had appeared—what to throw away.

When she'd nearly finished, Kate noticed the old Arturo Fuente cigar box in the corner of her old room. Opening it, she felt a smile tug her lips as she saw two diaries, an empty pack of cigarettes, the stub of a burned-down candle. Even the tattered, musty *Playgirl.* Surely her mother hadn't opened this box—the magazine would have been long discarded, otherwise.

The memory of prom night descended with the impact of a boulder on her heart. That night had marked the end of teenage illusions. It had enforced adult consciousness, made her see her mother as a woman not merely a parent. Over the years she'd come to accept that moment as something everyone had to go through. While she'd been deeply disappointed, it hadn't affected her strong feelings for Edie. She loved her as much now as she ever had. And, deep down, she was thankful for having learned the valuable lesson about the fickleness of relationships and the heartbreak of love by seeing what her mother had gone through. It had saved her from ever having to experience it firsthand.

"Glad you got out, Mom. Now, find some great retired guy down in Florida and grab yourself some happiness."

Flipping idly through the *Playgirl,* she cast a speculative glance at the centerfold. "Not bad." She liked her men long and lean, though not hairless and smooth-chested like this guy. Though flaccid, he definitely had a decent package, reminding her that it had been a long time since she'd had sex. She'd been surrounded by fake penises of all shapes, colors and sizes for so long, she hardly remembered what a real one looked like.

"No big loss," she mused out loud, still staring. She hadn't been kidding when she'd told Armand a small, clean vibrating one was her preference these days. She enjoyed sex. But it seemed to be an awful lot of work for an orgasm she could give herself in five minutes flat. Okay, so she'd never stayed with a man enough to really fall in love and couldn't judge how "making love" compared to sex. Frankly, deep down Kate suspected she would *never* fall in love—since love would have to involve trust and vulnerability. She wouldn't allow anyone to make her vulnerable, not after seeing what it had done to her mother for a couple of decades.

So sex it was. And sex alone had suited her fine for some time now. As a matter of fact, her favorite new toy—and a hot seller at her store, Bare Essentials—was a tiny vibrator that snapped to the end of her finger and handled things quite nicely. Small enough to carry in a tiny case in her purse, it was safely hidden in a side pocket right at this very minute.

She might just have to dig out her small friend tonight at the hotel. An orgasm would help blow off some tension. Though it had been a long time since she'd had sex with a man—more than a year…okay, *two*—Kate certainly hadn't lacked for orgasms. ''A woman owns her orgasms,'' she told the photo. ''She can take them anytime she wants and doesn't need to be gifted with them by some guy with a big dick, a little brain and no heart.''

Though, she had to admit, sometimes the real thing could be awfully nice. She closed her eyes, thinking of her day. Of Jack. Definitely not a little brain, judging by his quick wit and self-confidence. His friendly charm hinted at a man with a heart.

And, remembering the way he'd felt pressed against her body, he definitely had a big… ''Snap out of it, Kate.''

But she couldn't. Closing her eyes, she leaned against her old bed. She licked her lips, remembering how his tasted. She moved her hand to her breast, remembering how his chest had felt pressed against hers. She shifted on the floor, aroused again, her thoughts moving back to what she'd felt that afternoon.

She'd wanted him. Still did, judging by the hot dampness between her legs. Remembering she had brought her purse with her up to the bedroom, she reached for it, finding the zippered side pocket. Retrieving the vibrator, she snapped it onto the tip of her middle finger, and moved up onto the bed.

"Maybe it's been too long since the real thing," she said. There were benefits to sex with someone else. Touching. Deep, slow, wet kisses that curled her toes…like those she'd shared with Jack this afternoon. And she totally got off on having a man suck her breasts. Her nipples were hard now, just thinking about it. She envisioned a mouth. *His* mouth.

But her tiny friend would do for now. She moved her hand lower, down her body, under her skirt. Along the seam of her thigh-high stockings.

"Jack," she whispered as she brought the tiny, fluttering device to the lacy edge of her silk panties. "Who are you, really?"

3

A SHORT TIME LATER, after straightening herself up in the bathroom, Kate went back to work on her belongings. She grabbed the cigar box, snapped the lid closed and put it with the rest of her things. Loading everything in the car was a simple task, and she was finished a short time later.

Not even suppertime. In and out of Pleasantville in a matter of hours. A simple, unremarkable end to one long, painful chapter of her life. Well, unremarkable except for one thing. "Jack," she whispered. Did he live here in town? He must if the barber knew him. So he was best forgotten. She had no desire to get to know someone from Pleasantville. No matter how amazing a someone he might be.

Judging by what had happened in the bedroom, however, she imagined he'd be starring in her fantasies for a while. Her private interlude had done little to ease her tension. Orgasms were lovely. But she also found herself really wanting some hot and deep penetration. Unfortunately, she hadn't purchased any of the *larger* and more realistic-looking toys she sold at her store. "Might have to do something about that when I get home."

Before she left for the last time, she turned to look closer at the neighborhood. Her old street looked better than it had ten years ago. Obviously some new families had moved in. Most of the duplexes, which had once been considered the wrong side of the tracks, were neat and freshly painted. A rain-speckled kid's bike lay in front of a house up the block.

Pretty flowers bloomed in the beds across the street. It appeared the lower- to middle-class residents here refused to give in to the apathy and depression that had sucked dry the downtown area. She smiled, hoping the kids growing up here walked with their heads held high.

Out of curiosity, Kate went back up to the porch to peek into the window of Aunt Flo's duplex. It was, as she expected, empty. Her aunt had hooked up with the rich man she'd always wanted and had gone off to live with him somewhere in Europe.

Good for the Tremaine sisters.

Kate got into her SUV and drove away, fully intending to drive straight out of town. There was nowhere else she needed to go. Yes, she might see a friendly face, such as Mrs. Saginaw or Mr. Otis. But, with her luck, she'd run into someone who'd greet her with a smile, then whisper about her family behind her back. As had most of the people she'd gone to high school with.

But Kate hadn't counted on one last tug of nostalgia. As she pulled off Magnolia onto Blossom, she spied the sign for the Rialto Theater. She sighed over the boarded windows and dilapidated sign. "Oh, no." The one spot in town she remembered with genuine fondness, and it had obviously gone under long ago.

Some demon pushed her right foot against the brake pedal and she brought the car to a stop. The cloudy, murky afternoon had actually begun to give way to a partly sunny early evening. Lazy late-day sunlight flickered off the broken bits of glass and bulb remaining in the old marquis. Casting a quick glance up the street, she saw no one else around. Obviously whatever was left of Pleasantville's prosperity lingered up on Magnolia. Only closed storefronts and boarded-up buildings framed the sad-looking, historic theater.

She got out of the car, telling herself she'd just glance in the giant fishbowl of a box office, but she couldn't resist going to the front door. Rubbing her hand on the dirty glass, she cleared away a spot of grime and looked in. To her surprise, the door moved beneath her hand. Reaching for the handle, she pushed on it, and the door opened easily. It seemed unfathomable to her that the graceful historic building should be left abandoned, but to leave it unlocked and unprotected was downright criminal.

She bit the corner of her lip. It was still light enough out that she could see clearly into the lobby. A ladder and drop cloth stood near the old refreshment counter, along with tools, plywood and paint cans. Someone had obviously been working.

"Curiosity killed the Kate," she muttered out loud.

Then she walked inside.

JACK WASTED A GOOD BIT of the afternoon walking around downtown Pleasantville, looking for pleasant memories. There weren't many. For a town where the Winfield family was considered royalty, he had to say he had few fond remembrances of his childhood. His father had been mostly busy. His mother had been mostly teary-eyed. His sister…hell, he barely recognized the smiling, sweet-faced toddler in the surly blond woman.

The only real ray of sunshine from his childhood, their *maid,* had recently left Pleasantville and moved away. He wished he'd had a chance to say goodbye to Edie. Maybe he'd ask his mother if she had her new address. Then again, his mother seemed awfully skittish whenever Edie's name came up. He hoped she didn't owe the hardworking woman back wages. His mother had no conception of careful spending and was usually in debt, part of the reason his parents' marriage had been so rocky.

While he walked, he kept his eyes open for a brand-spanking-new SUV. He really didn't expect to see her. Since he knew he'd been looking Kate up when he got back to Chicago, he didn't feel it imperative to find her today. Then he glanced down a side street and saw it. Her silver car. Parked right in the open in front of the old movie theater.

Another opportunity—one too good to pass up. He headed for the theater entrance. When he saw one door was slightly ajar, he figured she'd gone inside, so he walked in, also.

Hearing some loud, off-key singing, he followed the sound through the lobby area. His steps echoed on the cracked-tile floor, the only sound other than the top-of-the-lungs belting coming from the theater. He barely spared a glance at the lobby, beyond noting that someone had been painting and cleaning up.

When he pushed open the door to enter the auditorium, he paused, figuring it would be dark and his eyes would need to adjust. Somehow, though, probably because there was repair work going on, the electricity worked. The theater wasn't dark at all down in front where work lights washed the stage with light. In the audience area, a few side fixtures made things visible.

He could see the rows upon rows of burgundy crushed-velvet seats. The thin, worn carpeting in the aisle hadn't changed, its pattern remained virtually indistinguishable after decades of wear. A pair of vast chandeliers still hung suspended over the audience—not lit, obviously. Even fifteen years ago when he'd come to see movies in this place, the chandeliers had been strictly decorative. The town was too cheap to electrify them, so they remained a sparklingly dark reminder of another era.

Finally he turned toward the stage, at the bottom of the theater, where the organist had played in the silent picture days. And he saw her. Kate. Singing as though there was no tomorrow.

Jack began to smile. Then to chuckle. He approached the stage, remaining quiet. She still hadn't seen him, so he took a seat a few rows from the front, watching her performance.

Lordy, the woman could *not* hold a tune. But what she lacked in pitch, she made up for in volume. The rafters nearly shook and he finally recognized the song. Vintage Pat Benatar. She even had the rocker's strut.

No, she couldn't sing, but damn, the woman had some moves.

"I would *definitely* like to hit you with my best shot," he murmured, knowing she couldn't hear over her own voice.

Her legs looked impossibly long beneath her short ivory skirt as she gyrated. She was bent at the waist, holding an imaginary microphone and singing into her fist. Her thick, dark hair fell forward, curtaining her face. From here, he had a magnificent view of the curve of her ass and hips as she bent lower, with parted legs, rocking on her high white heels. Then even lower, until the hem of her skirt rose higher, revealing the top of one thigh-high stocking.

Jack swallowed hard, knowing another inch or two and he'd be seeing whether Kate favored bikinis or thongs. Deciding to alert her to his presence, he prepared to stand. Before he could, however, she tossed her head back, and stood upright to finish the song. She thrust her chest forward. He shifted in his seat, watching the silkiness of her sleeveless blouse brush against the pronounced curves beneath.

When she finally finished, he simply had to applaud. She heard, obviously, and looked down toward the seats like a kid who'd been caught shoplifting bubblegum. "Who's out there?"

Jack rose to his feet, still bringing his hands together in a slow and lazy clap. "We meet again," he said as he walked down the aisle to greet her.

"Oh, no, did you hear me?" She looked thoroughly disgruntled as she narrowed her eyes and crossed her arms in front of her chest.

He climbed the steps leading up onto the stage. "Yep."

She cringed. "For your information, I know I can't sing. So don't even try to pretend you don't think I sounded like a howling female cat in heat."

Hmm. Interesting image—a female in heat. Particularly with the flush of color in her face, the sheen of sweat on her brow and the clinginess of her damp clothes against her amazing body.

She looked aroused. Sultry. Alive. He'd love to hear her purr. "You didn't sound like a cat."

"Well, then, a mutt braying at the moon," she continued with a surly frown. "Don't humor me."

"Not humoring you. Honey, you really can't sing. But, boy, you obviously know how to dance."

The compliment didn't ease her frown. Instead she practically glared. "So, are you following me? Should I worry I'm being stalked by the kissing bandit?"

"I wasn't stalking. I saw your SUV outside and came to investigate. Besides, I'm wounded. Here I thought you liked our kiss." Her cheeks flushed and she averted her eyes. *Gotcha!* He stepped closer until their bodies nearly touched. "I certainly did, and I've been thinking all afternoon about how much I wanted to see you again."

"You don't even know me."

"We could change that. Come have dinner with me, Kate."

"I'm really not hungry, thank you."

"Just coffee, then. Let's go sit somewhere and talk for

hours while we pretend we're not both thinking about what happened this afternoon.''

She raised a brow. ''Oh, you've been thinking about that? I'd nearly forgotten all about it.''

''Liar.''

''If it helps your male ego to think so, go right ahead.''

He laughed out loud. ''I'm not an egotistical man, Kate. But I know when I'm being kissed back.'' He stepped closer, into her space, but she wouldn't back down. ''Admit it. You *definitely* kissed me back.''

''Only to give the old biddies something to chew on with their tea and crumpets,'' she said with a determined frown.

''Ah, ah, you're breaking my heart here.'' He held his hands out at his sides, palms up in supplication.

''I somehow doubt that. You're a complete stranger. One who accosted me in public this afternoon.''

A definite overstatement. ''Not accosted. Surprised.''

''You surprised me all right. Don't guys like you usually wind up kissing a celebrity or streaking through the Academy Awards, then get committed to the funny farm sooner or later?''

He rolled his eyes. ''Do you always keep your guard up? Except when you're singing your heart out in an old abandoned theater, that is?''

''Do you always go around kissing women you see on the street?'' she countered.

He shook his head, becoming very serious. ''Never. Not until today. Not until you.''

She broke their eye contact first, suddenly looking nervous. ''Look, this is probably not a great idea, us being here. I don't even know you.''

''Would it help if I give my word I'm not a psycho serial killing…or serial kissing…nutcase?''

She shrugged. "If I'd thought that I woulda pushed you into the orchestra pit and run like crazy out of here."

"I'm glad to know you trust me. Now, about the coffee…"

"Don't you ever give up?"

"Not when I'm faced with something this important."

He didn't elaborate, and she didn't ask him to. They both knew what they meant. There was something happening here, something living and warm and vibrant flowing beneath them. She just wouldn't admit it.

"I won't say I'm not tempted. But I am on my way out of town," she said slowly. "Heading home."

"To Chicago?"

She paused. "How did you…"

"Well, I know there's no way you live in Pleasantville."

"True."

"And I recognized you."

"From where?"

"I'm from Chicago, too." He saw her eyes widen. In interest? Or maybe relief? "I saw the article in the business paper a few weeks back. You own some hot new women's store, right? The picture was striking." He looked down at her body, her chest still heaving as she brought her breathing back to normal. His mouth went dry. "But it didn't do you justice."

She froze as he looked at her, probably seeing the pulse in his temple as he stared. Beneath his gaze, two sharp points jutted against her silk blouse, telling him she was as aware of him as he was of her. "I liked that picture," she said, unable to disguise a shaky tremor in her voice.

"I did, too. For a businesswoman. A Katherine." He watched as she smoothed her skirt with her palms. She then checked the waistband to be sure her blouse was tucked in.

"But today, when you landed in my arms, you didn't look like a Katherine. Then...and now...you're Kate."

Almost as if she was unaware of her movements, she slid one hand up higher, up the smooth, soft-looking skin of her arm, until the tip of her finger rested in the hollow of her throat and her forearm on the curve of her breasts.

Her nipples jutted harder now, brought to tighter peaks by the scrape of her own arm across them. Did she realize it? Was she conscious of the silently seductive invitation she issued? As if she read his thoughts, she tapped her index finger against her throat. Lightly. Drawing his gaze there once again.

"So you read about me." She sounded breathless. Clearing her throat, she continued. "My store. Is that why you followed me? Why you kissed me?"

He shook his head, still watching the pulse tick away in her throat, right beneath the tip of her finger, wondering how she tasted right there. Wondering how she smelled. Wondering if she'd whimper when he gently licked the moist spot. And mostly wondering when he'd be able to take her in his arms again. Though, this time the decision would be hers. As much as she might believe otherwise, Jack didn't believe in *taking* what he wanted. It was much more pleasurable to be given such a gift.

"I followed you because of the way we looked at each other." Like they were looking at each other now. "I kissed you because you landed in my arms." As he wanted her to now. "What can I say? You were a beautifully wrapped present and I couldn't resist. Who could resist a beautiful woman so obviously in need of a kiss?" *Like now.*

She took a tiny, step back. He let her go. Not crowding. Not encroaching.

"You let me leave. You didn't try to stop me."

He smiled. "I let you go because after you told me your

name, I remembered your face and the article and knew I could find you again once I got home to Chicago.''

Her eyes widened. Tap went the index finger. Tick went the pulse. Down went the heat—through his gut, into his groin.

"So you read the article?''

He shook his head, being honest. "Not really. I just remember your face, your first name and something about a store. You sell women's lotion and things?''

She chuckled, a warm and truly amused laugh that rose from her throat. "And things.'' Before he could question the naughty twinkle in her eye, she'd turned and looked out into the dark auditorium. "When did the Rialto close?''

He shrugged. "I'm not sure, really. I don't come back too often. But I think it was seven or eight years ago.''

"You have family here?'' She lowered her voice, betraying her keen interest. "You're from Pleasantville?''

Jack nodded, but didn't offer more information. He certainly wasn't about to reveal who his family was. If Kate had spent time in town, she'd know the Winfield name. The last thing he wanted was someone else bringing up his father's death. And whatever scandal the town gossipmongers had been whispering about any time his back was turned in the past few days.

Besides, he liked the anonymity of this night. It seemed right, especially here, in the old abandoned theater, so rich with atmosphere and antique glamour.

"Yeah. But, like I said, I got out years ago, as soon as I could. And I avoid coming back as much as possible.''

Her rueful nod said she completely understood what he was saying. Then she smiled, a small, friendly smile that made him think for some reason she'd let down her guard. Because he'd admitted he didn't like this town?

"I used to love this building. It was my favorite place in

Pleasantville.'' She walked across the stage, her footsteps echoing loudly on the wooden planks. "I used to come for the first showing of a new movie, then hide in the bathroom to stay and watch it again and again."

"Ah, a daredevil," he said with a laugh.

A reminiscent smile curled her lips. "The ticket taker, the old one with the poofy black wig, caught me once."

"Miss Rose?"

She nodded. "Yes! That's it. Miss Rose. She was so funny, the way she'd talk about the movie stars, as if they were really here, living behind the screen."

"So what'd she do about you hiding?"

"From then on out I didn't have to hide—she always let me stay, but told me not to let on to anybody else." She looked down at her hands. "I'd forgotten about her."

Interesting. She looked happy and sad at the same time, as if it pained her to find positive memories about her years in Pleasantville. He could relate. Since his father's death, especially, Jack had tried to reconcile the kid Jack who'd left town with the man who'd come back.

Seeing a table right behind the partly open, red-velvet stage curtains, he pointed. "Anything interesting back there?"

Kate stepped between the curtains, and he followed her into the murky backstage area.

She picked up her purse, which was lying on the sturdy old wooden worktable beside the curtain. But, thankfully, she didn't immediately turn and try to leave. *"Flashdance,"* she said out loud, looking at a stack of papers lying on the table. "And *Dirty Dancing*. I think I actually saw that one in this theater."

"I could have guessed you liked dance movies."

She grinned. "What can I say? I can't hold a tune, but I can move to one."

"Did you take lessons?"

"Yeah, I started when I was really little, back in Florida."

"Florida? I thought you were from here."

"We moved here when I was six. After that, I took lessons when I could, before the only dance teacher in town got married and moved away."

He winced. "Don't remind me. My sister went into mourning and my mother wanted to sue the teacher for breaking her lease on the studio...just as a way to try to get her to stay."

As soon as he said it, he wished he hadn't. He still didn't want to get into any discussion about his family. Stepping closer to the table, he was easily able to distinguish the names on the old, crinkled, dusty advertisements. It wasn't completely dark back here—after all, the curtain remained open and the stage was brightly lit. Still, it felt very intimate. Almost cocooned.

"I wonder why no one ever took all these wonderful old movie posters. Look, here's Clint Eastwood."

He glanced at the title. "Don't think I've seen that one."

"*High Plains Drifter.* Not one of his most popular." She stared at the poster, looking deep in thought.

"Spaghetti western?"

"Sort of. He's a ghostly man who comes back to a horrid little town to get vengeance on the townspeople." Her eyes narrowed. "They think he's there to save them. In the end, he destroys them and rides away, disappearing into the mist."

He reached around her and pulled the poster away to see the next one. She didn't watch, appearing completely unaware of anything except the Eastwood picture, at which she still stared.

"Here's a James Bond one...from several Bonds ago."

She finally shook her head, ending her reverie, and

glanced at the poster in his hand. "Sean Connery. He's still so hot."

"You have a thing for older men?"

She cast a sideways glance at him. "No." Then she studied the poster again. "I think it's his mouth. He's got the kind of mouth that makes women wonder what he can do with it." She looked at Jack's lips, looking frankly interested.

"What he can *do* with it?"

She nodded. "Some men are strictly visual. While women might like being looked at, we're more elemental creatures. Some women like to be…tasted."

Jack dropped the poster, staring intently at her. "Are you one of them? Do you like to be…tasted?" He wondered if she'd dare to answer. If the color rising in her cheeks was brought about by sexual excitement, or simply nervousness.

"Yes, I do," she admitted, her voice husky and thick.

Definitely sexual excitement.

"And you? Do you like to *taste?*" she countered.

Yeah, he *really* did. Right now he wanted to dine on her as if she were an all-you-can-eat buffet and he a starving man.

Which was exactly the way she wanted it. She, the woman, in complete control. He, the drooling male, at her feet. He wasn't sure how he knew, but there was no doubt Kate liked being the one in charge when it came to sex. Perhaps that's why she'd kissed him the second time today. As if to say, "Okay, the first one was yours. Now, here's what *I've* got."

Two could play this sultry game. He shrugged, noncommittal. "I enjoy input from all my senses, Kate. Taste, of course. Good food. Cold beer. Sea air. Sweet, fragrant skin. The salty flavor of sweat on a woman's thigh after a vigorous workout."

She wobbled on her high-heeled shoes.

"And sight, of course. I think men are focused on the visual because we like to claim things. We like to see what we've claimed. Whether it's a continent, a car, a business contract. Or a beautiful woman in a red silk teddy."

She swallowed hard, then pursed her lips. "Some women don't want to be claimed."

He touched her chin, tilting it up with his index finger until she stared into his eyes. "Some women also *think* they don't want to be kissed by strangers in broad daylight."

She shuddered. "Touché."

"I'm a sensory man. I also enjoy subtle smells." He brushed a wisp of hair off her forehead. "Like the lemon scent of your hair, Kate. And sounds. Gentle moans and cries. Not to mention touch. Soft, moist heat against my skin."

Kate leaned back against the table, as if needing it for support. Her breathing deepened. He watched her chest rise and fall and color redden her cheeks.

"Yes, some men are definitely capable of appreciating all their senses." He crossed his arms, leaning against the table, next to her, so close their hips brushed. "So, Kate, tell me, a man who knows how to use his mouth. Is that really your *only* requirement?"

She licked her lips. "I suppose there are…other things."

"Other things?"

His fingers? His tongue? His dick, which was so hard he felt as though he was going to shoot off in his pants?

"His…" This time she ran her hand down her body, flattening her palm against her midriff, then lower, to her hip.

"Hands?" he prompted, staring at hers.

She nodded. "And one most important thing of all."

He waited.

"His brain."

Jack grinned but didn't pause for a second. "Did I tell you I graduated with honors from U.C.L.A. and have my masters in architectural design?"

She laughed again. A light, joyous laugh, considering they were having a heavy, sensual conversation about oral sex and other pleasures. He found himself laughing with her.

"I like you," she admitted, her smile making her eyes sparkle. Then she paused. Her smile faded, as if she'd just realized what she'd said and regretted saying it. A look of confusion crossed her face. It was quickly replaced by cool determination. As if tossing down a gauntlet, or trying to shock him into backing off, she tipped up her chin and said, "I mean, it's been a long time since I met a man who made me laugh and made me wet in the same sixty seconds."

Whoa. Yeah, definite challenge. Did she think she'd scare him off? Erect a wall that most men wouldn't have the guts to try to broach? He could have told her, had they known each other better, that he wasn't a man who was easily scared. And nothing turned him on as much as a woman who said what she wanted.

Holding her stare, he let a relaxed smile cross his lips, and let her have it right back. "I like you, too. It's been a long time since I've had to jerk off in the shower of my parents' house after meeting a beautiful, amazing, unattainable female."

Kate's heart jumped out of her chest and into her throat, then skipped two solid beats as she took in what he'd said. He'd answered her deliberate challenge with one of his own, without so much as a second's hesitation. Most men would have backed off, intimidated into retreat. A few would have thought about it, deciding whether or not they wanted a woman who knew what she wanted and said so. Some would have figured out a way to see if she really intended to put out. Played the standard game.

Not Jack. *He's too much. He's too much for you to handle.*

But, oh, my, how she wanted to *handle* him.

The realization surprised her. She'd thought she wanted him to back away. She'd figured her natural defense—that being a deliberately aggressive offense—would protect her as it had so many times in the past. It hadn't. Instead it had catapulted her right out of the frying pan and into the fire.

A seductive, intoxicating, all-consuming fire.

He didn't move closer, made no other suggestive comment, didn't try to kiss her or to persuade her in any way. They both knew what was at stake here. Good, hot, completely unexpected sex. A gift of pleasure from an attractive stranger.

She didn't think she'd had a more appealing opportunity in years. She'd never wanted anything so much in her entire life.

There really was no deciding.

"Now why on earth would you want to do something so terribly wasteful in your parents' shower?" His eyes widened as she reached up to touch his cheek, then pulled him close for a kiss. "And why would you possibly think I'm unattainable?"

She felt his shudder as he recognized her answer to his unvoiced invitation. To have him. To take him. To take this, now, to hell with what came afterward.

Yes. This wet kiss. This warm meeting of lips and tongue that stole her breath and rattled her senses. The touch of his hands, sliding around her waist, cupping her hip, then her bottom. He pulled her tighter against him and she ended the kiss, dropping her head back to moan at the feel of his rigid hard-on pressing insistently against the apex of her thighs.

"You're sure about this?" he asked, almost growling

against her neck as he nipped at her throat, then lower, to press a hot kiss in the hollow below.

Her answer emerged from both her energized, aroused body, and also from a lonely, empty place in her heart. She wanted to be close to someone. Held by someone.

Taken by someone.

"More sure than I've been about anything in a long time."

He didn't ask again. Lifting her at the waist, he sat her up on the table and continued to feast on her neck. Her earlobe. Her collarbone. Tangling his fingers in her hair. She parted her legs, and he stepped between them, making her hiss as his big erection came directly in contact with her thin, wet panties.

He couldn't seem to stop touching her. Her arms, her thighs, her face. She was just as greedy, tugging his shirt up so she could slip her hands beneath. She felt his washboard stomach, the light furring of hair, then tugged the shirt off.

He was glorious—a woman's erotic dream, with the kind of long, lean body she'd fantasized about earlier that afternoon.

"Can I tell you something?" she asked in a hazy whisper.

"Anything," he replied, pulling her blouse free of her skirt. He began to slip the buttons open, one by one, his fingers creating intense friction as they brushed against her bare belly and midriff. She shivered, lost her train of thought and strained toward his hands. Her breasts felt heavy and full and if he didn't touch them soon, she'd go crazy.

"Tell me, Kate," he said, finishing the unbuttoning and leaving her blouse hanging from her shoulders. He glanced down at her, his eyes darkening with desire.

Kate had never felt such a fierce sense of satisfaction about her own body. She did now, though. She liked herself because of the appreciation in his eyes as he studied her. Her skirt was pulled all the way up to her hips, exposing her thigh-high stockings and her tiny white silk panties. And the curves of her breasts, barely contained in the skimpy lacy bra.

But he still didn't touch them. Didn't caress them as she wanted him to. She whimpered and leaned into his hands. Offering herself. Hissing as her nipples brushed his index finger.

He moved his palms to cup her around the ribs. With his thumbs, he lightly touched her nipples, easily visible behind the lace of her bra. Then he moved them again, a tiny flick, a taunting caress. Knowing why he waited, she admitted, "I wanted you so much earlier today, I had to...to..."

"Yes?" Another flick, too gentle. She wanted more, wanted him to push the fabric away and take her nipples between his lips and suck deeply. Her breasts were ultra-sensitive; it wouldn't take much more than that for her to come.

"Tell me," he ordered.

"I had to touch myself," she admitted.

He rewarded her with a longer stroke, sliding two fingers into her bra and taking her nipple between them. Then he stopped again. "Where?"

"In my old bed."

He chuckled lazily and resumed the all too brief flicks of thumb against nipple, accompanying the touches with tantalizing love bites to her neck. "I meant where on your body?"

She groaned in frustration. "Where do you think?"

"Here?" he asked, covering her breasts with both hands, cupping their fullness.

"Oh, finally!"

"So you did touch your breasts?"

She shook her head, desperate for more. "No, but that's exactly where I want *you* to touch."

"You've got me curious, Kate." He kissed his way down her neck, pushing her back farther on the table until she was nearly reclining. Then he moved his lips down. Over the curve of her breast. Scraping his teeth along the lace, slipping his tongue beneath it to lick her nipple.

She jerked hard, her hot core grinding against him. "Curious? You've got me ready to sing the Hallelujah Chorus!"

"Hey, no singing," he scolded, lifting his mouth from her.

"I promise," she said between harsh pants. "No singing. But please, don't stop touching me or I'll scream."

"I want you to scream," he murmured, staring down into her face, his eyes lit with passion. "I want us both to scream because it feels so good there's no other way to express it."

Finally he deftly undid her bra, tugging it away and catching her fullness in his hands.

"Have I told you yet that I'm a visual man?" he asked as he moved lower to kiss her. "I love looking at these." Then he lifted her nipple to his lips and flicked his tongue over it with exquisite precision. "And feeling them."

"Thank heaven." She clutched his hair in her hands and pulled him closer, silently ordering him to stop fooling around and to get to some serious action. He complied, sucking her nipple deeply into his mouth as he caught the other between his fingers.

She had her second orgasm of the day a minute later. It made the first one in her old bedroom pale in comparison.

"I see we're well matched. You're very sensitive here, aren't you?" he asked, continuing his sensual assault on her chest. The pleasure began to build again, before she'd come down from her orgasmic high. "But we still haven't found the spot you touched yet, have we?'' He reached around to unzip her skirt.

Okay. This was good. Her nipples still tingled, but now other parts—lower parts—were ready for some action. She almost purred as he followed the path of skin exposed by the zipper, trailing his fingers down her tailbone until he slipped a hand under her panties to cup her bottom.

''Are you going to show me, Kate, where you touched?''

She nodded wordlessly, wondering how he'd stolen all thought, all will. He eased the skirt down, waiting for her to lift up so he could pull it all the way off and toss it to the floor. Then he stepped back and merely looked at her, clad only in panties, thigh-highs and strappy sandals. He looked his fill. ''I'm suddenly starting to hear strains of the Hallelujah Chorus myself. I think I've died and gone to heaven.''

Kate twisted and shifted restlessly, loving the way he ate her up with his eyes. Then she reached for the belt of his trousers. ''Well, angel, you're not going to get your wings, until you ring my bell.''

Chuckling, he pushed her hands away, undid his trousers and pushed them down. Kate bit her lip, watching through a curtain of her own hair as he pushed off his boxer briefs. When she saw his thick, erect penis spring free of them, she moaned out loud.

Vibrating fingertips just can't compare.

She found her voice. ''My purse. In my purse…''

He understood what she meant. He grabbed it, handing it to her while he shucked off the remainder of his clothes. Kate dug inside, grabbing one of the small foil packets in the bottom of the bag. She saw his curious expression. ''Freebies from my shop. Some stores give away matchbooks. We give away condoms.''

He looked as though he wanted to question her, but she

wouldn't have that. Ripping open the condom with her teeth, she reached for his penis to put it on, but had to pause, to feel the pulsing heat in her hands, to test the moisture at its tip with her fingers. *It's definitely been too long.*

But what a yummy way to get back in the saddle.

"Let me," he insisted, his voice thick and nearly out of control with need.

She did, turning her attention to her now-in-the-way panties. Pushing them off, she watched as he groaned at the sight of her. Glistening. Open and ready.

"Kate?"

"Yes?"

"Remember the discussion we had about the senses?"

Remember? She could barely remember her own name.

"I don't think I told you...I'm a visual man. But taste really is my favorite."

She only understood what he meant when he bent down and licked at her glistening curls.

Welcome her third orgasm of the day.

Before she'd even recovered from it, he stood, took her by the thighs and pulled her to the edge of the table. "Now?"

"Now," she cried, still heaving from the feel of his tongue inside her. "And, Jack? Don't even think about being gentle."

She had one moment to suck in a deep breath before he plunged into her. No hesitation. No sweet, thoughtful insertion.

Thank heaven.

He was giving her exactly what she wanted. She was being well and truly...

"Faster?" he asked when she jerked her hips harder and tugged him down for another wet kiss.

She couldn't talk, just nodded, delighting in the fullness,

in the thick, hard feel of him driving ever deeper into her body. And when he finally dropped his head back and groaned with the pleasure of his own fulfillment, she greeted orgasm number four.

Definitely a personal record.

4

IF THERE HAD EVER BEEN a time in Jack's life when he needed a bed, this was it. He wanted nothing more than to pull her body tightly against his, curl around her and languorously come back to earth after their pounding, exciting interlude. Instead he kept his hands on either side of her, holding himself above her, still connected below the waist. "You okay?"

Below him, Kate lay panting, with her eyes closed and her skin still flushed with pleasure. A sultry smile curved her lips, and he watched her pink tongue dart out to moisten them as she nodded. Though he couldn't imagine possibly having anything left in his body after exploding into hers a few minutes before, he felt a definite stirring of interest. God, she was glorious.

"Is that a gun in your condom or are you just happy to see me?"

She opened one eye and glanced down at their joined bodies.

He chuckled, again delighted by her wicked wit. "I can't seem to get enough of you. But, oh, I could use a bed. Or even a comfortable chair."

"Chaise longue," she said, a purr in her voice. "No sides."

Her suggestion definitely brought to mind some enticing images. Her, on top of him, straddling him and taking as much pleasure as she wanted. He held on to the mental picture, determined to one day make it a reality.

She wriggled beneath him, tightening herself deep inside and wringing a moan from him. "As flattering as this is, I don't think those things are reusable," she said, biting the corner of her kiss-swollen lip, trying unsuccessfully to hide a grin.

He gently pulled out of her. What he really wanted to do was grab another condom and go right back in. Make love to her slowly. Erotically. For hours. But this wasn't the time, place or soft flat surface for slow, sultry sex. *Chicago.*

"Any suggestions on where to, uh, dispose of the evidence?"

"I hadn't thought of that," she said with a giggle.

He chuckled, too. "It's been a long time since my teenage years in the back seats of cars, when this was a real issue."

"Teenage? Tsk, tsk. Don't tell me you were a bad boy."

"Actually, I was the golden boy," he replied, making no effort to hide his own disgust. "Which is why whenever I dated a girl, we'd have to go out of town if we didn't want a full report on our activities phoned in to our parents before our 1:00 a.m. curfew." Not wanting to get into a conversation about his family, he looked around backstage. "Now, I really should…"

"There." She nodded toward the workman's ladder standing in front of the partially drawn curtain. Jack followed her stare, seeing the big trash can standing nearby. Tugging his pants up to his hips, he said, "I'll be right back." He gave her a quick kiss on the lips before he walked away.

By the time he returned, after burying the used condom amid the remains of plastic, paint-speckled drop cloths and food wrappers, she was sitting up on the table, buttoning her blouse.

"So, wanna go see a movie sometime? I'm sure we could find something to do while we hide in the bathroom to sneak into the second show," he said with a grin.

She laughed again, not appearing at all nervous, having no second thoughts or regrets. He liked that, since he felt exactly the same way. Tonight was only the beginning. And he didn't regret one damn minute of it.

"I don't know if I'll ever be able to go into a theater again without thinking of this," she admitted, looking up from her buttoning to fix her brown-eyed stare on him. "I think we definitely made a memory tonight."

"Do you like making memories?"

She nodded. "I guess that's what my impromptu rock concert was all about. Throughout my childhood I'd wanted to get up on this stage. I always hoped somebody would buy it, forget about showing movies here and get down to business putting on some great plays in which I could be the star."

"Hopefully not musicals."

She responded with a light punch on his upper arm.

"I'm kidding," he said. "So, did that have something to do with why you decided to, uh, go for it with me? Not just a memory—but living out some childhood fantasy?"

"I don't know what kind of childhood you had, but I did not spend my third-grade year wanting to be stark naked, having the hottest sex of my life, on the stage of the Rialto."

He raised a brow. "Hottest of your life, huh?"

She looked away to reach for her skirt. "Well, hottest in the past year at least."

He crossed his arms. "Admit it. You haven't had sex in the past year. Have you."

Her face flushed. "How could you possibly know?"

"Let's call it a lucky guess."

"Well, what about you?" she asked as she hopped down

from the table and slid her feet into her shoes. "Can I hazard a guess and say it's been a while for you, too?"

"I guess it *was* over pretty fast."

She laughed, low and sultry. "It was perfect. Exactly the way I needed it. One to blow off steam..."

"And the next one?"

She paused. Then, lowering her voice, she said, "I wish there could be a next one."

Her honesty did not surprise him. No coyness, no shyness, no flirtation, just fabulous, forthright, honest Kate. No question, she was the most intoxicating woman he'd met in years.

She bent to hook her sandals, her hair brushing Jack's naked stomach. He heaved in a breath.

"Unfortunately," she continued, apparently not noticing his sudden inability to think a coherent thought, "there can't."

That woke him up and he bent to look at her. "Why can't there?"

She straightened immediately, almost cracking the top of her head into his chin. "You want there to be?"

Seeing the look of uncertainty in her rich brown eyes, Jack immediately took her into his arms. "Yeah. I definitely want there to be. And you're right, I haven't been involved with anyone for several months. I guess you and I met each other at precisely the right moment for volcanic sexual eruption."

She raised a brow. "Lucky us."

"By the way, the movie idea, and my dinner invitation, were very real. I want to see you again, beyond more of...*this*."

She hesitated, leading him to wonder if she really was out for sex and nothing else. For some reason that thought didn't hold as much appeal as it usually would for Jack. Sex and no strings had seemed fine for him up until a few months ago.

Hell, up until today. When he'd met her eyes across a nearly deserted street.

"We'd better go," she said softly. "The workman who left this stuff might remember he forgot to lock up and come back."

Sensing her desire to change the subject, Jack let it go. The subject of what they each were looking for in a relationship could be left for another time. Kate was unlike other women he'd known. She obviously knew what she wanted and wasn't afraid—nor apologetic—about going after it. Her cool exterior and calm demeanor hid a passionate woman with a naughty streak.

"Hope he didn't come back a while ago and quietly watch."

A decidedly wicked grin curved the corners of her lips up. "Well, what's a stage for, if there's no audience?"

Yes, a *definite* naughty streak. He could hardly wait to get to know her better.

After they dressed, they left the theater and stood outside, next to her SUV. Jack hated to see her leave, though he knew he'd see her soon. "So you'll get home sometime tomorrow?"

She nodded. "And you fly home late tonight."

He wished he didn't have to go back to his mother's house to pack. The simple solution to his regret at parting from this amazing woman was to drive back to Chicago with her. But he didn't suggest it. He sensed Kate wanted some time alone to sort things out. He didn't need any alone time. He had not one single doubt about what had happened. He was fully prepared to ride out this incredible wave to see what might happen next.

"I'll call you the day after tomorrow," he assured her.

"We'll see." She turned away, looking down the silent, shadowed street. "You don't have to, you know. You didn't do anything I didn't want you to. So there should be no guilt."

"I'm not feeling guilty." He brushed a strand of hair off her brow, wishing the streetlights around here worked so she could see the sincerity in his eyes. "I'm missing you already."

She shrugged, appearing unconvinced. Leaning forward, he pressed his lips to hers. Her hands snaked around his neck, and she deepened the kiss, as if making one of her memories—this time, the feel of him in her arms. He made one, too.

"I *will* call. So can you give me your number and save me from having to dig through my neighbor's recycling bins, trying to find a month-old newspaper with your name and store address?"

She chuckled. Reaching into her purse, she pulled out a small pink card and handed it to him. He palmed it. "Thanks."

She got into her car, then lowered the window. "I had a great time tonight, Jack. Thanks to you, from now on when I think of Pleasantville, I'll have much more pleasant memories."

He leaned in to kiss her one more time. "I'll see you in two days. I promise." He watched as she drove away.

Still holding the business card in his hand, he headed back to his mother's house. He hadn't even closed the door behind him when she waylaid him in the foyer. "Where have you been? And who were you kissing? Elmira Finley called this afternoon and said you and some stranger made a spectacle of yourselves outside the Tea Room!" She paused only long enough to take a long sip of her drink. Her favorite

cocktail—a glass of vodka with a thimbleful of orange juice
to turn the thing a murky peach color.

He walked past her. "I wouldn't call it a spectacle."

"How could you? And who was she? Nobody recognized
her."

His sister Angela entered from the living room and gave
him an amused look. "So, the golden boy gets a turn as
black sheep."

"Who, J.J.?" his mother stressed, ignoring Angela.

Jack glanced at the business card, which he'd tucked into
his pocket. Jones. Katherine Jones. Of course. Her thick,
long, dark hair and name had made him think of Catherine
Zeta-Jones when he saw the picture in the paper. "Her
name's Kate Jones."

The glass slid from his mother's fingers and crashed to
the tile floor, shattering into several sharp pieces.

"Mother?"

She shook her head, saying nothing. Angela, however,
didn't remain silent. "You've got to be kidding. Kate Jones
is back here? I can't believe she'd show her face in town
now."

He narrowed his eyes and stared at his sister.

"You know who she is, Jack. For heaven's sake, she's
one of those trashy Tremaine women."

Jack clenched his teeth. "I don't care what her connection
is to this town. She doesn't live here now, and neither do
I."

"You can't mean to see her again," his mother said,
sounding on the verge of tears. "Edie, her mother…"

He instantly understood. Kate was Edie's daughter. He'd
forgotten all about the fact that Edie had moved home to
Pleasantville as a widow with a little girl so many years
ago. He'd been only a kid of eleven or twelve himself.

His instant connection to Kate sure made sense. Edie was

one of the nicest people he'd ever known. "Mother, it's fine. Kate's wonderful, honest and open, like Edie. You'd like her."

Angela stepped over the broken glass until she stood next to him. "Honest? Open? Get real. How can you call the woman who'd been banging our father for twenty years honest and open?"

He narrowed his eyes. "You're on dangerous ground, Ang."

"Come on, Jack, the whole town knows it," Angela said. "Including Mom, who, if I'm not mistaken, was happy about it. Free maid service because Edie felt so guilty, plus you got to avoid any icky sex with Dad. Isn't that what you said, Mom?"

Jack looked at his mother, waiting for her to deny it. He expected her to faint, cry or yell. She did none of these. In fact, there was only one way to describe her expression.

Guilty as sin.

"So, HE STILL hasn't called?"

Kate looked up from her office computer screen and frowned at Armand. "I don't know who you're talking about."

He waved an airy hand. "Remember who you're talking to."

Kate smirked. "Your sexual preference is showing." Armand hated to be thought of as flaming, though he occasionally was.

"I don't really care, because for the first time in forever, we're talking about your sex life, not mine!"

"No, we're *not* talking about it." She walked past him onto the sales floor. The overhead lights were on, though they wouldn't open for an hour. Pretending she needed to check the bondage section, she busied herself counting leather masks and handcuffs. Big sellers, particularly around the holidays.

"Kate, stop pretending you don't care this guy didn't call. You've been moping for ten days, ever since you got home from Tortureville. Track the bastard down and confront him about it."

"I can't. The last words I said to him were there's no guilt, no regret, and he didn't have to call."

Armand rolled his eyes in disgust. "Well, of course, but you didn't *mean* it. Darling, all men—including the heterosexual ones—know that speech is complete bullshit."

She ignored him. "Besides, I don't know his last name."

"Stranger sex. I still can't believe you went for it."

She wished she'd never told him. But Armand was a sexual bloodhound. He could smell naughty secrets, even days later.

"So, you see, I can't track him down, even if I wanted to."

Which she didn't. Jack's silence in the past ten days spoke volumes. He knew where to find her and he hadn't looked. She'd cared at first. Too much. Then she'd reminded herself she knew what she was getting into. She could have walked away at any time, but she wanted great sex, with him, then and there. And she got it. So she couldn't now hate him for not following up on his promise to see her when he got back to Chicago.

"Please, Armand, let it drop," she said, rubbing a weary hand over her brow. "It was great, now it's done. I'm over it."

"You're such a phony, Katherine Jones," he replied. Then he stepped closer and took her in his arms, hugging her close. Kate allowed herself to be comforted, burrowing into Armand's hard, masculine chest the way she would with an older brother.

"It's really a shame you don't like women," Kate said, looking up at him. "You're funny, loyal and a total hottie."

Armand smiled, a heart-stopping smile that could make women try to reform him and gay men sit up and beg. "I *adore* women. I just don't want to sleep with them. Besides, I wouldn't want to be one of those men you push away as you close yourself up in your prickly, tough shell, keeping out anyone you think could hurt you. This way we can love each other without any sex or commitment stuff getting in the way."

"I love you, too," she said with a gentle smile, not acknowledging his probably all-too-accurate description of Kate's views on trust, love and relationships.

Before they could get any mushier, the phone rang. Kate answered, smiling as she heard her mom's voice. The smile faded as Edie told her some bad news about her Pleasantville house.

"Vandalized? How? Did the Keystone Kops do anything?"

"Sheriff Taggart assures me he'll do everything he can to catch those who did it," Edie said. "Tag's a nice young man, you'd like him. He and your cousin have apparently already met."

Kate snorted, still unable to believe Cassie had gone to Pleasantville. "Yeah, the son of a…I mean, the sheriff, gave her a ticket last night, her first night in town. Sounds like Pleasantville's as pleasant as ever to the Tremaines."

"It's not the whole town, Kate. Only a few bad apples."

"Enough to fill Mrs. Smith's pies for a decade."

Her mother tsked. "Obviously your cousin disagrees with you, since she's decided to spend the summer there."

Kate could have told her the *real* reason Cassie had gone to Pleasantville. But the cousins had agreed not to. Edie and Flo didn't need to know that Cassie was, in essence, hiding out from a troubling situation. A possibly dangerous situation.

At least Pleasantville is better than dead. Kinda.

"In any case, the real estate agent is having a handyman repaint," Edie said. "He also tells me he had a call asking if the house was available for short-term rental. What do you think?"

Kate, the accountant-at-heart, nodded. "Good idea. If you can rent it out to cover the mortgage until it sells, then do it."

After a few minutes' conversation she hung up and told Armand what had happened to her mother's house.

"What a horrid little burg," he said. "Who would paint graffiti on Edie's door? She's the nicest soul I know!"

Kate nodded, agreeing. Her mom was genuinely the nicest person she knew. Patient and understanding. Sweet-natured, helpful and modest. All the qualities Kate had wanted as a kid—which she now knew definitely had *not* swum across that gene pool from mother to daughter. She'd tried to pretend they had, while growing up in Ohio. But the sweet, modest, quiet genes had eluded her. She had to admit it…she liked herself better now that she was free to be herself. Prickly tough shell and all.

"I can't believe Cassie's vacationing there. Couldn't she have gone *anywhere* else but Nastyville?"

Kate shrugged. Yes, Cassie could have gone somewhere else, but fate and circumstance had pointed her to Pleasantville. There was Cassie's personal situation. Edie's departure. Flo's affair and decision to give Cassie several properties in their hometown—properties left to Flo by some of her more affluent lovers. That had amused Cassie to no end. And the diaries.

Kate had mailed Cassie's diary to her immediately after her return from Ohio, and the two of them had sat on the

phone for two hours one night, talking about them. They'd
relived all the slights, the hurts and their infamous prom
night. They'd even read over their "revenge lists." Then
and there, Cassie had decided the best place to hide out was
in a town that had never really seen her anyway. It made
sense, in a sad, twisted way.

THEIR DIARIES were still on Kate's mind late that night when
her phone rang at home. Cassie, needing a friendly voice.
They talked for several minutes about the pricey house on
Lilac Hill, which Flo had given Cassie. Then Kate asked
the inevitable. "So, did you go by Pansy Lane today?"

When Cassie went silent, Kate sighed. "You saw."

"Yeah. Your mom called, and I went to see how bad it
was."

"And?" When Cassie hesitated, Kate said, "Come on,
Cass, do you think I'll be shocked by anything the people
there do?"

"It's pretty bad. Horrible, ugly words, spray-painted
across the front of your mom's house." Cassie gave a hu-
morless chuckle. "And a few for Flo's house, just for good
measure."

Kate muttered an obscenity. "I'm thinking Pleasantville
could really use a High Plains Drifter," she muttered.
"Mom says the agent's going to have the damage fixed.
Let's talk about something else. Tell me how it's going for
you."

Cassie chuckled. "Did I tell you about the other building
Flo gave me? It was Mr. McIntyre's shop on Magnolia."

Kate gasped. "McIntyre's? No way! I never knew Flo
was involved with Darren's father. No wonder Mrs. Mc-
Intyre hated us. I guess that's why the men's shop closed
down."

Kate should have expected what came next. Cassie had

come up with the crazy idea to give Kate the building to open a store, a Bare Essentials, in Pleasantville! She laughed, loudly, as her cousin launched into reasons why it was a good idea.

They lightheartedly argued about it for a few minutes then Cassie said, ''And besides, it's right downtown. Right next door to the Tea Room. Are you following me here?''

While they kept discussing it, Kate's mind was somewhere else. Thinking of Edie. Of the vicious words that day in the Tea Room. Of the spite. Of the silly Clint Eastwood poster. Of the big overstock she had piling up in the backroom of her store, because of the going-out-of-business sale of a sex toy supplier from Texas. Of a big empty building and storefront, which, Cassie said, needed only a little elbow grease to get it ready to open. Which Cassie wanted to provide, if only to keep from going crazy with boredom. She thought of the cute girl she'd met in the nail salon, who'd longed for something to happen.

Mostly, she thought of Cassie. Alone, a sitting duck, in a town that didn't care a rat's ass for any of them and wouldn't lift a finger to help if her trouble followed her to Ohio.

Cassie urged, ''Come on, Kate. Opening a porn shop in Pleasantville. It doesn't get better than that.''

Kate rolled her eyes. ''Bare Essentials is not a porn shop. But you're right, it sure would cross number one off my revenge list, wouldn't it?'' Then she chuckled. ''And some of the Winfields are still in town to get even with, right?''

Cassie obviously understood. She knew what had happened on prom night, just as Kate knew what had happened to Cassie. They'd shared their most anguished secrets one night a few years ago over a bottle of cheap tequila and an entire key lime cheesecake. Then Cassie gasped. ''Oh, I can't believe I forgot. Did your mom tell you someone wants to rent her house?''

"Yeah. I guess *if* I come back to town, I'd better ask her not to so I'll have someplace to stay.''

"Don't be silly. You can stay with me. It's too late, anyway, your mom told me she heard from the renter today. It's J. J. Winfield. He's renting her place in a couple of weeks.''

Kate reeled. J. J. Winfield was going to be living in her mother's house? Why would he stay on the *seedy* side of town when his family lived on the sunny one? "Impossible!''

"Swear to God. Your mom seemed really touched by it.''

Kate wasn't surprised her mother hadn't called her back to tell her. Kate had never admitted knowing about her affair, but Edie knew she couldn't stand the Winfields, anyway.

Kate suddenly saw an opportunity. Mayor John Winfield was gone, but there would soon be another John Winfield in Pleasantville. Could she possibly get vengeance on the late Mayor Winfield through his son? Seduce him, break his heart, get some serious payback on behalf of the Tremaine women?

She wondered if she could really go through with it. Physically, yes. Kate wasn't vain. But she knew something about sex and seduction. It was her stock in trade. So yes, she could do it. It was the emotional part she worried about.

But men did that kind of thing every day, didn't they? Look at what had happened to her in good old Pea-Ville ten days before. A man had taken what he wanted—admittedly giving her some pleasure, too—and walked away without a single word since. Hurting her. Though, damn it, she'd never admit that to anyone!

Her decision was easy. With a few shipments of goods,

and some vacation time this summer, she could look out for Cassie, give a major screw-you to the old guard in Pleasantville…and seduce and break the heart of the son of the man who'd broken her mother's. Throw in a humiliating moment for Darren and Angela, and she'd make all her teenage dreams come true.

"Cassie," she finally said, knowing her cousin awaited her decision. "Do you think Flo would let me stay in her old place?"

5

JACK COULD HAVE CHOSEN the master bedroom when he moved into Edie Jones's house. Since he'd be in town for at least a month settling his father's tangled financial affairs, he probably should have made himself comfortable in the larger bed. He didn't, for several reasons, but mostly because of the image of his own father—and Edie—in it. He shuddered at the thought.

He still couldn't believe it. His father and Edie had been lovers for two decades. He hadn't just taken Angela's word; his mother had admitted it. That was when he'd decided he couldn't stay in his parents' house during his trip home this summer.

Most sons would probably have felt as much anger toward Edie as toward his father. Jack felt only pity and regret for the woman, who'd been the kindest part of his boyhood. His parents' marriage had been as convoluted as his father's finances, and Edie had been a victim more than anything else. Looking through his father's records, it became obvious the pittance he'd left Edie in his will didn't come near to covering her paychecks, some of which she hadn't cashed over the years.

His family owed Edie something. Staying here, fixing up her house, doing repairs and maintenance so she could sell the place and make a new life for herself, was the least Jack could do.

"Sleep, Jack." He glanced at the clock, which showed

the hour had moved past one. Sleep proved elusive here, especially because Kate had told him how she'd spent her last afternoon in this house. Lying on her bed. Thinking of him. Touching herself. "Knock it off, moron," he said. He couldn't allow himself to think about Kate. Not until he'd figured out how to make up for the damage his parents had caused to her and her mother.

"God, I'm sorry," he muttered. Sorry for Edie, who, he'd learned, had been ridden out of town like a scarlet woman by the old guard of Pleasantville. Sorry for Kate, who'd grown up in this tiny house, on Edie's small income, made smaller by his parents' selfishness. Sorry for himself, because what he wanted more than anything was to find Kate and to tell her how hard he'd fallen for her on the day they'd met, just over a month ago.

But he couldn't. His family had done enough to hurt the Jones women. Until he could find some way to right the wrong, he couldn't let himself see Kate again.

It had been impossible to stay away from her. He'd been drawn to her, easily locating her store on Michigan Avenue. Twice he'd watched her from outside, trying to figure out how to go in and face her. The second time he'd had his hand on the door handle, prepared to go inside. Then he'd seen her in the closed shop in the arms of a tall, dark-haired man. He'd driven away, never finding out whether the guy had been friend or lover. But the image of her with another man had given him some long, sleepless nights.

Like now.

He closed his eyes again, determined to sleep, then opened them as he heard a noise through the wall. A bang. A low curse. Both came from next door, inside what should have been the *empty* half of the duplex, which belonged to Edie's sister.

"Son of a bitch." Jumping up, he grabbed some sweat-pants and ran downstairs, figuring the vandals had returned.

Whoever the vandals were, they weren't very smart. The front door to the adjoining unit was wide open. He easily made out the beam of a flashlight moving around upstairs. Ready to transfer all his unexpended sexual energy into some violence against the intruders, Jack took the stairs two at a time. In the upstairs hall he turned toward the room directly beside the one in which he'd been lying next door. As he burst in, the beam of a flashlight, held by a dark-clothed person, swung toward him.

"Stop right there, you rat bastard," Jack snarled as he tackled the person and took him to the floor.

"Ow, get off me!"

A female voice had spoken. Definitely a soft, curvy fe-male body cushioned his against the hard floor. A mass of thick, dark hair spilled across his hands and brushed against his bare chest. Catching the achingly familiar sweet scent of lemon, he knew even before he saw her who it was. "Kate?"

The flashlight thunked as it rolled out of her hands, swinging around to shine on her face.

She stopped struggling beneath him and stared up, finally recognizing him in the shadowy darkness. "Jack?"

"I'm sorry." He rolled off her. "Did I hurt you?"

She sat up, sucking in deep breaths, but didn't answer. When Jack reached toward her, to make sure she was real and all right, she flinched away as if she couldn't bear his touch.

He probably deserved it. He couldn't imagine what she'd made of his silence since their meeting. "Are you all right?"

"I'm fine," she finally answered, her voice shaky and her breathing still shallow. "What are *you* doing here?"

"I could ask the same of you."

"This is my aunt's house. She knows I'm here, she told me I could stay for a while."

Kate staying right next door? Sleeping in this room, directly next to the one where he'd be sleeping? Moving around in this house behind one all-too-thin wall so he'd be able to hear her sigh in her sleep or step into the shower?

God help him.

"Now, answer my question, Jack. Why are you here in the middle of the night?" She glanced down, as if just noticing his bare chest and loose sweats. Her eyes immediately shifted away, but not before he saw her lips part so she could suck in a deep, shaky breath.

"I'm staying here."

She jerked her attention back to his face. "Staying? *Here?*"

"I mean, next door. I'm renting the duplex next door." He paused. "Your mother's place."

"My mother's...wait, you know my mother?" She paused. "You know who I am?"

"Yes. To both questions."

"How? And what do you mean, you're renting Mom's duplex? That's not possible. You can't be living in her house."

"You didn't know she'd rented it out?"

"Well, of course, but to J. J. Winfield..." Her voice softened. Even in the low lighting provided by the flashlight and the moon shining in through the bare front window, he saw her cheeks go pale and her mouth drop open. "Oh, no. Tell me your name is not J. J. Winfield."

He shook his head, sending a bolt of relief shooting through her body. "No, it's not." Her relief quickly disintegrated when he continued. "No one except my parents and your mother have called me J.J. since I was a teenager. I go by Jack now.''

Kate couldn't breathe. Couldn't think. Certainly she couldn't speak. The man she'd had fabulous sex with in the theater several weeks ago was J. J. Winfield—the son of Mayor John Winfield? The man she'd come back to town to seduce and to destroy was the one who'd already hurt her so badly by breaking his promise to call after their amazing encounter? She covered her eyes. ''This is a nightmare.''

''Kate, I'm sorry, I had no idea you were coming back to Ohio. Your mother never mentioned it.''

She didn't know which was worse. That he was here and she had to face her inattentive lover, or that he was John Winfield Junior. Somehow, the memory of all those long, silent, lonely weeks since she'd seen him last seemed the more devastating now.

''No, of course you didn't know I was coming.''

Her mother couldn't have told him, because even *she* hadn't known. Kate and Cassie hadn't told Edie because Kate knew her mother too well. She'd be on the first plane back here if she thought Kate was coming to stay in town.

Cassie was one thing—everyone in the family knew Cassie could take care of herself. With her looks, brains and her self-confidence, Cassie had never really had to rely on anyone for anything. Except love and loyalty, which the Tremaine women were always quick to provide to one another.

But, to Kate's eternal annoyance, her mother seemed to think Kate was too easily hurt, too vulnerable, and in need of protection. Which really sucked when she wanted people to see a hardworking, intelligent, kick-ass businesswoman. Not the girl who'd cried into her teddy bear after so many childhood hurts, the girl who'd hidden in her tree house and made up stories about how her father hadn't really died and would one day come back.

Not the girl who'd been dumped on prom night.

Jack couldn't have heard about her return from anybody else, either. Kate and Cassie had been careful to keep their plans quiet, to avoid the inevitable protests and backlash. She was sure many people had known Cassie had been working in the old storefront for the past three weeks, preparing to open a ladies' shop, but not the exact *nature* of the ladies' shop.

"No, you couldn't have known I'd show up. You never would have stayed here, in this house, had you known," she said. "Because, you couldn't very well avoid me if we were practically roomies. And obviously, you had no intention of seeing me again. Right?" She couldn't keep the accusation out of her voice. She wondered if he heard the tinge of hurt there, too.

She waited for him to run the usual male line. *I meant to call you, babe, just lost your number...forgot to pay my phone bill...broke my dialing finger...was sent away on a deadly, top-secret government mission.*

"I should go," he said, not even acknowledging her justified anger.

His lack of response angered her even more. He couldn't even *attempt* to make up a lame excuse? He wasn't going to be courteous enough to give her the chance to tell him what she thought of him? Wasn't going to try to sweet talk her so she could tell him he could touch her again when hogs started flying over Pleasantville, leaving the appropriate droppings right down the middle of Magnolia Avenue?

That wasn't how the game worked. Uh-uh. No way was he getting off so easily. "Oh, sure, I know you must be a busy man. Too busy to even, oh, I dunno, pick up a phone once in a while?"

"Kate…"

"What, Jack? You expect me to be like your Lilac Hill girlfriends? Like your sister, *Angela?*" She spat out the name, not caring if he heard her dislike. "I'm supposed to be brushed off quietly, like a lady, not bring up the fact that I'm *unhappy* you lied?"

"I didn't lie…"

"You shouldn't have promised, Jack. You shouldn't have made a big deal out of swearing you'd see me in two days. I was willing to let it end right then and there outside the Rialto. But you had to be Mr. Noble, Mr. Good Guy. You made me think of what happened as something more than it was. You hurt me and, damn it, you have no business hurting me!" To her horror, she heard her voice break. If one tear fell down her cheek, she mentally swore she'd poke her own eye out.

"Kate, honey, I'm sorry. Listen…"

"Forget it," she snapped. "Forget I said anything."

"I thought about you all the time," Jack said, his voice low and throaty in the near darkness. "But things got…complicated."

She snorted. "Complicated. Uh-huh." She started to rise. "Look, I don't really care. You shouldn't have said you wanted to see me again if you didn't plan to, that's all." Swallowing hard, she continued. "We're both adults. We both knew it didn't mean anything."

Her words seemed to anger him. He grabbed her wrist and held her, not letting her get up beyond her knees. "Like hell. It meant a lot, Kate, and you know it."

His green eyes sparkled with intensity in the near darkness, and she could almost believe him. Then she remembered his name. His lineage. And knew she could never trust a word that came out of his heartbreaking mouth.

"No, *Mr. Winfield.* It didn't mean anything more than

any other sexual encounter between two strangers.'' She
jerked her arm away, stood and brushed off her jeans, wincing as she realized he'd knocked her hipbone right into the
floor with his tackle. It already ached.

''We're not strangers.'' He stood, as well, standing so
near she could feel his warm breath against her hair. She
bit her lip, trying not to look at him, trying not to remember
the feel of his hot, hard chest pressing against hers. Trying
to erase the mental picture of him standing above her, his
face filled with need and passion, as he thrust into her while
she lay on the table at the Rialto.

''We recognized something in each other from the minute
our eyes met,'' he continued. ''That's never happened to me
before.''

From out of the near darkness, she felt his hand move to
her cheek. She pushed it away. ''Back off, J.J. Don't touch
me.''

''Ouch. I don't know which is worse, hearing you tell me
not to touch you, or hearing you call me J.J. Please call me
Jack.'' His voice moved lower. She realized he'd bent to
pick up the flashlight only when he brought it up and shone
it on them both.

The light looked pretty damn good on him. His chest. His
tousled, right-out-of-bed hair. His thick, muscular arms and
broad shoulders. His green eyes, not twinkling with humor
now, but dark and confused. His mouth…

She gulped, then crossed her arms in front of her chest,
looking for a defense mechanism when there was really
none to be found that could halt her physical attraction to
him. Finally she said, ''What kind of stupid nickname is
Jack, anyway?''

''What?''

She knew she sounded like a belligerent kid, but couldn't
help herself. Sarcasm was her only defense. ''I mean, come

on, aren't nicknames supposed to *shorten* your real name? Like Kate instead of Katherine? What genius decided to change a four-letter word like John into a four-letter word like Jack?" *Four-letter word being the operative phrase, here.*

She saw his lips turn up as he shook his head and gave a rueful chuckle.

"Oh, I amuse you now? You break in here, tackle me, almost break my back..." *Almost break my heart...* "And now you're laughing at me?"

"No, I'm actually agreeing with you. It doesn't make much sense, does it? But anything's better than J.J."

"So what's wrong with plain old John? It's good enough for your average, everyday toilet, isn't it?"

"Ouch. You're really pissed."

She clenched her jaw, mad at herself for letting him see her anger, which he would rightly assume had to have evolved out of hurt. She took a few deep breaths, trying to regain control. Where was her infamous control? *Gone, baby. Gone for weeks, since that kiss on the steps of Mrs. McIntyre's Tea Room.*

Finally she forced a shrug. "No, I'm not, not angry at all." A strained laugh emerged from between her clenched teeth. "I'm just tired and cranky from getting knocked on my rear by a six-foot-tall man in the middle of the night."

"I'm so sorry about knocking you down. I had no idea it was you moving around over here. I was afraid someone had come back to cause more problems for your mother. I told her I'd look after the house for her. Both houses, actually."

"Why would you do that?" she asked, still not able to comprehend him being here. "Why would you, a mighty Winfield, care what happens to your trashy Tremaine maid's house?"

He stepped closer, holding her chin and forcing her to look up at him in the semidarkness. She remembered, suddenly, how tall he was. How petite and feminine he'd made her feel.

Their bodies were only inches apart and she could smell his musky, clean scent, and feel warmth radiating from his hard, bare chest. Her body reacted instinctively, getting hot and achy. Her nipples felt incredibly sensitive against the cotton of her sleeveless tank top, and her jeans were suddenly uncomfortably snug. She wanted nothing more than to taste him. All over.

"Your mother was the nicest person I knew growing up," he said, his voice thick with emotion. "And I hated to hear what this town had done to her because of my father."

Kate's eyes widened. Did he know? Could he possibly know about Edie's affair with the mayor? She took a deep breath and carefully asked, "Your father?"

He let go of her face, walking over to stare out the undraped window at the shadowy front lawn. "My father left her a small amount of money, when by rights he owed her more." He cleared his throat and shook his head. "A *lot* more. As usual, the town looked for scandal and decided to crucify her with spite and innuendo because of it."

No. He didn't know. He didn't understand the truth. Kate, Cassie and Edie were still the only ones who knew the Pleasantville gossipmongers really had the story right.

And that's the way it was going to stay.

"Okay, you liked her. You wanted to help her. Why does that equal you living here, in her house, instead of with your mother and Angela at your family's place?" Her voice dripped dislike. "Don't tell me you're not one big, happy, rich Winfield family?" She could tell by the look in his eyes, and the way his jaw clenched, that he was mentally arguing over how to answer. "Come on, Jack, what's the story?"

Finally his eyes shifted away from her face and he muttered, "You know my father died only a few months ago."

She bit the corner of her lip, trying hard to remember Mayor Winfield had actually been someone's father. Swallowing her dislike, she murmured, "Yes, I know. I'm sure that's been painful for you."

"It's been difficult. I never realized…"

"What?" she prompted.

"I don't know. How much I cared about him, I guess?" He gave a sad laugh. "How much I'd miss him, even as I find out day by day how very little I knew him."

Having lost her dad at a young age, Kate could understand that feeling of wishing she'd had a chance to know a parent. "I'm sorry, Jack. I know how it is to lose your father."

"I know you do. You were a kid when you lost yours, right?"

She nodded. "Six."

He shook his head. "Awful. Your mom was so young to be a widow." He lowered his voice. "And she never remarried."

No, Edie had never remarried. She'd instead wasted decades on a man who was married to someone else. Kate rubbed a weary hand over her brow. "No. But we're talking about your father."

"Yes, we are," Jack replied. "He left a mess behind him."

More than you could possibly know.

"I told my mother I'd come help her out this summer, sell some real estate, get some paperwork taken care of."

"And you can't do that on Lilac Hill?"

"I'm a grown man, Kate. Can you picture me living in

my mother's house for a month, being scolded not to let my shoes scuff up her tile floor, and to be careful not to rumple the plastic on the sofa in the parlor?''

She couldn't help it. She burst into laughter. ''She has plastic on the sofa?''

A faint smile crossed his lips. ''Yeah.''

''Does it ever come off?''

He shook his head.

''Not even if the First Lady came over?''

''Well, maybe the current one. But definitely not a Democrat. And certainly it wouldn't come off for me!''

Suddenly his childhood sounded less golden than she'd always imagined. ''Sounds like you were the classic poor little rich kid.''

''I did okay. Thankfully, your mother was around a lot.''

Kate's smile faded. Yeah, her mother had been around the Winfields a lot more than he knew. She wondered what he'd think about that.

In her heart she knew it would hurt him, just as it had hurt her to learn a parent she loved really hadn't been perfect. Maybe if she were a vindictive person…or maybe if Jack weren't already mourning his father's death…she'd have told him. As it was, she simply couldn't. No matter what he'd done to her, no matter how much his broken promises had hurt her, she couldn't repay him with that kind of spite.

His sister was much better at that, she recalled.

''Anyway, I wanted to be on my own,'' he continued. ''There aren't a lot of furnished short-term rentals around. Your mom seemed happy to let me stay here for a month. End of story.''

Kate sensed it wasn't really the end of the story, but she was too tired to think about it tonight. She still hadn't quite absorbed the fact that she was here, back in Pleasantville, this time not only for an afternoon, but for weeks.

And Mr. Gorgeous was her next-door neighbor. Oh, joy.

"You need to leave," she finally said, wanting him out of here before she did something terribly stupid. Such as kick him, kill him. Or even worse, kiss him. "I'm tired and I want to go to sleep."

He looked around the empty room. "Uh, where?"

"I brought a sleeping bag for tonight."

"The power's not even on and it's hot as blazes in here. You'll roast."

"I'll be fine. Just go, please? I'm really beat, it was a long drive from Chicago."

He turned to leave, then hesitated. "Look, your mom's furniture is all still in her house. Why don't you stay over there tonight? It'll be more comfortable than the floor."

Stay there? With him? And give him another chance to use her again? *Do I have I'm A Sucker stamped on my forehead? No, thanks, mister.*

Then she thought about her revenge plan, one of her main reasons for coming back here. Hadn't she intended all along to get involved with J. J. Winfield? Seduce and destroy. Entice and evade. It appeared he was handing her the prime opportunity to do exactly that.

But that was with J. J. Winfield. The spoiled, weak, pale and pasty-faced J. J. Winfield she'd pictured in her mind for so long. Not Jack. Definitely not golden-haired, laughing-eyed Jack with the strong hands, the perfect mouth and the big...

"What do you say, Kate? Just for one night." He raised a brow and gave her a wicked smile. "It could be fun."

One night. One more night like the one they'd shared at the Rialto? She might never survive it. Though, there was no doubt in her mind she'd love every minute of it. Every deep, sweaty, hot, pounding, orgasmic minute of it.

Get your mind out of your pants, Kate! This man could hurt her. She was already too vulnerable to him, too attracted to him. Damn it, she already liked him too much. Or at least she had before she'd decided he was a creep and a user. Another interlude with Jack and she might find herself forgetting she wasn't allowed to like him anymore. She could be the one with the broken heart if she followed through on her seduction idea.

No, there had to be another way—a less dangerous way—to even the score with the Winfields. One that wouldn't risk her own emotions. Emotions she'd become quite adept at protecting over the years. After all, with the examples set by women in her family, emotional self-preservation was a requirement. Nobody else looked after a Tremaine woman...except a Tremaine woman.

"I'll be fine. I can open a window."

"What about the vandals?"

She shrugged. "My mother told me the sheriff caught the kids who sprayed her house. They'd apparently hit a lot of other houses in town with the paint cans, and now they're doing five hundred hours community service each."

"Good. Still, you don't need to stay here. Come on, it makes sense. Your mom's place is furnished, and lit. Aren't you achy from your drive? Don't you feel like taking a long shower?"

"I know what you do in showers," she snapped, remembering his comment from the theater.

He thought about it and chuckled. "I just moved in today."

"Doesn't take too long for some men."

"Zing. Was that another comment about how quickly it was over the first time?"

Quick? Ha! In her memory she could *still* feel him making love to her. Riding her, filling her, rolling orgasm after orgasm over her body. She'd felt him inside her for weeks.

"No," she finally replied. "And I think you mean *only* time. First implies there could be a second." *Or a twentieth.*

But there wouldn't!

He ignored her comment. "I promise the shower's clean, Kate. As for anything happening between us…"

She waited, wondering if he'd make some flirtatious, sexy suggestion that they pick up where they'd left off weeks before. If he did, she'd have to kick him, she really would.

He shook his head. "Don't worry. Strictly platonic."

She found herself wanting to kick him anyway.

As if his silence in the past weeks wasn't bad enough, now he'd basically admitted he didn't want her even though she'd practically fallen right back into his arms? She hated to admit it, but her femininity took a definite hit.

"Well, maybe a shower would be nice," she mused out loud, suddenly wanting some payback, wanting to remind him what he was missing out on. She tilted her head from side to side to work out some imaginary kinks in her neck, then raised her arms above her head to stretch. Arching her back so her breasts pushed tight against the cotton tank top, she hid a look of satisfaction as Jack stared, long and hard.

"Okay," he finally said, his voice low and shaky. "Do you need any help with your stuff? A suitcase?"

"No, thanks. I'll only need my purse and my toiletry case." Some devil made her add, "I don't wear anything to bed, anyway."

He closed his eyes.

"It'll be funny, going back to sleeping in my old room for one night. At my place in Chicago, I have a huge California King bed." *Liar.* She had a queen. "With black satin sheets." *Double liar.* They were percale. And pink.

Rather than looking even more hot and bothered, as she'd hoped, Jack gave her an amused look. Finally he said, "Sorry, Kate, your room's taken. 'Fraid you'll have to take the master bedroom…or the foldout."

"You're staying in my room? Why?"

He nodded. "You're not the only one who remembers everything we talked about that night at the Rialto."

She didn't follow.

He stepped closer, invading her space again so their bodies were separated by only a bit of air and moonlight. "You might know what I do in the shower," he whispered, reaching out to scrape the tip of one index finger along her shoulder, playing with her bra strap, which had somehow slipped out. His touch made her shake and she could barely keep herself focused on his words.

"But I also remember what *you* did in your old bed."

By the time she understood, and felt hot blood rush into her cheeks, Jack had already turned and left the room.

6

OFFERING A SHOWER and a bed to a woman he couldn't
have—but wanted so much his nuts ached—had to rank up
there among the stupidest things Jack had ever done in his
life. Maybe not as stupid as the time he'd tried bungee
jumping off a bridge in California, or when he'd scuba dived
with sharks in Australia, but pretty stupid all the same.

The house had only one bathroom. It was upstairs, between the two bedrooms, and he listened to every move
Kate made in there. He could swear he heard a metallic hiss
as she unfastened the zipper of her jeans, followed by a
whoosh of air as she dropped her clothes to the floor. Then
the rustling of the shower curtain as it opened, the water
starting, her tiny gasp as she tested the temperature and
found it too hot. Or too cold.

Jack gave up trying to sleep. Sliding closer to the wall in
her small, twin-size bed, he listened intently. The gurgling
rush of the water from the faucet changed to a sizzling
stream emerging from the showerhead. She stepped into the
tub, closing the curtain behind her. Then she dropped something—the soap? As she retrieved it, her hand knocked
against the tub just inches from his head. He swallowed
hard.

She began to hum. Off-key. Not Benatar now, but some
other old rock tune he couldn't place.

Soon there was nothing but the pounding cascade of water, muted when her body was beneath it, harder as it struck the tub when she had stepped out of the stream to wash.

That was the hardest. Imagining her rubbing a soapy washcloth, or, better yet, her bare hand, over her skin. Easing the tight muscles of her neck. Kneading the kinks out of her shoulders. He closed his eyes and pictured the slide of her hands down her body. The way her fingers would look on her throat, her breasts, her thighs. And between them.

He shuddered. Probably the only thing he could imagine being as arousing as touching her himself would be to watch Kate's hands on her own body. Giving herself pleasure, the way she said she had here, in this very bed, a few weeks back.

He groaned and pulled the pillow over his face, dying for sleep...for release. Both thoroughly eluded him.

Her long shower continued. *Hurry up, would you?* He had a feeling he was going to need to take a cold one of his own.

Jack imagined sharing one with her. It would be incredible. He'd barely gotten to taste her at the theater and his mind flooded with images of sitting beneath her in the shower. Looking up at her. Holding her hips in his hands and tilting her soft thatch of dark curls toward his hungry mouth to taste her, indulge in her, positively inhale her.

Only after he'd had his fill would he stand up, turning her to face away while he stood behind her. She'd lift one foot, resting it on the side of the tub. He could picture her hand, flat against the tile wall for support, her red-tinted nails a stark contrast to the cream-colored tiles. Her fingers would clench then widen as he stepped closer and she felt his body press against her back, his hard-on slipping between her legs.

He'd have to touch her. He'd reach his hand around, caressing her breast, then her belly. Then lower, until he could slide his fingers into her slick crevice, testing her readiness. Pleased at how wet she was for him.

She'd bend forward slightly, arching her back, turning to look over her shoulder at him with wide, passion-filled eyes that screamed "Take me now." He'd tease her, not giving in to her demands yet, taking time to kiss the tiny little bones on her spine until he heard her whimper in anticipation.

Then he'd give her what she wanted, sliding into her from behind, slowly, until he was so deep inside her they couldn't distinguish their bodies from one another.

They'd pause, the hot water pelting them as they savored the connection. They'd be inundated with the scent of the soap and her lemon shampoo. And the thick, heady smell of sex.

She'd bend lower, tempting him with the curve of her hips and her perfect rear. The visual would join with all his other senses to overwhelm him and he'd have to move. Faster. Getting caught up in her tight heat, having to bend over her, holding her hips and driving them both into oblivion.

"Stop, you idiot," he muttered with a gasp.

He almost came in her bed. It took all his concentration to grab his last bit of control to prevent his body's reaction. Calling himself an asshole, he lay there for a few moments, thinking of prostate exams, Brussels sprouts and wrinkled geriatric patients. Anything unappealing.

It wasn't easy; it didn't help his erection subside, but he managed to avoid having to make a sneaky, middle of the night sheet change as he had a few times during puberty.

Jack couldn't remember the last time he'd come so close to climaxing just from thinking about a woman. Considering

Kate was all he'd thought about for weeks, maybe it wasn't so surprising.

He still couldn't believe she was here, not only here in this house, but in Pleasantville at all. From some of the things he'd heard, Kate and the rest of her family hadn't been treated too nicely in the old days. He only hoped she wouldn't hear any of the rumors about her mother while she was in town. He knew she couldn't possibly be aware of the truth…if she were, she'd never have spoken to him once she found out who he was.

If she ever did find out, she'd hate his guts, thinking him just another snobby Winfield out to nail a trashy Tremaine.

Wrong. So wrong. He'd been fascinated by her, wildly attracted to her, dazzled by her, back when he didn't even know her name. He didn't remember another better sexual encounter in his life than the one they'd shared on the stage. Completely spontaneous, passionate, fulfilling. If her last name—or his—had been anything else, he would have spent every night since then in her bed. Guaran-damn-tee it.

And during each one of those nights, he would have worked to remove the sadness he sometimes saw in her eyes, and the anger he'd heard in her voice. Particularly tonight, next door, when her sarcasm hadn't been able to disguise her hurt.

He made it his goal, then and there, to do exactly that. But not here, not in her mother's house, in this town that sucked the soul right out of her. The only place he'd seen her truly happy, passionate and excited was at the Rialto. That was the Kate he wanted to seduce—but he had a feeling he wouldn't find her again until they returned to Chicago.

And until Jack wiped the slate clean regarding his father.

In the meantime he'd control himself, keeping his libido firmly in check. "Yeah, right," he muttered.

Just when he wondered if she was ever going to get out of the shower, he heard the water turn off. "Thank God," he muttered.

The plastic rings clinked against the metal rod as she pulled back the curtain. Then silence, for one long moment, until he heard her voice. "Jack? You awake?"

Was he awake? How could he *not* be awake when three-quarters of his blood supply was centered in his groin? It was a miracle he hadn't passed out from lack of blood flow to the brain.

"Yeah," he said. Realizing he'd spoken in a whisper, he cleared his throat. "Yeah, Kate, did you need me?"

"I don't have a towel."

No towel. Perfect.

Tempted to tell her to stay in there and drip dry—quietly—until he could get control over his raging libido, he sighed and sat up in the bed. Throwing back the sheet, which had felt cumbersome and heavy against his naked body anyway, he reached for his sweatpants. He couldn't find them.

"They're too hot, anyway," he muttered in disgust. Instead, he grabbed a pair of gray boxer briefs and tugged them on. It wasn't as if the woman hadn't seen him naked already.

They were uncomfortably tight. Too damn bad.

Walking out of the bedroom to the small linen closet out on the landing, he grabbed the top two towels on a stack and knocked on the bathroom door. "I've got two for you, just in case."

"Great. I don't have a robe, so I can wrap up in one."

Jack gritted his teeth.

"You can leave them on the counter," she continued.

Pushing the door open several inches, he reached in, intending to drop the towels and go. The shower was behind the door, no way would he see anything. He figured she was hiding in there, fully covered by the flowery plastic curtain, and certainly didn't consider trying to sneak a peek. He was already horny enough, thanks so very much. Even a glimpse at her naked body behind the curtain could have him coming in his briefs.

Jack hadn't counted on the mirror. As he dropped the towels, he glanced up and met her eyes in the reflection. The cold air from the hall had seeped in when he opened the door. Where it met the glass, the misty steam rapidly began to evaporate. She was *not* cowering behind the curtain, probably having assumed he couldn't see her from around the nearly closed door. But see her he did.

Her brown eyes widened in her creamy pale face as their stares met in the mirror. Her lips were parted, droplets of moisture falling down her cheeks toward them. She slowly licked one away. He had to clutch the doorknob for balance.

Swallowing and taking in a deep, shaky breath, he lowered his eyes, staring at the long, wet hair that hung over her shoulders. Jack couldn't have prevented his gaze from shifting even lower if someone held a gun to his head. So he looked, seeing a few strands of hair draping her breasts, though not completely covering them. Her dark, puckered nipples were easily visible. His mouth went dry as his pulse sped up.

She said nothing, didn't make a move, just watched him watch her. He kept looking, at the curve of her waist, that wet thatch of brown curls between her slim thighs.

Then his stare shifted to her hip where a purplish bruise marred the pale perfection of her skin. "What happened to you?"

She seemed to awaken from her daze. Snatching the edge of the curtain, she pulled it over herself, until only her face was visible. He wondered what she'd do if she knew he had a perfect view of one breast and puckered nipple peeking between the leaves of two roses on the plastic curtain. He thought it wise not to point it out. "Tell me."

"You can leave now."

"I mean it, Kate, what happened to your hip? You've got a horrible bruise." He clenched his fists. "Did someone hurt you?"

Obviously seeing he wasn't going to go away until she explained, she said, "You did, you big jerk. When you tackled me earlier."

"Oh, God, I'm so sorry." Pushing the door farther, he stepped inside and turned to face her. "I didn't realize I'd injured you. Let me see it."

She didn't answer. Her attention was firmly fixed low on his body. Her lips parted as she saw the erection he couldn't hide. "I think you should go." Her voice was thin and reedy.

Seeing her injury had nearly made him forget the almost painful urge between his own legs. He could only imagine what she thought. He thrust the concern away, not caring right now if she wondered what he'd been doing in her old bedroom while she'd showered. "Let me see your hip."

She shook her head, slowly, not saying anything. But she didn't resist as he gently pulled the edge of the shower curtain from her fingers and tugged it over a few inches so he could see the side of her body. She still said nothing as he dropped to his knees to examine the reddish-purple bruise on her hipbone.

The size of his palm, it must have hurt like hell. "I'm so sorry. Can I get you some ice for it?"

"No," she whispered. "I'll be fine. Thanks for the towel."

"Why didn't you say something?"

"It's not a big deal, Jack. I'm fair-skinned, I bruise easily." Her voice still sounded shaky. "I can barely feel it."

He touched the bruise with the tip of his index finger. When she winced, he yanked his finger away. "Liar."

Then, almost unable to resist, he leaned forward to place a gentle kiss on the bruise. When she moaned, he pulled back. "Did I hurt you again?"

"No. You didn't...hurt me."

He leaned forward again to gently kiss her skin. He avoided the tender bruised area. Instead he kissed her all around it, caressing her waist, her upper thigh. Unable to resist, he moved to that vulnerable hollow of flesh between her pelvic bone and the still-concealed dark thatch of curls hiding her feminine secrets. The curtain shifted slightly, as if she'd let go of it. When he glanced up, he saw her eyes closed, her head tipped back and her hand on her throat.

"Better?"

She groaned. "You're trying to kiss it and make it better?"

He nodded, his lips still brushing her skin as he inhaled her, breathing in the smell of her clean skin. And the unmistakable, musky scent of aroused woman. "Is it working?"

"I can't tell yet."

He chuckled, knowing she wanted more. He gave it to her, now kissing her more deeply, flicking his tongue over her moist body, licking the water off her hip and thigh. She shuddered and he moved his hand up to steady her. He held her leg, then higher, to cup her rear. Her scent filled his brain, drawing his mouth closer to the edge of the plastic curtain, which barely concealed her curls. He remembered the hot, sweet taste of her on his tongue, the tenderness of that beautiful pink flesh between her legs. He wanted to taste her again. Wanted to feel her, touch her, have her. He pulled her tighter against him, unable to resist the feel of her skin against his cheek, fighting a battle deep within himself.

His mind told him no even after his body had decided yes.

When she hissed, he realized he'd pressed too hard against her bruise. ''I'm sorry, you really are in pain.'' He looked up and saw her flushed face, her parted lips.

Well, she didn't look *entirely* pained. She also looked very aroused, very...*close*. Hot satisfaction at having brought her to the brink swept through him. He'd seen her this way in his dreams. Every night since the night they'd met.

Shit.

Unless he was prepared to forget all about his decision to be a decent guy and not make love to her again while they were here in Pleasantville, he needed to exit stage left. Immediately if not sooner.

He stood, trying not to notice that the curtain had moved farther to the side, completely baring one perfect breast and delicious puckered nipple. Remembering how sensitive she was there made his feet freeze and his hands clench.

''I'm going to get you some ice,'' he finally said tightly. He somehow found the strength to turn and walk out of the bathroom.

Kate watched him leave, then let out a long, shuddery breath. ''Not one of your brightest ideas, Kate Jones.''

No. Not smart. She'd come into the bathroom knowing full well there were no towels. She'd had one thing in mind. Okay, two, if she counted washing away the grime of several hours' worth of driving. Even more than cleanliness, however, she'd wanted payback. Just a tiny bit of satisfaction by way of some brief shower exhibitionism. The way Jack had walked away from her next door—after commenting on how she'd had to pleasure herself in her bed the day they'd met—had pricked her ego. Not to mention her libido.

Damned if she hadn't wanted to prick his, too.

Hence the naked-in-the-shower-without-a-towel bit. Okay, so it was sneaky, though, she really hadn't intended for him to see her reflection completely. She'd figured there would be only a foggy image to get his imagination racing and give him some sleepless hours tonight.

Once their eyes had met and she'd seen the heat in his stare, her will had fled as quickly as the steam on the mirror.

She'd certainly been repaid in full. Because, man, oh man, she'd been the one left shaking and unfulfilled. Yes, she'd brought him to his knees, literally. But looking down, seeing him with his mouth and tongue on her body, so warm, so tender, so *close* to where she'd wanted him to be—had been agony.

"I can't believe you just left," she whispered angrily as she got out of the tub, grabbed one of the towels off the counter and began drying off.

His quick departure rankled. No, she wasn't going to sleep with him, she'd already decided. Getting further involved with him would be about as stupid as sitting in a tub full of water and turning on the hair dryer.

Good analogy. He could fry her brains and she knew it.

Of course, that didn't mean she didn't want him to want her. She had to admit, if only to herself in the quiet bathroom—it bugged her that he'd walked away, that he'd been *able* to walk away. If the fit of his briefs was any indication, he had not been physically unaffected by her.

Which meant he didn't want her mentally.

"Well, doesn't this suck eggs," she muttered. The first guy she'd had sex with in two years, and it wasn't even good enough to make him want seconds, not even when she had been wet and naked right in front of him.

Frowning, she moved faster, drying her body in quick, almost rough strokes. She winced as the cotton scraped across her bruised hip. Biting her lip, she looked at it in the mirror and winced. *Okay, yes, an ice pack would be good.*

Tucking the towel around her body, sarong-style, she reached for the other one and used it to dry her hair.

"I can think of a better use for an ice pack," she muttered. If she truly wanted to feel better, she should put the damn thing between her legs to try to cool herself off where she was *really* aching.

But cold, hard ice wasn't what she wanted between her legs. She wanted hot, hard man. One big, hot, hard man.

"No way, Kate. It's a Hugh Jackman fantasy and a vibrating fingertip for you tonight," she muttered as she bent to wrap the towel around her hair.

"Vibrating fingertip?"

Still bent at the waist, she winced, hoping those weren't Jack's sexy bare feet she spied right outside the partly open doorway. Praying that hadn't been his voice and he hadn't heard her comment about needing to get herself off with an actor fantasy and a vibrator.

She squeezed her eyes shut. When she opened them, the feet were still there. And she was still bent in front of him like some kowtowing servant. He'd heard.

Kate knew she had three choices—ignore him, pretend he'd misunderstood or be bold and shameless about the whole thing. Knowing what Cassie would do—what any self-respecting Tremaine woman *should* do—she took a deep breath. *Brazen it out.*

"Yeah, a vibrating fingertip," she said, standing and twisting the towel so it would stay on her hair. Her upraised arm caused the towel wrapped around her body to loosen. As it began to slip, she caught it at the tip of her breasts, and tucked it back together. Then she risked a glance at

Jack. His chest was moving rapidly, as if he had to struggle to breathe.

She had a feeling it wasn't the lingering steam in the bathroom making him gasp.

Thank heaven.

"It's actually a clever little vibrator that slips over your finger and feels…mmm…so good." She licked her lips. "I have it right here in my purse, and can take care of myself anytime I want," she added, not knowing how she could be stupid enough to step even closer to the fire in which he could consume her. But step she did. Then even closer. "Would you like me to show it to you?" She lowered her voice. "I remember you're the kind of man who appreciates visual images."

Jack's jaw clenched and his eyes narrowed. "Sit down."

"Excuse me?"

"You heard me," he said, his voice low and thick. "Sit down, Kate."

He stepped closer. Not waiting for her to obey, he instead pushed her with the tip of his index finger until she backed up against the bathroom counter. Sliding up to sit on it, she held her breath, wondering what he would do next, wondering what she'd begun…and if she dared to finish it.

Had she gone too far? Her intention had been to taunt, to arouse, then to walk away leaving him to imagine her touching herself in another room in the house. Somehow, though, things had changed. He'd taken control of the situation.

She didn't pause to evaluate why she didn't care.

He reached for her thighs, tugging her closer to the edge of the counter. Then he gently eased her knees apart.

She shuddered. "Jack, I…"

"You don't have to take care of yourself."

Her eyes widened and her heart pounded with the primal rhythms of a tribal drum in her chest.

"I'm going to take care of you this time," he whispered.

She held her breath as he reached for her towel, tugging it open at the bottom, exposing one thigh all the way up to her hip. The other flap of the towel remained over her lap, caught almost coyly between her thighs. He made no effort to tug it free, instead trailing his fingers on her flesh in a slow, gentle caress.

Kate closed her eyes, waiting for a voice to scream in her head, telling her to stop, to not be taken in by him again. *Great sex and a whole bunch of earth-shaking orgasms won't cancel out the hurt of his disinterest later.*

Who the hell was she kidding? Right now, at this very moment, great sex and a whole bunch of orgasms would be worth just about anything, including a kidney or her first-born child.

It was only when she felt the frigidly cold water splash on her leg, and the colder ice pack connect with her aching bruise, that she realized what he'd meant by *taking care* of her.

"You're taking care of my hip."

He nodded. Only a tiny twitch of his lips told her he knew what she'd been picturing him taking care of.

Touché. Score one for Mr. Gorgeous. She almost groaned out loud. But she didn't. This game wasn't over yet. Especially because he did not simply leave the pack in her capable hands and walk out of the room. No. He stayed, holding it against her skin, still standing between her knees. His jaw remained rigid as he sucked in deep breaths, as if he were trying to control himself by sheer force of will.

She dared a quick glance down. *Those tight briefs can't lie, sweetheart.* She almost purred with satisfaction at the sight of his immense hard-on. A small spot of moisture on the gray cotton tempted her beyond belief. She wanted to touch it, taste it with her tongue. Wanted to have him explosive, hot and wet in her hand. Her mouth. Her body. *All three.*

Smiling slightly, she murmured, "Thank you for the ice."

"I really am sorry I hurt you," he rasped.

Her hip? Her heart? Her feelings? He didn't clarify. She didn't ask.

"Funny thing, ice. So cold, it's almost painful. Yet it's…pleasurable in a way. Makes me feel tingly."

"Tingly?"

"Yeah. Almost…hot. As strange as that sounds."

"Shut up, Kate, you're breaking my concentration."

She grinned. "Uh, sure. I know it takes a lot of concentration to hold an ice pack on someone. I mean, I'm sure that's why there's such a high turnover rate in the candy striper field…all that ice pack holding. Sheer torture."

His bare shoulders—so thick, broad and toned—shook as he chuckled. Darn, he'd succeeded in distracting her. The laughter hadn't changed the way she felt, though. She shifted, not feigning her discomfort on the hard surface of the small counter. She was wet and throbbing, sensitive and needy, and the countertop didn't help things. "This isn't the most comfortable place to sit. It's almost as hard as that table at the Rialto."

His eyes narrowed as he continued to stare at the ice pack, holding it steady. Now and then, though, she'd feel his fingers shift, feel him touch her, just the tip of an index finger on her hipbone. So light and fleeting at first she thought she'd imagined it. Now she ached for it.

"So, you never answered my question, Jack."

"What question?"

"About whether you want to see my little toy."

"I thought you were joking."

Reaching for her purse, she unzipped a side pouch and pulled out the small carrying case.

"You weren't kidding," he said, staring at the plastic pouch. His stare never wavered as she flicked the snap open with her thumb.

"One of the hottest sellers at Bare Essentials."

"Your store?"

Nodding, she ran her fingers along the tip of the vibrator, knowing he paid very close attention.

"You *sell* vibrators in your ladies' shop?"

She tsked. "You never did go back and find that article, did you, Jack? If you had, you'd know that Bare Essentials isn't a typical ladies store. We sell intimate items for women."

"Like that," he said, nodding toward the vibrator.

Smiling lazily. "Like this. And other things. Lots of delightful...other things."

He raised a brow. "So, you own a porn shop?"

She sniffed. "Bare Essentials does not sell pornography. We have lots of fun, sexy toys for ladies and couples. People come from other cities to shop for our lingerie, which is designed by my partner. We have a media section, with tasteful, instructional books. Plus erotic videos geared for women and couples. But nothing X-rated."

"I'm not criticizing, Kate," he said, obviously sensing her defensive reaction. "I'm fascinated. You have obviously made a big success for yourself. It's not often you see the owner of a sex shop on the cover of the Chicago *Business Journal*. You should be very proud."

Sensing he really wasn't being judgmental, and finding herself refreshed by his attitude, she relaxed slightly. "We found a niche. A clean, tasteful, brightly lit place for women and monogamous but adventurous couples—who are our biggest client base—to shop for special items. Bringing sex out of the seedy dark rooms or brown-paper-wrapped catalogs, and into the bright light of Michigan Avenue." Some demon made her add, "Complete with guest sex therapist lecturers, and the best selection of dildoes and cock rings in the state."

"Oh, so we're back to that, are we?"

"What?"

"This game of up the ante again. Trying to shock and tempt me some more."

Heat rose in her cheeks. "I don't know what you mean."

A slow smile spread across his lips. "Sure you do. The way you're running your fingers over that thing, like you don't know I'm watching, as if you don't think I'm picturing you touching yourself like that." His voice lowered. "Turning it on and moving it over every sensitive inch of your body."

Taking in a shaky breath, she pulled the vibrator out of the pouch. "Are you?"

"You know damn well I am."

She clipped it onto her middle finger.

He continued. "Just like you knew how I'd react to you naked in the shower. The forgotten towel. The vibrating finger comment."

"I really didn't know you were there when I said that," she murmured. Turning the vibrator on, she ran it across her shoulder to her collarbone, then her throat. Lower, over the curves of her breasts. Goose bumps rose on her skin. Beneath the towel, she felt her nipples grow even harder, until they scraped almost painfully against the cotton fabric.

Heat, stark and intense, flashed in Jack's eyes as he watched her. He silently dared her on, and she answered his challenge. Running the tiny device down the edge of the towel, she followed the seam down to her stomach. Lower. Until her hand rested on her lap and the vibrator kissed the inside of her thigh. Its hum was the only sound in the room, other than the faint rasp of Jack's labored breathing. And her own.

Pausing, she curled her lips into a sultry smile, warning him that she wasn't going to stop. Not unless he stopped her.

He didn't move a muscle.

Kate slid her hand beneath the towel.

"Mmm." She moaned as she scraped her fingertip across the curls between her legs.

"Enough." He dropped the ice pack and caught her wrist in his hand, clenching it tightly.

"I've barely started." She knew he could hear both the challenge and the promise in her voice.

He shook his head. "You've done what you set out to do, Kate. Hell, you did that the minute I saw you next door earlier." He let go of her wrist and took a step back. "You want me to want you. You want me crazy with wanting you."

Well, yeah!

"Mission accomplished."

He didn't try to do anything about it. He'd admitted it, but made no move to kiss her, to touch her.

"You've won. I concede. Now you need to stop."

His lips said stop. His eyes begged her to proceed. She moved her fingertip, letting her lips fall open in a pleasureful sigh as the vibrator skimmed across her throbbing clitoris. She knew he was going crazy, imagining what she was doing, but not really able to tell because of the discreet draping of the towel over her hand. "You're sure you want me...to stop?"

He closed his eyes. "Yes."

Liar. With a quick glance down, she saw that his body was still raring to go.

"The timing's bad on this, Kate," he said. "Really bad."

Obviously his mind was *not* raring to go.

"Bad timing. Right. There's a good reason for me not to give myself the orgasm I'm dying for," Kate said. "This has nothing to do with you, anyway."

"It has everything to do with me." He stepped closer, putting both his hands flat on the counter on each side of her hips. Leaning in until his face was inches from hers, he admitted, "I want to take you right here and now, fast and hard and furious, just like you're *begging* for…like it was that first night." His gaze dropped to her lips, to the towel, which had loosened again and barely clung to her body. As if he couldn't resist, his hands moved closer, until they touched her thighs. His fingers were cold from the ice pack, but it wasn't cold that made her gasp. It was the heat of his touch.

"Then I want to take you to bed, kiss away the pain on your hip, spend hours exploring your body and make love to you in ways you've never even dreamed of," he finally said, his voice ragged and full of need.

His expression told her he could, too. *So do it.*

"But not tonight, Kate. Not now." He straightened and stepped back. "Definitely not *here*."

Once she was able to think again—once her heart started beating again—she told herself it didn't matter, that she had never planned to have sex with him tonight anyway. And he was right, she couldn't imagine a worse place to have sex with Jack Winfield than in the same house where their parents had probably spent intimate time together.

She flipped off the vibrator. "Sure." After tightening the towel around her chest, she slid off the counter. "Look, maybe I wasn't playing nicely. Maybe I was being unfair, trying to pay you back a little for not calling."

"I figured as much. And I'm sorry."

He didn't try to explain. Made no effort to tell her what

had happened, what had changed between that night in the theater and two days later when he *hadn't* called her.

She couldn't ask him, of course. She instead relied on false bravado. "It really doesn't matter. I got what I wanted. A little payback." She glanced down at his body, making them both fully aware of his need for her. Then she smiled seductively.

"You go back to bed. Alone." Stepping closer to walk around him and out the door, she continued. "While I go back to bed, too. With the mental image of a shirtless Hugh Jackman." Holding up her hand, she glanced at the vibrator.

"And this."

7

JACK SLEPT LATE the next morning. That wasn't a big surprise since he'd lain awake in her bed until at least 5:00 a.m., wondering what she was doing. If she was touching herself. If she ached, the way he did. He'd listened for hours, torturing himself, waiting to see if she'd cry out when she came, as she had the night in the theater.

He wasn't sure if he ever heard her cry out, or if he just imagined the cries of ecstasy throughout the long night hours.

Enough of that.

Rising, he pulled on some jeans, then walked down the short hallway to the master bedroom. Though the door was partially open, he knocked quietly in case she was still asleep. When there was no answer, he glanced in and saw the stripped bed.

Kate hadn't slept in her mother's old room.

Curious, he went downstairs and saw the pile of folded linens and a pillow on the living room sofa. Hearing a voice through the thin wall, he stepped out onto the patio and walked over to the open door of the adjoining duplex.

Kate was inside, talking on a cell phone, sounding more than a little irritated. "Look, the power was supposed to be turned on yesterday. I have my confirmation numbers, you already charged my credit card, so why am I sitting in the dark, sweaty, and unable to take a shower this morning?"

He couldn't imagine how she could be dirty after the

endless shower she'd taken the night before. She looked fresh and chipper, dressed in tight jean shorts and another of those flimsy, sleeveless tank tops. Red and wicked, it hugged her curves and made his heart skip a beat. There'd obviously been no sleepless night for her. She'd probably slept like a baby with her play toy clipped to her finger, her hand curled in her lap.

"Yes, I know it's a Saturday," she continued. "But please try to get someone out here this morning."

Jack would be willing to pay any after-hour fees the company might charge if it meant getting her into her own place by that night. No way could he take another night like the previous one.

"Problems?"

She almost dropped the phone when she heard his voice. "Hi. Yes, problems. The power company's as efficient as ever around here. They lost the work order to get the electricity back on for me before yesterday."

Without waiting for an invitation, he entered the living room of the small house. It was a mirror image of the one next door, though held not a stick of furniture. "You never did tell me why you're here, anyway. I had the impression visiting Pleasantville isn't your favorite thing to do."

"I suppose it's better than being buried up to my neck in a red ant nest," she muttered.

He chuckled. "So why're you here?"

"Business."

Interesting, given her line of work. "*Your* kind of business?"

"The private kind."

"Okay," he said with a shrug. "Is this business going to keep you in town long?"

"A few weeks at least."

Weeks. Damn. He'd really hoped she was making a quick

trip. If she stayed, he'd be in for lots of long, sleepless nights. Even worse, it would be nearly impossible for her to avoid hearing the gossip about Edie and his father.

Jack suddenly found himself willing to do just about anything to prevent that. As sorry as he felt for Edie, he knew she'd made her choices. She'd dealt with them in her own way.

Kate hadn't chosen to be the target of gossip, scorn and spite from this town. Yet that was about all she'd gotten here as a kid. And, he feared, about all she'd find here now.

If his sister Angela's comments were anything to go on, Kate and her cousin hadn't had the best time in high school. Kate hadn't let that stop her in the least. She'd gotten out, made a life for herself, created a new world where she had the power, the money and the upper hand.

Much as he had done.

No wonder he liked her so much. After all, in spite of their dissimilar childhoods, they had a lot in common. Hadn't they each been put into a mold by this town, and done whatever they could to break out of it? They'd both left after high school—her opening a sex shop and him focusing on career and casual relationships with a lot of different women. And they'd both come back, still wanting to rebel and shock, until they'd found each other and fallen headfirst into a hot kiss on a public street. Not to mention what had happened in the theater.

"Do you want something to eat?" he finally asked, figuring she couldn't possibly have any groceries in the house.

"I already had a donut and a warm diet Coke, thanks."

"How nutritious."

"It's not exactly the breakfast of champions, but it will do."

Glancing toward the floor, she bent to get something out of her purse. Jack tried not to notice the way her shorts hugged her ass, the way they rode up on her thighs until he could see the hem of her panties.

Well, no, he didn't really try not to look. He just tried not to let it affect him. Which was impossible.

After grabbing a brush, she straightened and gathered her hair into a ponytail at the back of her neck. Her shirt pulled tighter against her curves as she lifted her arms. Jack again wished he'd stayed in bed, avoiding her for the day.

"Did you sleep okay? I noticed you stayed downstairs on the couch. You could have used your mom's room."

She looked away, busying her hands putting the brush back into her purse. "The couch was fine."

"Sure there was enough room for all three of you?"

"Three of us?"

"You know. You, Hugh and your little friend?" he asked, wondering what demon made him bring the subject back to what had happened last night when they'd parted.

She laughed softly.

"So what is it with Hugh Jackman? A mouth, like Connery? Dangerous glint in his eye, like Eastwood? Or that schmaltzy chick-flick-time-travel with him and Meg Ryan?"

She shook her head, licking her lips. "Wolverine in *X-Men.* I just love a lean-looking man who can kick ass." She shrugged, obviously being honest and not trying to torment him sexually as she had the night before. "What can I say? I like men who can move their bodies gracefully while being seriously dangerous."

If he were going to pursue a sexual relationship with her—which he absolutely was *not,* not *yet* anyway—he'd have contemplated inviting her to one of his Tae Kwon Do classes, which he taught three nights a week. Instead he changed the subject. "So, are you planning to sleep on the floor for weeks?"

She glanced around the empty room. "Some of my aunt's old furniture is stored in the garage of her new place. My cousin, Cassie, is going to help me load some up and bring it here."

"Cousin? Your cousin's back in town, too?"

She shot him a look from half-lowered lashes. "She's been here in town for several weeks already. Do you know her?"

He shook his head. "No, I don't remember her at all. But I know the two of you lived here, in these houses. Is she going to stay here with you?"

"No. Her mom owns some other property around here. Cassie's staying at Aunt Flo's other place up on Lilac Hill."

Jack raised a questioning brow.

"Aunt Flo had a lot of admirers in this town. Male admirers. A couple of them liked to give her presents."

He understood. "Someone *gave* her a house on Lilac Hill?" At her nod, he whistled. "Some present. Who was it?"

"Mr. Miller, the banker."

A grin tickled the corners of Jack's lips. "He was old as dirt when I was born."

"Flo's not age discriminatory."

"He was a widower with no family for as long as I can remember." Jack thought about it. "I'm glad your aunt gave him a little bit of happiness. He was a nice old guy. You know he lived only two doors down from us."

Her chuckle was decidedly wicked. "There goes the neighborhood."

Knowing how his mother and sister felt about the Tremaine family, he had to wonder why he hadn't heard anything about this latest insult upon the glory that was Winfield.

"So, Cassie stays on the hill and you're staying here."

"Right. Is there a problem?"

"I'm wondering why you're not staying there with her."

"Let's just say the snob set's not exactly my cup of tea."

"But they are your cousin's?"

Kate shrugged. "Cassie fits in anywhere. She's very successful. You'll probably recognize her when you see her."

"Why?"

"She's a lingerie model. Poses in sexy underclothes for catalogs that pretend they're for women, but which men swipe from their wives and hide in the bathroom to look at."

He shrugged. "And you're a super successful store owner who makes front-page news. Sounds like both of you got away from here and made good." He glanced around the room. "I'm sure you have more expensive tastes these days, too."

"This is fine for me." She raised a hand, gesturing to the small room. "Part of Cassie's reason for staying up there was out of her innate need to be as outrageous as possible."

"I somehow think your cousin hasn't cornered the market on being outrageous in your family."

Rolling her eyes, she sat on the floor, draping her arms on her upraised knees. "No, I'm the smart, quiet, *sweet* one." She sounded thoroughly disgusted.

He couldn't help it—he let out a loud bark of laughter. Her glare told him she didn't appreciate his amusement.

"Honey, I can think of a lot of words to describe you, but something as insipid as sweet definitely isn't on the list."

She frowned at him. "You're saying I'm not sweet?"

"No, you're definitely not sweet, Kate." Stepping across the room, he bent to sit directly in front of her. "Smart, yes. Quiet—well, only in the way that smart people are because they're always thinking. Deciding their course of action before they act on it. Like you did at the theater.''

Her jaw tightened. "Get back to the part where you tell me why I'm not a nice person.''

He wagged an index finger at her. "Uh-uh, I didn't say you're not a nice person. You're a fascinating, charming, *nice* woman, Kate. But not anything as simple as sweet. There are such depths to you…." He stared intently at her face, losing himself again in those dark brown eyes, wondering what was going on in that beautiful mind of hers. "I'd like to know what makes you tick,'' he admitted softly.

Color rose in her cheeks and her lips parted. He'd gone too far, treaded back into personal, intimate territory. He backpedaled. "So, tell me, why do you think you're sweet and quiet?''

"Because my family has told me I am for twenty-eight years.'' She blew out a frustrated breath. "Cassie was the wild, tempestuous child. I was the sweet, good girl. The little ballerina, the straight-A student.''

"I imagine you got quite a reaction with your store.''

"My mother left during the grand opening reception. Never came back again until after I started sending her copies of my bank statements.'' She paused. "Of course, my aunt Flo sent a huge bouquet of orchids and told me she never thought I had a wicked streak in me. I guess they thought Cassie and I were destined to be exact replicas of them. They expected it even before we were ever born.''

Knowing how difficult it was to break out of the position in which every family tried to paint its members, he nodded in agreement. "I would be willing to bet Cassie is not nearly as wild as she's said to be.'' He leaned closer to her. "And I know you're not exactly a good girl.''

"Really?'' She looked at him so hopefully he almost laughed. He didn't, though, not wanting to hurt her feelings.

"No, I don't think good girls own sex shops or carry tiny vibrators around in their purses. Nor do they often go for it when offered the chance to do something as wildly impulsive as what we did at the theater."

He waited for her to look away, to break the stare, but she didn't. Her eyes looked softer, dreamier, as her lips parted. A tiny sigh preceded her reply. "Thank you."

"For?"

"For seeing the Kate I see...not the one everyone else sees. For letting me be myself, not who everyone thinks I am." She paused. "Even if who I am is sometimes a not-so-nice, not-so-sweet person."

Jack leaned close and pressed a kiss to her temple, then brushed her hair away. He saw her pulse ticking in her throat as she looked up at him. "Sweet is boring, Kate," he whispered. "I much prefer spicy...even if I know I'm going to get burned."

Her moist lips parted and she tilted her head back as she took in a deep breath. He'd never seen a more clear invitation to go further. Kissing her temple wasn't enough for either of them. He had to taste her, just once more, or else he'd go crazy wondering if her mouth was as soft as he remembered. He leaned closer, brushing his lips across her temple again, then her cheek, and her jaw. She sighed, but didn't pull away.

"I take it back, Kate," he murmured as he moved lower, to kiss her earlobe and the side of her neck. "You taste very sweet." Then, unable to resist, he moved his mouth to hers. Their lips met and parted as instinctively as the beating of a heart. He licked lazily at her tongue, dipping his own into her mouth to taste her more thoroughly. She kissed him back, curling against him, tilting her head, inviting him deeper.

When they finally pulled apart, neither spoke for a moment. Then she narrowed her eyes. "Don't you do that again."

Her shaky voice held a warning and a challenge. He wondered if, as usual, she was trying to scare him into backing off. He mentally tsked. Obviously she didn't remember what had happened when she'd tried that at the Rialto.

Finally, Jack smiled. "Yeah, there's definitely both sweet and spicy to you, Kate Jones. I can't decide which side I like better."

Before she could reply, he got up and left the duplex.

WHEN KATE ARRIVED at Cassie's house up on the hill that afternoon, her cousin greeted her with a big hug and a humongous margarita. "A pea-green drink in honor of your return to Pea-Ville." Cassie held up her salt-rimmed glass to clink a toast.

Kate clinked back, then sipped deeply. The electric company still hadn't gotten her power on by the time she'd left the house, and the drink went down like a powerful blast of air-conditioning. Besides, she'd been all hot and bothered ever since Jack had kissed her then walked out. "Ah, perfect. I'd forgotten how hot it is here in the pits of hell in the summer."

"I guess I'm getting used to it."

Hearing an unexpected note of warmth in Cassie's voice, Kate raised a brow. "The heat? Or the town?"

Cassie shrugged. "Maybe a little of both."

"Well, I can see you don't have a scarlet letter on your shirt, so maybe things aren't as bad as I'd expected."

"Believe it or not, I haven't heard one person call me a tramp since I got here." She winked. "At least not to my face."

Her cousin led Kate into the house, then gave her a quick

tour, including a stop in Flo's outrageously decorated boudoir.

Going back downstairs, they sat in the kitchen, drinking their margaritas and gabbing for an hour. Kate didn't like the tired, dark circles under Cassie's eyes—though, they certainly didn't distract from her beauty. Since Cassie never brought up the trouble she was in, trouble that involved an over-amorous man who hadn't taken her rejection too well, Kate didn't, either. There would be time enough to talk about it, and to give Cassie her mail, which had been forwarded to Kate in Chicago while Cassie hid out. Kate wanted to put off handing over the dozen or more letters. "So the store's really coming along okay?"

"Absolutely. I've got a couple of high school boys who've helped with the painting and repairs. The shelving units and cabinetry were already there from when the men's shop was open. Carpet goes in Monday, and the stock you sent arrives daily."

"Well, I'm here now to help with the inventory, at least, now that you did the hard stuff. The permit was approved, right? I still don't know how you pulled it off."

Cassie gave her an evil smile. "It's called boobs. A low-cut shirt and a pair of breasts leaning on the desk of a city worker's office can accomplish a lot. Including rubber-stamping an application for a business license."

"Boobs and brains. Cassie Tremaine Montgomery, you're a force to be reckoned with." Kate sipped her drink.

"It's only fair I got the bigger boobs, since you got the bigger brain," Cassie pointed out.

Kate sighed. "But we both got the big hips."

Cassie gave her a Cheshire-cat smile. "Most men who look at my pictures in the catalog like curvy hips."

Kate agreed. "I'll bet the permit guy is a fan."

"Even if he's not, I didn't lie on the business app. We *are* going to open a lovely, tasteful little ladies' shop...."

"With King Kong Dong featured prominently in the front display window," Kate interjected with a snorty laugh.

They clinked their glasses again.

Cassie got up to make them a couple of sandwiches for lunch. "Speaking of King Kong Dong, or dongs in general, have you met your new neighbor yet?"

Kate didn't answer right away, drawing a curious stare from Cassie. In spite of how close they were, Kate hadn't told Cassie about her interlude with Jack at the Rialto. So she couldn't exactly explain what had happened the night before when she'd discovered he was really J. J. Winfield. "We've met."

"And?"

Kate got up to wash lettuce for the sandwiches.

"Come on, what gives? Aren't you going to make him your love slave, then trample all over his heart with the heels of your six-inch-high, slut-puppy boots?"

"I don't own slut-puppy boots."

"You sell them."

"I sell a lot of things that I don't own or use myself," she said as she sipped.

"Aw, gee. Here I figured you gave a personal testimonial with every dildo, clit ring and butt plug you peddle."

Kate laughed so hard some of her margarita spilled from the corner of her lips. "You are as bad as Armand."

"So tell me about the Winfield prince," Cassie said.

"I don't know about Jack—J.J. He's not what I expected."

"Meaning?"

"Meaning he might be more than I can handle."

Cassie lifted a brow. There probably wasn't a man alive who her cousin couldn't handle. But Kate wasn't Cassie.

"Maybe I'd better start out a little easier. Focus on some of my other goals. Like the shop. Or Angela and Darren."

"Hmm, yeah, I forgot about them. I saw Angela one day, walking out to her car. She and her mom live up the street."

"Please tell me she's fat."

"Sorry, hon. She looks pretty good. Still looks like a total bitch, but not a Jenny Craig-bound one."

Rats.

"What about Darren?"

"Works at a car dealership and lives downtown in an apartment over the Tea Room. Did you know he and Angela were married for a while right after high school? The rumor mill says she got knocked up on prom night. They married that summer. Then when she lost the baby, he divorced her and went into the army."

Kate winced. "Maybe I should thank her for stealing him on prom night." She couldn't imagine how her life might have ended up if she'd been the pregnant teen. Probably she'd be living here, bitter and sour with a poochy belly, saggy breasts and four kids who looked like moon-faced Darren clinging to her skirts.

Kate met Cassie's eye, knowing she was thinking along the same lines. They exchanged shaky smiles. "Here's to what *didn't* happen to us on prom night," Kate said softly.

Cassie nodded. "Hear, hear."

JACK LUCKED OUT and arrived at his mother's house after she'd left for her Saturday hair appointment. Closing himself in his father's office—to the chagrin of Leonardo the bulldog—he spent two hours balancing bank statements, sorting out documents. He heard his sister Angela moving around, once stopping to have a long phone conversation in the next room.

He didn't get his sister. Angela was pretty and had been

given every advantage. She'd been the apple of their parents' eye, and had once had a genuine sweetness to her personality. Sure, she was spoiled. She'd shown signs of that, even as a toddler. But at least before, when she'd been a kid, she'd had an infectious laugh and a beautiful smile. In the fifteen years he'd been gone, she'd lost them both. Probably three failed marriages and two miscarriages could do that to a person.

Resolving to get along better with her, he forced a look of welcome to his face when she walked into the office. "Hi."

"You busy?"

He nodded and rubbed his weary eyes. "Dad left a mess."

Her laugh could only be described as bitter. "Yeah. As usual." She sat on a chair next to the window. "I don't suppose you've changed your mind and plan to stay here."

He shook his head. "I'm sorry, Ang. I don't know how you can stand it. I can't breathe in this place."

"Even after he died Dad still managed to drive you away."

Jack pushed his chair back. "What are you talking about?"

"I mean, you took off fifteen years ago because of him. Because of how he pressured you to follow in his footsteps."

"Most fathers do."

Angela continued as if he hadn't spoken. "And as soon as it looks like you're going to come back, you find out about his dirty little secret and won't stay here now, either."

Jack shook his head. "It's more complicated than that. How did you find out about Dad and Edie, anyway?"

She glanced out the window. "I saw them kissing once. Not long after you'd gone away to college."

She'd been thirteen. He swallowed, hard. "What'd you do?"

"Nothing. I didn't confront him, or tell Mother, or anybody else. I was afraid if she found out, they'd get a divorce and I'd be shuffled back and forth between them forever."

A wave of guilt washed over him as he acknowledged he'd left her here without an ally in his hurry to escape from home. "I'm sorry, Angela. But maybe now it's time to move on. Have you thought about getting out of here, too?"

"I've been dying to move out, get my own place downtown, but Mother plays the guilt card whenever I mention it."

"I meant, maybe it's time to get out of Pleasantville."

"I can't. I don't want to leave him...I mean, leave here."

Him? He didn't think Angela was seeing anyone, though she'd been divorced from her third husband for over a year.

She stood abruptly. "I have to go. I have a nail appointment. Be sure to lock up when you leave, okay? Mother doesn't trust Sophie to secure the house." Her jaw clenched. "After all, she's not nearly as trustworthy as *Edie* was."

Judging by the way she spat out the other woman's name, Jack surmised his sister had not been able to forgive and forget.

As Angela left the room his parents' ever-hopeful dog, Leonardo, slunk in and strolled over to the desk. At Leonardo's longing glance at his jeans-clad leg, Jack shot him a suspicious glare. "Dog, how many years is it gonna take for you to figure out you've got no balls?"

Leonardo gave him a sheepish glance from his wrinkled face. Walking around in circles once or twice, he appeared to be looking for something—or someone. He finally curled up at Jack's feet and looked up at him with sad eyes.

"Okay," Jack said with a sigh. "I guess you miss him, too."

A half hour later he straightened up to leave, determined to get out before his mother got back. After making sure the mutt had enough water, he locked up and headed for his father's pickup truck, which he'd been driving during his stay.

As he drove down the street, he glanced toward old Mr. Miller's house and saw a shapely brunette in a red tank top trying to drag a big mattress across the driveway.

He immediately stopped the truck. "Kate, are you trying to break your back? Put that down."

She dropped the end of the mattress and frowned at him. "You distracted me. Do you know how long it took to tug that thing out of the garage?"

He trotted across the driveway to her side. "I thought your cousin was going to help you."

"She is. She's had a bunch of phone calls to deal with. Problems with her agent."

"And Miss Have-To-Do-It-Now can't wait for her?"

"I'm not helpless. I've gotten a bunch of other stuff by myself." She gestured toward her SUV, which already held a couple of chairs. And, judging by the upraised legs that nearly reached the interior roof, a small kitchen table.

He couldn't believe she'd done it all alone. "I suppose you plan to unload all this stuff without help when you get back home, too?"

She scuffed the toe of her sneaker on the driveway and mumbled, "Well, I kinda figured you'd be back sooner or later."

"Back to help you unload it, or to make you another ice pack and take care of you again after you slip a disc?"

Wrong thing to say. They both instantly remembered how he'd taken care of her the night before. Awareness hummed between them, as always, now not below the surface, but right out in the open again.

She bit the corner of her lip. "Look," she finally said, "I'm almost done, are you going to help me or criticize me?"

He glanced at the open hatch and the mattress. "Honey, I hate to tell you this, but you've got a size problem here. I don't think something this big is going to fit in there."

"You sound like a conceited teenage boy about to get laid for the first time."

Not recognizing the sultry voice of the woman who'd spoken, he turned and saw a shapely blonde standing just behind them on the driveway. She had her head cocked to the side and her hand on one hip, smiling wickedly. With her eye-popping build, sunny-blond hair and outrageous words, he immediately assumed she was the cousin.

Frowning, he ignored her comment. "I hope your call was important, since your cousin nearly gave herself a hernia out here."

The blonde's brow shot up. She immediately turned to Kate. "Katey, I told you to wait for me. Good grief, how'd you carry all that stuff by yourself?"

Kate didn't answer. She was too busy looking back and forth between Jack and Cassie, a confused frown scrunching her brow.

Jack grabbed the end of the mattress. "Let me throw this in the truck and take it for you, Kate. I'm going home anyway."

"Home?" the blonde—Cassie—asked. Then understanding crossed her face. "Oh, my, you're J. J. Winfield, aren't you?"

He swallowed a groan. "Jack. Jack Winfield."

The blonde didn't reply, just looked him over, head to toe, very intently. Smiling, she extended her hand. "Hi, Jack. I'm Cassie. The truck's a great idea. Can you take a few other things, too?"

"Sure," he said, still wondering why Kate looked so befuddled and hadn't said a single word since her cousin had come out of the house. "Is that all right with you, Kate?"

After she nodded, he hoisted the queen-size mattress up with both hands. He saw Cassie's eyes widen as she stared at his arms, chest and shoulders. As he walked away, he heard her whisper, "Too much to handle, indeed. But oh, Kate, wouldn't you have fun trying?"

They loaded up his truck with the few remaining pieces of furniture and were finished within a half hour of his arrival. Cassie disappeared into the house again, after thanking Jack once more for his help.

"Are you heading back now? Or do you want me to drive this stuff back, then wait for you to get there to unload it?"

"Let me say goodbye to Cassie and I'll come back so we can unload it this afternoon." She turned to go into the house, then paused. "Jack? Thanks a lot for stopping to help. I really do appreciate it."

He shrugged. "Just being neighborly."

She glanced up and down the block, at the manicured lawns, the gated driveways that were filled with expensive cars. "Yeah. Right. I'm sure there were bunches of other neighbors lacing up their deck shoes to come out and help when you stopped. I bet they're still peering out their windows, waiting for the chance to lend a hand."

He followed her stare, figuring she was probably right, but not admitting it. "It's not all bad here."

"I guess Cassie likes it. But I wouldn't be able to stand the quiet sense of knowing everyone on the block is watching every move you make." She brushed an errant, damp strand of hair off her brow. "It'd be like living in a goldfish bowl, some big fat cat always waiting to pounce on you if you leap out of the safe waters where you belong."

"Yeah, that's exactly what it was like growing up."

Their eyes met. She looked surprised that he agreed.

As for Jack, he thought it remarkable how quickly Kate had nailed what his childhood had been like on this block. In this town.

"Can I venture a guess that living on Pansy Lane was something like a fishbowl, too?"

Her slow nod was his only answer.

He reached out to brush away the blowing strand of hair again. His fingers connected with her temple, sending heat through his body. Heat that had absolutely nothing to do with the blazing sunshine overhead.

"Then I guess it's a good thing we both like to live a little dangerously."

WHEN THEY GOT BACK to the duplex, Kate first went inside to check the power, then leaned out to give him a thumbs-up. "Yes! Houston, we have ignition."

"Good, now you can take a shower in your own bathroom tonight," he muttered.

They unloaded the truck, making several trips.

"So," she asked as they carried some chairs into the kitchen. "Did you get a lot done at your mother's house today?"

She seemed to be making an effort to be polite, social and absolutely impersonal. He followed her lead. "Barely made a dent. My father had accounts all over the state, with at least a dozen banks. He owned property I didn't know about, held mortgages my *mother* didn't even know about. I haven't even gotten to the stuff in a file marked Private that I found in his desk drawer."

"Well, if you need any help, I do have some accounting background." At his look of surprise, she hurried on. "What? I mean, I do owe you one for helping me today."

"I'll keep that in mind," he said with a smile. "Though, maybe I'll choose the way you repay me."

They left the queen-size mattress for last. It would be the trickiest, since it had to go up the narrow staircase to the bedroom. "Hope you sleep really well to make it worth lugging this thing all over town," he said as they hoisted the thing through the doorway. They dropped it right on the floor as Kate hadn't bothered with a bed frame.

"At least it's not a twin," she said with a smile, obviously referring to the way he spent his own nights. "Nice and roomy."

He frowned. "You're not planning on sharing it, are you?"

"Huh?" She looked truly puzzled and he felt like an idiot for his instant of jealousy. "Wait a second." She pointed an index finger at him. "You want to know if another man is going to be staying over here occasionally."

He crossed his arms, not saying anything. She chuckled. "Uh, I don't think so, Jack. In spite of what you might think, given the way I acted on the day we met, I'm not a bed hopper." She paused. "I don't think I could even be called a bed crawler, these days."

Good.

"Not that it's any of your business."

"No, of course not." *Damn right it was his business.*

"If I did choose to bring someone here, you'd have absolutely no say in the matter," she continued, almost challenging him to deny it.

He stepped closer, tipping her chin up with his index finger until she met his eye. "I wouldn't say a word." Her lashes lowered as she tried to look down. "I can promise I wouldn't say anything to him as I threw him out the window, Kate."

She bit her lip, looking both confused and a little bit

pleased. Unable to resist, he bent to kiss her mouth. Lightly. Playfully.

"What was that for?" She brought her shaking fingers to her mouth when he ended the kiss and stepped away.

"Just to remind you."

"Remind me of what?"

He walked toward the door, but glanced over his shoulder.

"That I'm the only man you want."

8

_____

KATE DECIDED to spend her first few days in Pleasantville devoting all her thoughts to the new store. And none to her love life, such as it was. That didn't count her dreams, of course, over which she had no control.

Jack starred in them every night, damn it.

On Saturday night, after Jack had helped her unload some furniture at the duplex and given her the playful kiss that had left her reeling, she went downtown to see the shop for the first time. Cassie and her high school helpers had done a great job. Sure, there were some lighting problems, but the old dressing room area was perfect, with lots of mirrors so customers could get addicted to Armand's luxurious lingerie. And the store had adequate air-conditioning and plenty of display shelves, with discreet alcoves for some of their more risqué items. If this store were in some other town, she could envision it thriving.

Kate and Cassie enjoyed eating pizza, listening to loud music, drinking wine and examining sex toys until late Saturday night. At least until the sheriff, Sean Taggart, showed up.

As soon as Kate saw him, she understood why Cassie got such a strange look on her face whenever his name came up. The man was pure, rugged manna from tough-guy heaven. Maybe not movie-star gorgeous, like Jack, but with his lean body, thick brown hair and dangerous smile, she could see why Cassie might find him distracting. So distracting that Kate immediately decided to leave the two of them alone. After all, it wasn't often she saw her cousin nearly blushing around a man.

It also wasn't every day she came across a man who did not turn into a tongue-tied, drooling idiot around her cousin. Jack hadn't. On Saturday, when Cassie had been at her Cassie-est, all blond, leggy and saucy, he'd barely glanced in her direction.

She hadn't known whether to kiss him or to take his pulse to see if he was still alive and breathing. In any case, she could almost love him for it. "Love him?" Insane. She barely liked him.

Well, she conceded, that was a big lie. She did like him, she'd liked him from the minute they met, in spite of who his father had been. He was charming and sexy, playful and self-confident. She liked that he didn't swagger, and he felt no need to play tough guy. He was a flirt, a man who liked women. Right now he liked her, she knew it, in spite of his failure to call. She could see the heat in his eyes when he looked at her. He wanted her every bit as much as he had their first day. But something was holding him back.

If his last name were different, and if he'd come up with a reasonable excuse for not calling her, she might have tried to find out what was stopping him. And maybe she would have tried to change his mind.

The realization floored her. How strange that for the first time in nearly forever, she'd found someone who tempted her to let him get closer. She could conceive of lowering some of her guard, taking a chance on what could be a fabulously erotic, exciting relationship. But he'd erected barriers even taller than her own.

She supposed it was just as well there were insurmountable walls between them right up front. Jack obviously liked to play. A lot. He wasn't the stick-around type and she knew it. While Kate believed if there ever did come a time when she found that one right guy—her true love—she'd be a goner for life.

Much like her mother had been, unfortunately.

Over the next couple of days Kate refrained from pumping Cassie about her problems—either her old ones, or her new one, in the form of the hunky sheriff. Somehow, while they priced, ordered and set up displays, she found herself getting excited as she had before the opening of her shop in Chicago.

Knock it off, this isn't the same thing at all!

Nope, it definitely wasn't. In Chicago, she'd wanted her shop to be a wild success. Here, she fully expected it to be a grand failure. But at least they'd have fun failing, doing it publicly, right on the main street of Pleasantville. And, as they failed, she'd be right here in case Cassie needed her. She knew her cousin too well…if Kate had stayed in Chicago, Cassie would never have come to her if things got bad. Here, she couldn't very well avoid it!

She managed to avoid Jack for the most part—not an easy feat considering their close living quarters. But he was usually gone during the day, and so was she. That suited her fine.

Nights were tougher. They slept mere inches apart, separated only by the width of one slim, interior wall. There were times when she thought she heard his hand brush the wall behind her head, when he'd roll over in her old bed next door. She knew from childhood experience that at times she and Cassie had heard each other's late-night bad dream cries.

On Wednesday morning she stepped outside on the porch as soon as she got up, glad for the fresh early-morning air. Down the block, a mother rode a bicycle, with a toddler in the child seat. The woman waved as she rode by.

A nice, peaceful morning. She didn't remember those from when she'd lived here, though, she supposed there must have been some. At least for Edie. Otherwise, why would her mother have ever come back here when Kate's dad died?

Hearing sounds coming from next door, she stepped closer and peered into the front window of her mother's duplex. She wished she hadn't. Jack stood in his living room, bare-chested, wearing only a pair of loose white pants. He was stretching, moving his body with fluidity and grace. And power. It took a second for her muddled brain to realize that he was running through some type of karate moves.

He had no idea she was there. So she watched for several minutes. The sweat gleamed on his bare chest and thick arms as he swung and kicked and arched. He moved his body like a sleek animal, a finely tuned—but dangerous—machine.

Walk away before he sees you. She couldn't, though. She couldn't turn and walk into her house. *Just one more moment of watching....* One moment stretched into five or ten minutes until finally, inevitably, he glanced up and saw her there.

He immediately stopped. They stared at each other through the glass for a minute, then Jack lifted his hand and pointed toward her with his index finger, wagging it back and forth like a parent to a kid who'd done something naughty.

Act innocent. She gave him a "Who me?" shrug.

He crossed his arms and raised his brow, waiting for her to admit she'd been spying on him.

"Oh, all right," she muttered. As she entered the front door she immediately launched into an explanation. "I didn't mean to watch you working out. I just stepped out for some fresh air, and couldn't help noticing.''

"Uh-huh," he said as he began to stretch his arms out, slowly rolling his shoulders as if cooling down from his workout.

"I mean, the curtains were open. I just caught a glimpse.''

"Right."

His one-word answers did nothing to hide his amusement.

"Really, Jack, I do respect your privacy.''

He finally stopped moving all those yummy muscles long enough to meet her eye. "Kate, you've been standing there for almost ten minutes.''

She fisted her hands and put them on her hips. "You saw me?''

"No," he admitted. Then he grinned. "But I heard your front door open, and that board on the front porch really creaks.''

She was surprised he'd been able to hear anything except his own churning pulse as he'd flexed and stretched all those lovely, hard muscles. She forced herself to look away, wondering if she'd been drooling while she'd watched from the window. She surreptitiously lifted her fingers to her chin to check.

"So, uh, were you doing some kind of karate?" she finally asked, wanting to fill the charged silence. "I've thought about taking some self-defense courses.''

"Tae Kwon Do. If you're serious, I teach at a studio in Chicago. I can give you the address.''

That implied they'd see one another after they left Pleasantville, something Kate hadn't really allowed herself to consider. "Well, I don't know…..''

"If you don't feel comfortable in a class," he said with

a cajoling smile, "I'd be happy to work with you one on one."

Work with her. One on one. *How about one you on one me?*

She gulped. "I'd better go."

He grabbed a white towel and draped it over his shoulders. "Don't go. I'll make you some breakfast. I can't promise gourmet food like diet Coke and donuts, but I can do a decent omelet."

Considering she hadn't bothered to do a grocery shopping trip, and had been living off fast food and 7-Eleven burritos for the past few days, Kate's stomach overruled her brain. "Great."

"Lemme change."

You don't have to on my account!

While he was upstairs, Kate went into the kitchen, glad to see Jack was keeping the place spotless, just as it had been when her mother had lived here. Kate, unfortunately, was more the slob type. And the world's greatest chef—or even a competent one—she was not. She did, however, know how to crack an egg and was hard at it when he returned, dressed in jeans and a T-shirt.

"So tell me why you want to take self-defense courses," he said as he began making their breakfast.

"I dunno, I live in a big city and run a rather infamous store. I got a few wacky phone calls after that article."

Jack's shoulders stiffened. "Did anyone threaten you?"

"Oh, no. I just got asked on some unusual dates—to strip clubs, S and M hangouts and the Circus."

"Circus sounds pretty normal."

"I thought so, too, at first. Turns out there's a sex show called the Circus where the animals are all people in costume who offer *rides* to members of the audience."

"I think I'd rather not have known that," he said with a groan as he diced some ham for the omelets.

"Me, too." She made herself at home, finding his coffee supply and filling the coffeepot. "I guess some people heard about my shop and instantly thought the worst of me."

He put the knife down to study her. "You've had to deal with that before, haven't you?"

She knew he meant here, in Pleasantville. "Ancient history."

"So how does it measure up now? How has the town treated you these first few days?"

So far, she had to admit, things had been okay. Then again, she hadn't been out too much, staying mostly at home, at Cassie's place or at the store. "Fine, actually. How about you? Has the red carpet been rolled out for the return of the prodigal son?"

"I'm keeping a low profile, though one of my father's friends asked me to move back and run for mayor next year."

"Will you?" She held her breath waiting for his answer.

"Not on your *life*."

She nearly sighed in relief. *Why would it matter to you if he came back here, married the local big-haired town princess and stayed forever?* She didn't know why, she only knew it *would* matter.

Somehow, even though she'd told herself nothing was going to happen between them, Kate couldn't imagine being in Chicago, knowing Jack wasn't there somewhere, in that big bustling city, stopping traffic on the street with his smile and teaching his Tae Kwon Do classes. Tackling intruders and doing fix-it work on a needy woman's house.

Their eyes met, and somehow Kate knew Jack had read her thoughts. He knew she liked him, and she felt drawn to him.

Kate's eyes widened as Jack stepped close, until she was backed up against the kitchen counter, and he pressed almost neck to toe against her body. "I'm looking forward to a lot of things changing when I get back to Chicago, Kate." He lifted a hand to her face, softly caressing her cheekbone, then touching a strand of her hair. "Changing for both of us."

Before she could ask him to explain, he'd turned back to the stove. Kate clutched the counter and sucked in a few deep breaths, trying to regain her composure. By the time breakfast was ready, she felt completely calm and relaxed, or at least she thought she looked that way—no point in wondering if he knew she was still edgy and aware, and now very curious about what he'd meant about things changing between them.

"So, Jack, what else do you do in your real life. You're an architect. Ever designed anything I've actually heard of?"

He answered with a question. "Like to go shopping?"

"Does Imelda Marcos like shoes?"

He chuckled. "My firm designed the new Great Lakes Mall. I managed the project."

She gave a little whistle of appreciation. "Nice. Anything else?"

He named a few more buildings Kate instantly recognized, particularly the stores and shopping centers. "Sounds like retail's your niche."

"Mmm-hmm. If you ever decide to open a new Bare Essentials, let me know."

If only you knew...

"How'd you get into architecture? Didn't Daddy want you to follow in his footsteps and become a lawyer?"

"I prefer to build things, not tear them apart, which is what lawyers seem to spend a lot of their time doing." He flipped their omelets onto two plates and carried them to the table. "I really built things when I was going to college. I worked for a construction company in L.A. every summer."

"I somehow pictured you surfing your way through college."

"Ha! I tried it once and the damn board almost tore my ear off. After I wiped out, it hit me in the head. I still have the scar." He turned his head, pushing his hair up with his fingers. Kate bit her lip. Unable to resist, she stepped closer, until the toes of her sandals nearly touched his bare feet.

His hair was still slightly damp with sweat from his workout, and his skin still glowed with energy. She gulped, trying to ignore her response, and examined the thin scar that ran from just under his earlobe into his hairline.

If she wasn't mistaken, she might have kissed that spot during their interlude at the theater. Her heart skipped a beat.

"Ouch," she murmured.

He seemed to notice her sudden intensity, and her closeness. Her face was inches from his neck, and she inhaled deeply, smelling his musky warmth. She closed her eyes briefly, remembering what it had been like to kiss him. To touch him.

Lord help her, she still wanted him so much she could barely stand up. She wanted to nibble on his neck, to taste his earlobe, to feel his body get all sweaty again—preferably while it was on top of hers. Inside hers.

"You ready?" he asked, letting his hand fall to his side. She nodded dumbly. "Uh-huh." *Ready for just about anything.*

"Do you like it spicy?"

Spicy? Oh, yeah, she *loved* it spicy. "Yeah. Real spicy."

"I think there's Tabasco sauce in the fridge."

Tabasco? Kate shook her head, hard, and realized Jack

was watching her with an amused, knowing look on his face.

He'd been talking about hot and spicy eggs.

She'd been thinking about hot and spicy sex.

Please, floor, open up under me and swallow me whole.
"Kate?"

She raised a brow, trying to pretend she hadn't been picturing some of the spicy things the two of them could do on the kitchen table. Or counter. Or floor. "Huh?"

He reached for her, his hand brushing past her hip as he touched the handle on the refrigerator door. She jumped out of the way, noticing the way his hand tightened on the handle, as if he were exerting some great effort. Possibly for control? Was he as affected as she by their closeness?

There was only one way to find out. She reached out and touched the thin scar on his neck. He flinched and glanced at her. "It must have hurt," she said softly.

Jack didn't pull away as she moved closer, standing on tiptoes until her lips brushed his neck. Remembering the way he'd kissed her hip in the shower, she couldn't help kissing that hot, damp, male skin. Slipping her tongue out, she savored the faint salty flavor of sweat from his workout. She sighed at how good he tasted to her. Her touch elicited an answering groan from him, but he didn't move away. "I'm sorry I wasn't there to kiss it and make it better," she murmured as she moved her lips higher, kissing a path up to his earlobe. She stepped closer, for better access, sliding one foot between his, until his thigh was nestled between her legs. Kate closed her eyes briefly at the very intimate contact.

He muttered a soft curse, as if he could take no more. Catching her around the waist, he lifted her higher, pressing his leg tighter against her sex as he lowered his mouth to hers. Their kiss was explosive. Hot and wet. Deep and hungry. Kate met every thrust of his tongue, loving the way he tasted, the way he explored her mouth as if he couldn't get enough of her. She jerked her hips, needing the strength of his hard thigh against the crotch of her jean shorts.

When they finally broke apart, Jack stared down at her, warmth and tenderness shining through the passion of his gaze. "I invited you to breakfast. I didn't intend to leap on you at the first opportunity."

To be honest, she'd done the leaping. But she didn't point that out. "I wasn't playing any get-back-at-you games," she admitted softly. "Like Friday."

"Good. I wasn't playing games, either. But I think we should probably sit down and eat."

Nodding, she took a few deep breaths, trying to forget the way he'd kissed her, the way the strong muscles of his thigh had felt against her still-aroused body. She was too thankful that he wasn't going to tease her about her momentary lapse into mindless lust to argue.

As they sat to eat, Jack apparently looked for a quick way to change the subject. "Hey, I know what I forgot to tell you. I heard some news about the Rialto yesterday."

"Really?"

"Apparently the city now owns it, due to a loan default. It's sat there empty for years, but now a group of concerned citizens has announced they're going to work on renovating it, then open it as a public playhouse."

She smiled. "Wonderful."

"It gets better. Rose Madison is leading the effort."

"Miss Rose?"

He nodded. "She's the one who told me about it. I ran into her. I mentioned we were both happy to see some work being done on the old place."

"Did she remember me?"

"Yes. She said if you want to pay for those free movies, you're welcome to come down anytime with a paintbrush."

"I think I can wield a paintbrush."

"Hopefully better than you can crack an egg," he said with a grin as he picked a tiny white piece of shell off his tongue.

"You got me. I'm a lousy cook. But if you want me to tell you how to save money at the grocery store, I'm your woman."

"Absolutely," he said softly.

Absolutely? What did that mean? Absolutely he wanted to learn how to save money grocery shopping?

Or…absolutely, she was his woman?

Too chicken to ask which he meant, since she wasn't sure what she wanted his answer to be, Kate finished her breakfast, thanked him and then left.

But she wondered about his comment all day long. Not to mention their kiss.

JACK SPENT THE AFTERNOON out of the area, visiting some of his late father's properties in nearby towns. They were mostly rentals, small tract houses for young families. His father hadn't been a slumlord, but some of the buildings were old and in need of repair. The agent who was handling the sales told him he'd take care of it.

When he got back to Pleasantville that afternoon, he found the duplex empty. Kate's SUV was not parked outside. She'd probably gone back to her cousin's place on Lilac Hill, which was the reason Jack decided not to go to his mother's house.

He told himself he wasn't avoiding *her*. No, he was just trying to avoid temptation. He hadn't been kidding in the kitchen when he'd said he wanted things to change between them once they got back to Chicago. That day couldn't come soon enough for him, particularly after that kiss they'd shared.

He had also been fully aware of her desire for him. Hell, she'd worn it as if it were perfume, oozing from her every pore. So staying away from her seemed to be the smart choice.

Needing something to do, he remembered Rose's request for help at the Rialto. He'd developed a real affection for the old theater, particularly since the day he'd met Kate. Changing into some old clothes, he drove downtown and pulled up outside the Rialto.

Right behind a silver SUV.

Drive away. Of course he didn't. Seeing her might be foolish, since he already spent way too much of his time thinking about her, but he parked and got out of his truck, anyway.

As he entered the building he heard loud music blaring from a boom box and saw a pair of bare legs, complete with paint-speckled sneakers, dangling from a scaffold. "What do you think you're doing?" he asked, recognizing the curve of Kate's calves.

He realized he probably should not have startled her only after he saw her drop the paintbrush. Right toward his head.

A quick step back saved his skull, but not his shorts.

"Jack," she cried as the brush careened down his leg, leaving squishy beige marks in its path.

"I'm really sorry," she muttered. She shimmied on her hands and knees across the wood plank of the scaffolding, doing very interesting things to her black gym shorts. Well, black and beige gym shorts, considering all the paint stains.

She reached the built-in metal ladder on the side of the scaffold and swung around to it. Not wanting her to drop anything else—including herself—Jack went over and steadied her as she descended.

"Did you get any paint on the walls?" he asked her, looking down at her speckled clothes. And her skin. Not to mention her face and hair. "You are a complete mess."

"That's what long showers are for."

Oh, great. Kate was taking another long shower. Maybe he should just shoot himself now.

Looking around the empty lobby, he said, "You here alone?"

She nodded. "Miss Rose and her brother were here when I arrived. They were just getting ready to go for a dinner break, but said if I wanted to I could keep working on this wall."

Jack followed her gaze and looked at the interior wall that she'd been painting. It extended up all the way to the top of the open, two-story lobby. Where Kate had been working, he saw a big circle of paint. "Didn't anyone teach you to do the trim first?"

"Since you're the construction genius, why don't you do it?" She bent, grabbed another brush and tossed it to him. Though not paint covered, the brush was wet and as he caught it on the bristle-side, it oozed beige-tinged water between his fingers.

"Nice," he said as he shook the moisture off. "I think you've been selling body paint at your store too long. This kind doesn't come off so easily."

She stepped closer, a laugh on her lips. "Oh, so you're saying I shouldn't do…this?" She lifted her completely white hand and cupped his cheek.

He cringed, then realized he didn't feel moisture against his skin. "If that paint on your hand had been wet, I'd be turning you over my knee and spanking you right now."

Her eyes widened. "Oooh, sounds kinky. I didn't know you were into that sort of thing."

"I'm not," he replied. He had to know. "Are you?"

She turned her head slightly and peeked at him through lowered lashes. "Light S and M? Well, lots of my customers are."

He couldn't resist asking, "*Light* S and M? How, exactly, would that differ from the heavy variety?"

She shrugged. "It's more playful, not for seriously weirded-out people. We don't sell whips, belts or paddles. But some couples enjoy the occasional black leather dominatrix outfit."

He had a sudden mental picture of her wearing black leather and clenched his jaw.

"And, of course, there's also light bondage. Handcuffs, silk scarves, blindfolds. It's all part of the fantasy."

"Fantasy?" God help him. Even though it might give him another long, sleepless night, he really wanted to know her fantasies. "Like?"

"Like being overwhelmed," she admitted softly. "Letting yourself be overcome by passion, even made helpless when you're with someone you can trust." She bit the corner of her lip, as if deciding to continue. "Exploring every possibility, going as far as your body can go, without being able to stop, because someone you know would never hurt you is in complete control."

Kate was nearly covered with paint from head to toe. Her thick, dark hair was pulled haphazardly into a ponytail at the back of her neck. She wore no makeup and she held a drippy paint roller plopping little drops of paint on the plastic drop cloth every time she moved it.

He'd never wanted her more.

Jack had walked hip-deep into this conversation, so he had no one else to blame. And he couldn't quite find a way to get out of it. Nor was he sure he wanted to.

"Is that your fantasy?" He heard the thick tone in his voice. "Being overwhelmed? Letting someone you trust give you pleasure without any mental barriers, any restrictions, taking because you have no other choice but to take?''

"I think so," she murmured. "Being free to wring every ounce of gratification you can because it's beyond your control to stop it."

In twenty seconds Kate had just made him understand the appeal of silk scarves and handcuffs.

"You must be really good at your job," he said softly. "Though, I still don't get the whole spanking thing."

She gave him a wicked grin. "Well, I don't particularly care for pain, but I have to say you are *very* good at kissing and making all better."

Remembering kissing her hip in the shower the other night, he knew exactly what she meant. His body reacted instinctively, another sudden rush of heat rushing southward from his gut to his groin. "Now, I *could* take that the wrong way and be offended," he said, stepping closer.

"Oh?"

He nodded. "You just basically told me to kiss your ass. I could take it as an insult." He lowered his voice to a whisper. "Or a really tempting invitation."

Her lips parted and her tongue snaked out to moisten them.

"Which do you think it was?"

Unable to resist, he lifted a hand to her throat, running his finger down and touching its hollow. "I think if this were a week ago, it'd be an insult. Today, I'm not so sure."

She closed her eyes, tilting her head back as he traced a path around her neck, to her collarbone, touching her only with the tips of his fingers. "Me, neither," she admitted.

Needing to feel her in his arms again, Jack tilted her chin up and caught her mouth with his own. She moaned, parting her lips, inviting him deeper, and he accepted her invitation.

He loved kissing Kate. Every time was better than the last, hot and sweet, carnal and tender. He made love to her mouth, tasting her, drinking of her, making no effort to step away to disguise his body's reaction. She pressed against him, moaning again as he moved his mouth to press kisses on her jaw. "It's hard to find a clean spot," he said with a chuckle.

"Here's one," she whispered, pushing the sleeve of her tank top, and her bra strap, to the edge of her shoulder. A naughty invitation, which he immediately accepted. He kissed down her neck, to her collarbone, and right below it.

"Where else?" he asked, nudging the cotton top down even lower. She answered with only a soft sigh and an arch in her back, telling him to proceed. He did, scraping his tongue down to the top curve of her breast, then sliding it lower to flick at her pebbled nipple.

She quivered in his arms, and leaned back against the old refreshment counter. Appropriate. He wanted to completely gobble her up. But first he wanted to see her.

As if he had no control over them, his hands moved to the waistband of her shorts and tugged her shirt free. He lifted it up, slowly, watching as the toned, creamy-colored skin of her stomach was revealed inch by inch. Until finally he saw the lace of her bra and the bottom curves of her breasts. His mouth went dry with hunger. "You are so beautiful," he whispered as he moved his hands higher. She didn't reply, just arched into his touch, twisting until he slipped his fingers beneath her bra. She hissed when he touched her nipples, tweaking them lightly, stroking and teasing the way he knew she'd liked when they'd made love before.

"I have to taste you," he muttered.

Before Kate responded, Jack heard the front door of the theater open. Footsteps echoed on the tile floor. Acting instinctively, he yanked Kate's shirt down, and turned to shield her behind him while she put herself back together.

"Get a lot of work done?" someone called. Wincing,

Jack watched as Miss Rose and her grinning brother entered
the lobby. The older woman gave Jack and Kate a pointed
glance. "If Jack wants to be covered with paint, he's welcome to get on the scaffold and make a mess of himself,
just like you have," Rose said with a chuckle. "There was
no need to share yours, Kate."

Kate scrunched her eyes closed, obviously embarrassed
as hell. Jack chuckled and reached for a paint tray. "Okay,
Kate, you were good enough to teach me one or two things
this afternoon." He winked. "How about I teach you how
to paint?"

THROUGHOUT THE NEXT DAY, as Kate worked in the store
with Cassie and some high school boys who followed her
cousin around like puppy dogs, she kept wondering if she
should move and stay with Cassie up on Lilac Hill. Even
after everyone else left, leaving her alone in the shop to
finish up some paperwork and cleaning, she thought about
it. Cassie's house would be safer. Having Jack next door
was impossible, especially now, after what had happened
yesterday. Their kiss in the theater had been intoxicating. If
Miss Rose hadn't come back when she did, they might have
ended up rolling around on the floor, covering their naked
bodies with the specks of paint littering the drop cloth.

She should move. Jack was simply too tempting. Too
disturbing. Sooner or later they were going to end up back
in bed together, and she didn't know if either of them was
prepared for the consequences of that.

One other thing disturbed her about being back in town.

"Hiya, Kate! How's the store coming along?"

Friendliness. Damn, she really couldn't get used to that.

Pausing with her hand filled with the paper towels she'd
been using to clean the front window of the store early
Thursday evening, she turned around. Diane. New owner of
the Downtown Deli, whom Kate had met during her one-

day trip to town, then again when she'd gone in for lunch Monday. "Good, thanks."

"I remember when we were gearing up to open," the sweet-faced strawberry-blonde continued, as if not noticing Kate's less-than-welcoming reply. "We got a chilly reception from some of the other merchants, let me tell you." She cast a critical glance toward the Tea Room. "You'd have thought we murdered Mr. Simmons, instead of just buying the deli from him."

"I can't believe he finally decided to retire. He was as crusty as his sub rolls." Kate chuckled. "I bet he wanted you to promise never to put mayonnaise on an Italian sub, didn't he?"

Diane's eyes widened. "Yes, he did!"

"He called it a sacrilege whenever I ordered one for Mom."

"Well, I waited on your mother more times than I can count, and I never once deprived her of her mayonnaise," the other woman replied. "How's she doing down there in sunny Florida, anyway? We sure do miss her at the Bunko Club."

Kate's eyes widened. They missed her? At the Bunko Club? And what the hell was a Bunko Club? "I didn't realize you knew her."

Diane snorted. "Darlin', you've been gone a long time if you've forgotten that everyone knows everyone here. Edie was the first one at my door with a home-made apple pie when me and Will moved into the apartment above the deli. She's a real doll."

From behind Diane, Kate heard another voice. "Edie? You bet your life she is. Although, it sure was a nightmare getting her raggedy nails fixed all up. The woman worked too hard!"

Kate looked past Diane to see the young woman she'd met her first day in town. The friendly one from the nail salon. She looked different—her hair now being purple instead of a reddish orange. And the number of earrings had increased. But the welcoming grin was the same.

"Hi, again," Kate offered, unable to resist the smile.

"I sure never expected to see you here washing windows. Get in there and get some gloves on before you ruin that manicure."

Kate glanced down at her hands.

"On second thought, don't. Come by my shop after you're done and we'll fix you right up. And we'll have a long gab. Okay?"

"This is Josie," Diane interjected. "Don't make any pussycat jokes or she'll use too much glue on your acrylics then refuse to fill 'em. You'll have to pry them off with a crowbar."

Josie stuck her tongue out at the other woman, then turned her attention to Kate. "And you're Kate Jones. Edie's long-lost, super-successful daughter, cousin of the supermodel who has Sheriff Taggart going around in circles."

She talked so fast Kate had a hard time keeping up.

"Oh, really?"

Diane nodded. "His ex-girlfriend, Annie—she's the dispatcher—says Tag starts acting like a grizzly bear with a burr in his butt whenever he has a run-in with your cousin."

He hadn't looked like a grizzly Saturday night when he'd come to the shop at 1:00 a.m. No, he'd looked more like a panther. Dark and dangerous. She hoped Cassie knew what she was doing.

"Uh, can I ask a stupid question?"

"Anything," Diane replied.

"What's Bunko?"

The other woman linked her arm in Kate's. "You've never played Bunko? It's the woman's version of poker night. The Lilac Hill types have their bridge club. We prefer Bunko. A dice game, rotated among the homes of the club members. Twice a month we meet to talk, laugh and play. The hostess provides the prizes."

"The members provide the bourbon," Josie added helpfully.

Kate laughed out loud. "Sounds like fun." Surprisingly, she meant it. She could see how her mother would have enjoyed something so simple yet charming.

"Then it's settled, you come to our next game, which happens to be tomorrow night at Eileen Saginaw's house."

Kate's smile widened in genuine pleasure. "Eileen is my mom's best friend. I'd love to see her again."

And as easy as that, Kate found herself committed to a social event with some of the women of Pleasantville.

What is wrong with this picture?

"Now, tell us what you're going to sell in your store," Diane said. "Pretty please? Nobody knows anything more than it's a ladies' shop, and everybody's going crazy trying to find out."

Kate bit her lip. These two were the nicest people she'd met so far in Pleasantville, but that didn't mean they were going to welcome sex toys on the main drag of town.

"It's gotta be something good," Josie said. "Tell me it's real shoes. Real, decent shoes that don't have rubber soles and plastic uppers. If you say you're gonna carry Dr. Martens I'll get down on the ground and kiss your toes. And I'll give you a free pedicure while I'm down there."

Kate shook her head. "Sorry. Not shoes."

"Clothes. Oh, please let it be clothes," Diane said. "The closest store to buy a decent dress is twenty miles away. And that's not even one of those new super Wal-Marts, it's just a plain old regular one."

Kate bit her lip and shook her head at Diane's genuine consternation. "Sorry. Not clothes." *Not unless you counted crotchless panties and leather bustiers!*

Josie bounced on the toes of her chunky black boots like a kid waiting in line for Santa. "Then what?"

"You'll have to wait until our grand opening to find out."

"Grand opening?"

She recognized that voice. Wincing, Kate turned around to see Jack standing right behind her. The man was quiet as a cat—she'd never even heard him approaching.

Obviously neither had the other two women. Because she felt sure she'd have noticed those matching holy-cannoli-take-me-big-boy looks on their faces.

"Hi, Jack," she murmured. Her voice didn't even shake. Amazing, since her heart had started racing like an out of control freight train speeding toward heartbreak junction.

The man was too handsome. His smile too adorably sexy to be real, the twinkle in his brilliant green eyes too charming. He made women want to hug him. Then *do* him. Including Kate. Especially Kate.

Diane and Josie spoke in unison. "Introduce us."

After she'd made introductions all the way around, and listened to Josie and Diane pump Jack for information about why on earth he'd waited so long to come back for a visit to Pleasantville, she tried to slide away. Evening was approaching, though it was still light out. She wanted to get inside and lock up. Mainly she wanted to get away before Jack started asking any more questions about her store.

Just when she thought she might make a clean getaway, however, an old, beige Cadillac pulled up on the street and parked one building down, in front of the Tea Room.

"Great," Jack muttered. "It's my ex-brother-in-law."

"Which one?" Josie said under her breath, her voice holding a definite note of sarcasm. Obviously she knew Angela.

As Kate watched the man emerge from the Cadillac, she answered softly, "Darren."

9

DARREN HADN'T CHANGED a great deal, though his face was rounder and his hair thinner than it had been in high school. His belly was rounder, too. He wasn't fat, just soft and mellow-looking. Like a salesman.

He nodded to Diane and Josie, barely glanced at Kate, then noticed Jack. His face paled and for a second Kate thought he was going to get back in his car and drive away. Then his shoulders straightened as he locked the car and walked around it to the sidewalk.

Okay, so the jerk wasn't a complete wimp. He wasn't going to try to avoid his ex's brother.

"Hello, Jack, Josie. Diane." Then he glanced toward Kate, as if waiting for an introduction. His eyes narrowed as he tilted his head. "You…my God, it's Kate Jones."

"Hello, Darren."

"I had no idea you were back in town."

"Well, you know what they say about bad pennies."

"You look…wow, you look *great*," he said, his eyes wide as he stared her up and down.

Next door, the door to the Tea Room opened. Darren glanced past Kate, his face growing red. She knew darn well who stood there. "It was *so* nice seeing you, Darren. Be sure to say hi to your mom for me, okay?"

She turned around. Mrs. McIntyre stood on the porch next door, all stiff-necked, righteous indignation. Another woman, one Kate didn't recognize, stood with her. The two of them immediately started speaking in low voices. She couldn't hear their words, but she got the message loud and clear.

Kate gave them a forced but saccharine-sweet smile as she strode inside her store, as if she hadn't a care in the world.

Jack watched Kate leave, and made no attempt to stop her. He'd seen the silent exchange between Kate and Darren's mother. The glassiness in her eyes and the quiver of her lush, beautiful bottom lip, said she was holding on by a thin thread.

He'd also read the tension between his ex brother-in-law and the woman he now considered his. He didn't stop to evaluate that, knowing Kate would resent the hell out of him thinking that way. Particularly since he'd wondered if it was best to stay away from her, for his own sanity and reproductive health. He'd come to the conclusion that walking around with a hard-on eighteen hours a day could really be bad for his future children.

Josie and Diane seemed to notice the tension in the air, as well. Telling Jack how nice it was to meet him, they both walked down the street, their heads close together as they talked.

Once they were gone, Jack eyed his sister's former husband. "How's it going, Darren?"

Darren was still looking at the door to the building that had once belonged to his father. "I can't believe Kate came back. I haven't seen her since graduation."

"You knew her in high school?"

Darren nodded. "We dated for a while, during senior year. She was my prom date."

Prom night. The night, if he wasn't mistaken, when his kid sister had gotten pregnant by this little prick, who'd walked out on her as soon as she'd miscarried their baby.

Jack's teeth clenched. "I thought Angela was your prom date."

"Oh, no, we just left together afterward..." Darren seemed to realize who he was speaking to, because his face went redder. "I mean, well, Angela and I had dated the year before. And we kind of got back together that night at prom."

"What about Kate? You know, your *date?*"

Darren stood there looking hopeless, helpless and regretful. He finally shrugged. "High school, man. I was a kid."

Jack shook his head. "Some people don't have to wait till they grow up to become dickless assholes." He prepared to walk away, but paused. "Darren?"

Darren finally looked him full in the face.

"If you like breathing, you'll stay away from Kate." Not waiting for an answer, he turned to follow Kate into her shop.

The doorknob didn't jiggle in his hand, she'd obviously flicked the lock when she went inside. He knocked, figuring she wouldn't answer. To his surprise, the door moved. Pushing at it, he watched as it swung open. The lock was apparently broken, lucky for him.

After he got inside, and closed the door firmly behind him, Jack noticed the smell of paint and new carpet. The overhead lights in the shop were off, but recessed ones above the shelves cast illumination throughout the shadowy store. A bit of late-afternoon sunlight peeked in through the sheers on the windows.

He didn't see Kate. He did hear a voice, however. Following the sound of a radio, he walked through the sales area and back to the offices and storage rooms. He found Kate sitting in the center of a cement-floored room, surrounded by boxes, staring mindlessly into the air.

"Kate," he said softly. "Are you okay?"

She slowly nodded. "How'd you get in? I locked the door."

"Something's obviously wrong with the lock. You should have someone look at that. Are you all right?"

A small smile widened her lips, and surprisingly, no tears marred her cheeks. "I'm fine, Jack. Just wondering..."

"Wondering what?"

She hesitated, and he thought for a moment she wouldn't answer. Finally she admitted, "Wondering whether it's right to go on resenting someone for doing only what you yourself have done for much of your life."

He waited but she didn't explain. He somehow suspected she had no intention of talking about whatever it was she was thinking. "So you're really okay?"

She nodded. Rising, she brushed some dust from the floor off her butt, calling his attention to the miniscule white shorts she wore. He closed his eyes briefly. No wonder Darren had been unable to stop staring. Kate looked amazing. "I see you got all the paint washed off."

She nodded. "For now. Though I promised to go back and help some more tomorrow at the Rialto."

"Me, too," he admitted. "Now, you want to tell me what grand opening you were talking about." He glanced around the storage room at all the boxes. "Are you going into business here?"

"Yep," she replied as she grabbed a box and moved past him, exiting the storage room.

He followed her through a short hallway, into the store area. She continued, through an arched doorway toward the dressing rooms and a mirrored alcove. She dropped the box near several others already lined up beneath rows of shelves.

"Your kind of business?" he asked, repeating his question from Saturday.

She tilted her head and gave him an arched glance out of the corner of her eye. "What do you think?"

When she bent and retrieved a filmy white bra from one box, then what appeared to be a black leather bustier from another, his eyes narrowed. "I think you've decided to play Clint Eastwood."

He'd nailed it. He saw by the shock in her eyes, and the way she gasped as she dropped the two pieces of sexy lingerie, that he'd hit the truth dead-on.

"You're out for a little revenge."

"How could you possibly…"

"Come on, Kate, opening a new Bare Essentials right here in Pleasantville? Next door to the Tea Room?" He paused, letting the concept sink in, then reluctantly began to chuckle. "Damn, you really are something."

"You…you're not shocked?" she whispered.

Shocked? No. He'd already learned that Kate Jones was like no woman he'd ever known. He shook his head. "Not shocked. I think you're crazy, and you're going to lose your shirt." He cast a heated glance at her body. "I mean figuratively speaking. Literally, I wouldn't mind in the least."

She rolled her eyes.

"If you ever open your doors, that is. I'm sure there'll be a protest from certain quarters. You could lose everything you've already put into this place."

"Which wasn't much. It cost only some sweat equity— mostly Cassie's—and shipping charges to ship stuff here." She shrugged. "Besides, it's not about money."

"Of course not."

She stepped closer and her smile faded. "It's not some silly revenge plot, Jack. I had to be here…I needed to come back to town this summer."

He couldn't imagine what could possibly be important

enough to bring Kate back to a place she quite obviously hated, and told her so.

"I can't really talk about it," she said. "A lot of things happened all at once." She crossed her arms in front of her chest and rubbed her hands up and down, as if chilly.

"Kate, whatever is going on, whatever this is about…"

"Yes?"

"Just be careful. Sometimes things don't work out the way you think they will."

"I somehow think this will," she said, "because I don't have unrealistic expectations. I fully expect to fail here."

He raised a brow.

"We'll open, we'll cause a lot of chest-clutching, a lot of scandalous whispering, and then, when Cassie's safe…" She cleared her throat. "I mean, when Cassie's ready to leave…we'll close and go away. Cassie will sell this building and everything else she owns here and we'll never come back. No ties, no bad memories, just a laugh when we think back on our one last hurrah."

"Cassie's in trouble?"

"No. Forget it, okay? Cassie's fine." She looked at her nails, obviously feigning nonchalance. "Did you like her?"

"Like her? I barely spoke to her."

"Most men don't have to *speak* to her to form an impression."

Jack shrugged. "She's beautiful, of course. Flamboyant and probably too sexy for her own good. She'll drive any man who loves her to the verge of insanity."

She waited. When he didn't continue, she prompted, "That's all? You weren't…interested?"

He shook his head. "Do you think I'm a total scumbag? What kind of guy would lust after the cousin of the woman he's involved with?"

"We are not involved."

"Bullshit. We are very much involved," he admitted, confirming that not only to her, but to himself.

He waited for her to deny it. She couldn't. Who could deny the inevitable? They might not have done much about their relationship since they'd been back in town, except for a few hot kisses and that one close encounter yesterday. But there's no question they would. Sooner or later.

Judging by the look in her eye, and the expectancy in the air, he suspected it was going to be sooner.

He waited for a mental voice to tell him no, waited for his feet to instinctively turn toward the door. Waited to hear from the nice-guy voice of reason who'd been whispering in his ear for weeks.

That voice had been growing weaker as each day passed. He'd been listening to her from the other side of the duplex, seeing her shining, dark hair as she left in the morning, hearing her off-key singing as she showered. Every day another chunk had disappeared out of the wall of willpower he'd tried to erect between them. And after yesterday, it had come down like the last remnants of the Berlin Wall.

Sure he'd had good intentions, but all the good intentions in the world couldn't stop what was happening between them. No more than a surfer could stop a wave on which he was riding.

Sometimes he had to ride it out to see where it took him.

"So are you going to tell me what's wrong? Is your cousin in some kind of trouble or not?"

"Jack, let it go, okay?"

He didn't press her on the Cassie issue, sensing she wouldn't tell him what was going on, anyway. "So, back to your shop and your revenge plan. Anything else on the agenda?"

"No, I think I've summed it up."

"Not much revenge there. I mean, you're not having the population paint every building red?"

She chuckled. "You rented *High Plains Drifter*."

He nodded.

"Okay, so it's not the greatest revenge." Her smile was mischievous and it made her brown eyes sparkle. "Must be that rotten sweetness everybody says is somewhere inside me. I'm great at fantasizing, just not so great at execution."

Hearing her laugh at herself, Jack found her as captivating as she'd been the day they'd met. As if here, in a shop like the one she owned in Chicago, she was free to be herself. She'd let the negative elements of Pleasantville—her hurts, her misgivings, her sarcasm—disappear.

He found himself doing the same. As if nothing outside the building mattered. They could have been meeting for the first time in Chicago, as far as he was concerned.

She sighed. "Our plan seemed a lot more dramatic and outrageous when we fantasized about it as teenagers."

"You fantasized about opening a sex shop in Pleasantville?"

"Yep, we even wrote it down in our diaries on prom night."

His smile faded. "I heard about your prom night."

"It's fine. Water under the bridge," she insisted. But she wouldn't meet his eye.

"Should I even ask who else was on that revenge list you made that night?"

She pursed her lips. "No, you probably shouldn't."

As he'd thought—his own sister had probably been a pretty large target. Not to mention Darren.

"So, can I assume this shop will satisfy your need for revenge? I mean, I don't have to worry bodies are going to start flying out the upstairs windows over the Tea Room, right?"

She sidestepped the question. "Oh, look, the store's not even revenge at all. It's more…I don't know…like the old song. They talked about us throughout our childhoods, well, now we'll *really* give them something to talk about! And they'll never forget the Tremaines."

"What if you fail to fail?"

"Excuse me?"

"You know, what if the store's a big fat success? What then?"

Her laughter echoed in the small alcove. "Not a chance. That'll never happen."

"You never know. Your store is a big hit in Chicago."

"This is *so* not Chicago." She bent, opening a box at her feet. "Can you see Mrs. McIntyre buying one of these?"

She pulled out what looked like a foot-long hot dog. Then he realized it was a dildo. "Now, there's something you don't see every day in Pleasantville," he mused out loud, not at all shocked, as she'd obviously intended.

"Gee, ya think?" She giggled like a kid as she grabbed something else out of the box. "I'm thinking of these in the display case right by the cash register."

He raised a brow. "Anal beads?"

Holding the strand of beads between her thumb and index finger, she swung them around, a wicked look in her eye. When he said nothing, she dropped them, reached back into the box and pulled out something else. He instantly knew what the black, rubbery circle was for.

The playful laughter faded as she caught the heat in his eyes. It was answered by her own aware expression.

His groin tightened as he imagined using the item during sex with Kate. The way she'd slide it down his dick, her cool hand holding his balls as she tightened the cock ring around him. Then climbing on top of him and riding him, letting the ring keep him engorged and rock-hard. Building the pressure until he'd have to grab her by the hips and thrust up into her until they both came together in one strong, fiery blast of sexual pleasure.

"Ever used one?" she finally asked.

He wondered if she'd be shocked by his reply, and decided to find out. "Yeah. Have you?"

Her lips parted as she sucked in a deep, shuddery breath. She obviously hadn't expected that, hadn't been prepared for him to answer with blatant honesty. Even from several feet away, he could see the goose bumps on her chest, and the sudden jut of her nipples against her tight blue T-shirt.

"No," she finally answered. "I, uh…don't try everything we sell in the store."

His stare shifted to the huge dildo.

She shook her head slowly, as if dazed.

He reached over and picked up a pair of handcuffs from a pile on a nearby shelf. Remembering their conversation from yesterday, he asked, "What about these?"

She shook her head again.

"Just as well," he murmured as he put them back. "They'll chafe your pretty wrists when you thrash around on the bed."

He wasn't speaking in general terms. And felt sure she knew it. This wasn't an *if* conversation—it was a *when*.

The inside of the store began to feel steamy hot.

"We do sell faux-fur-lined ones," she admitted, her voice shaky and breathless.

Did she even know she'd issued him a blatant invitation? Of course she knew. This was Kate, after all.

"What *have* you tried?" he asked, unable to stop this sensual self-torture. "I know you've got your little finger vibrator. But what else can you personally recommend for your shoppers…based on your own experience?"

She hesitated.

"Come on, Kate," he said as he stepped closer and dropped his voice to a whisper. "Show me your wares."

He wondered if she'd leave, if she'd back away from the sultry atmosphere into which they'd once again fallen together.

He should have known better.

"There's a nifty vibrating tongue…"

He groaned softly.

"It's not wet enough, though," she continued slowly, obviously knowing full well what she was doing to him. "Not like a real one. But powerful. It doesn't get tired, doesn't veer off at the last second and ruin everything just before climax."

Neither had he. Not that he reminded her of that.

"What else do you like? Any other replicas of body parts?"

She shook her head. "Not really. My favorite thing we sell is probably the lingerie. My partner has real talent. Bare Essentials goes well beyond your average teddies, thongs and push-up bras."

He managed not to come in his pants at the image of Kate in any or all of these seductive items. "Oh?"

Nodding, she pointed to a stack of folded cloth. She picked up something off the top and shook it out. It took him a moment to realize what it was. "Crotchless tights?"

"A big hit in Chicago in the winter. It's too cold for thigh-highs, or even regular panty hose. And, for some reason, men seem to get off on women in tights." She shrugged. "I think it's the same reason men like blondes on trampolines."

He understood. "Or cheerleaders. It reminds them of that whole teenage thing where boys are one six-foot-tall pile of testosterone and the girls know it."

She laughed.

"So, do you wear them?"

She gave him a coy look out of the corner of her eye. "Maybe. Most women who do like the naughtiness of it. They like knowing that even if it's twenty degrees outside, they can go for something outrageous in the back of a limo if the right man happens to be around."

His smile tightened. "Speaking from experience?"

She didn't try to lie. "No." Raising her hands, palms up, she shrugged. "What can I say? I live a pretty boring life in Chicago, in spite of being the sex toy queen of Michigan Avenue."

He was damn glad of that. He hated even thinking of Kate with another man. His own possessiveness surprised him. Jack had been involved in enough casual relationships to know women had as much sexual drive as men. Where they chose to fill that need had never been any of his business, once they'd left his bed.

Kate was a different story. He had a feeling he could get damn near violent thinking of her with anyone else.

Which completely floored him.

"There are some pieces of lingerie I've used." She bent at the knee, almost kneeling at his feet. Looking down, seeing the top of her head about level with his groin, Jack had to fist his hands to try to gain control.

She hunted around in a box, then said, "Aha." Standing, she showed him what she'd found. "My favorite."

She held a pretty, lacy, pale blue bra. It had straps, underwire, a satiny strip of material to go beneath a woman's breasts—but nothing to cover the rest. A front-less bra.

"You, uh, wear those things?"

"Sometimes. Especially when I'm wearing cotton or silk."

They both glanced at her cotton T-shirt.

Though almost afraid to ask, he had to. "Why?"

"The different textures of fabric feel amazing against my nipples," she admitted, something dark and erotic flashing in her eyes. "It's empowering to give yourself a thrill throughout the day, without anyone ever being aware of it. Like the tights."

He swallowed. Hard. Then he stepped closer, until their bodies nearly touched from neck to knee. Looking down at the sharp points of her breasts, he finally managed to ask, "Are you wearing one of those bras now?"

"Maybe." She didn't step back. Instead, she reached for his hand and pulled it toward her body. Dropping her voice to a purr, she said, "Why don't you see if you can tell?"

Dangerous. Like reaching out to touch a blazing red burner on a stove...you know you're going to get burned, but you just can't shake yourself out of the spell.

Jack didn't care.

He touched.

10
_____

"YES, I THINK YOU MIGHT be wearing one now," he murmured.

Kate didn't reply, couldn't even speak as he traced the tips of his fingers across her sensitive nipple. Then he moved his hand lower, to cup her breast. Stepping even closer, until their hips brushed, he brought his other hand up. When he passed his open palm against her other breast, making the fabric of her top scrape the other distended nipple, she shuddered.

"Jack…"

"Shh," he whispered, his mouth so close to her hair she felt the warmth of his breath. "I'm not sure yet. I think I need to test some more before I decide if you are."

"Please do," she said with a tiny whimper.

He did, cupping, squeezing lightly. He caught her nipples between fingers on each hand, tweaking them, making sparks shoot from there straight down to her crotch. Her legs shook as heat and moisture flooded her shorts.

"Yes, you are," he finally said. Thankfully he didn't pull his hands away.

"So, Kate, let's recap. You wear seductive lingerie for your own pleasure. You carry a vibrator in your purse and use a battery-powered tongue whenever you want an orgasm."

She nodded mindlessly, agreeing, anything as long as he continued the stroking of her breasts.

"There's one thing you haven't mentioned. Something I know you like."

She instantly knew what he meant and whimpered.

"Penetration," he continued, dragging out the word as if it were a caress. "Deep, hard, erotic penetration."

"Yes." She arched her back, offering more of herself, her fingers itching to grab the bottom hem of her shirt and lift it so she could get even more of his intimate attention.

His hands moved away, caressing her waist, her back, her hip. "Can you get that from your toys or playthings?" he asked, as if he didn't know she was about to crawl out of her own skin out of sheer, undiluted need.

"No." Aroused to the point of pain, she shifted, pushing her pelvis toward his and grinding against the huge erection she could easily feel against her body. The moisture between her legs doubled, the electric awareness thrumming through her body quadrupled. Not questioning the impulse, knowing she had to touch him or die, she slipped her hand between their bodies to cup him through his jeans. "Nothing compares to this."

He hissed as her fingers tightened around him.

He suddenly got serious, obviously realizing she wasn't playing sexy games anymore. "You're sure?"

"Oh, yeah."

"Here?"

"Uh-huh. But there's no table," she said as she continued to caress him.

"Floor'll do," he muttered before catching her mouth in a wet, carnal kiss. She melted against him, rapidly refamiliarizing herself with the taste of his mouth, the sweetness of his tongue. The feel of his long, hard body pressed against hers.

One hand slipped from her breast down to the waistband of her shorts. He tugged it free, stroking her belly, her waist, then higher until his fingers were inches from her nipples. No cloth barrier this time, she knew it wouldn't take much and she'd be coming right then and there.

That would be lovely. But this time she didn't want to be the only one completely out of control, brought to ever higher peaks of ecstasy by Jack.

She wanted to be the one turning *him* into a raging, living, breathing hormone.

"I love kissing you," she said with a whimper when their lips parted. "I want to kiss you *everywhere.*"

His eyes widened in understanding as she dropped to her knees in front of him. "Kate…"

"Hush."

Her hand trembled as she unbuttoned, then unzipped, his jeans. He wore white boxer briefs, which did little to hold back his erect penis. Her mouth watered, then went dry as she savored that long moment of anticipation that probably lasted no longer than a few erratic beats of her heart.

Finally, once again, she would see him. Touch him. Taste him. Working the briefs down, she held her breath, watching as his hard-on was revealed. She moaned at the sight, remembering how it had given her such pleasure their first time. Knowing he'd give her more pleasure tonight.

But not yet. Not until he was completely out of control.

Jack didn't want her to proceed. He'd been walking around in a state of arousal for weeks, and as she leaned closer to his cock, her lips brushing the sensitive skin at its tip, he nearly lost it. "Kate…" he said with a moan as her tongue flicked out, just a touch, a tiny caress to taste the moisture there.

"Remember what you said that day on the stage, Jack? Well, fair's fair. I like taste, too."

Then she moved her lips over him and took him into her mouth. "Ah, Kate." He moaned, dropping his head back.

He clenched his fists, let her suck him, surrounding him with hot, wet sweetness and gentle pressure. When he felt her hand slide between his legs to cup his balls, his eyes shot open and he looked down at her.

Her head moved slowly, back and forth, sucking him deep, then pulling away until she'd almost released him completely.

"Kate, please, you've got to let me…"

"Watch," she murmured between one smooth stroke of her mouth and the next. When she tilted her head and glanced to the right, toward the mirror, he followed her gaze.

And nearly lost his mind.

Feeling her wet strokes. Hearing her coos of pleasure that said she really *liked* what she was doing. Seeing part of his body disappearing between those beautiful lips of hers.

He couldn't take another second.

"Enough," he growled, taking her by the shoulders and pushing her back.

Their clothes—with the exception of Kate's front-less bra—were gone within twenty seconds. He was between her upraised legs ten beyond that.

"Condoms are in there," she muttered, pointing to a box near his hip.

Jack didn't even look as reached for it, feeling around with his hand while he kissed Kate senseless. "You knew what that would do to me," he whispered against her lips.

"I kinda hoped," she said with a sultry chuckle. "I wasn't ready to stop."

"Not now," he told her. She panted as he sucked her earlobe, and hissed when he caught her breast in his hand. "Our first time back together…we'll go at the same time."

She gasped and arched up, grinding her hips into him.

"Go at the same time? Do you mean...in the *numerical* sense?"

It took him a second to grasp her meaning. When he did, the image she suggested—giving each other oral pleasure at the same time—flooded his mind, making him even harder. Even more frantic.

"Hate to have to break it to you, but you're definitely *not* sweet, Kate Jones," he said with a ragged laugh.

"Thank heaven."

He ran the flat of his palm down her body to her hip. Then he slid his fingers into her curls, into the slick, hot crevice, knowing she was ready. "Except maybe here," he whispered as he slid his finger into her.

She tightened around him, moaning and bumping against his hand. He gave her what she wanted, flicking her tight little clit with his thumb until she cooed, then inserting another finger into her, stroking her G-spot from within. "Yeah, you're very sweet here." He could tell by her cries she was within seconds of climaxing.

"No fair. We're supposed to go together this time," she said with a whimper.

Before he knew what she was doing, she'd pushed him, rolled him over so she could straddle him on the floor. "Better."

Looking up at what had to be the most glorious sight on the planet, he had to agree.

Kate stared down at him, seeing the passion and admiration he could never have feigned. He was hard beneath her bottom, and close to where she wanted him. She shifted slightly until his penis slid into the wet folds of skin concealing her opening.

He growled.

"What? Not good?" She knew damn well it was.

"You know it's good. It's just not enough."

"Anxious, are we?"

He ripped open the condom with his teeth, showing her how anxious he was. She took a glance at their reflection, amazed at the sensuality of the moment. She slid back and forth over him, using his hardness to stroke her clitoris until she gasped.

"You like watching, too." Jack's stare met hers in the mirror.

She nodded. Then, knowing he watched her every move, Kate slid her hands up her body, until she cupped her own breasts.

"Keep going."

She did, catching her nipples between her fingers. "Mmm. But not as good as your hands."

He complied, replacing her hands with his own, then leaning up to suck one nipple deeply into his mouth.

Kate had her first orgasm instantaneously. She was still shuddering from it as she plucked the condom from his fingers and moved out of the way to roll it down over him.

When he was fully sheathed, she held herself above him. She caught his stare and held it. Then, with aching precision and slowness, she slid down on him, taking him completely into her body, inch by endless inch, until he'd filled her up so much she felt complete for the first time in ages.

"Yes," she said with a contented sigh.

"Yes," he echoed.

She didn't move at first, just sat there, absorbing him, stroking him with muscles deep within her body. She saw him clench his fist and tilt his head back in pleasure.

"More?"

He nodded, reaching for her hips. "Definitely more, Kate."

Then he started to move below her, thrusting upward. She

met every stroke with one of her own, amazed at how quickly their bodies synchronized to one another.

It was hot. Energetic. Frenzied.

But also something else. There were moments when they'd meet each other's eyes and smile. When he'd reach up to brush her hair off her sweat-dampened cheek. Or he'd rub his thumb across her lower lip, then tug her down for a slow, wet kiss that somehow felt even more personal than the mating of their lower bodies.

He'd slow the pace, drag out the pleasure, until Kate felt her legs tremble with near exhaustion.

"Let me," he said as he held her around the waist. He rolled her over, staying inside her, his face inches from hers. Another kiss. Another stroke.

She turned her head and saw them in the mirror. Saw him holding his beautifully hard body above hers on his thick, strong arms. Saw his shoulders flex, his back strain, his gorgeous, tight butt move up and down as he pumped into her over and over again, so deep she had to gasp for breath. She clutched his shoulders, wrapped her legs around his hips and met him thrust for thrust.

She sensed the minute he'd gone too far to hold back. And as soon as he had, he braced himself on one arm, bringing his other hand between their bodies. "Come with me, honey."

And, of course, Kate did.

"I'M SORRY I didn't call," he whispered a few minutes later. They lay together on the newly carpeted floor, wrapped in each other's arms, exchanging lazy kisses and slow caresses.

He felt her stiffen against him. Then she asked, "Sorry because you had to wait for this?"

"No, I'm not sorry that way. I mean, I *apologize* for not calling you, Kate. I thought I had good reasons—and maybe

I did. But I thought about you constantly and I never stopped wanting to see you again.''

She tilted her head back to study his face. ''Good reasons. And that's all you're going to say?''

He nodded once, knowing he couldn't elaborate. The truth of the long-term relationship between his father and her mother was tough enough for him to deal with. He didn't want to burden Kate with it. Her mother was still alive—the past needed to die.

''Just tell me one thing, okay? Tell me it wasn't because you're involved with someone else. If I find out you're married, engaged or engaged to be engaged, I won't be responsible for my actions.''

He chuckled. ''No. I'm completely unattached. Or, rather, I was until I met you.''

She smiled languorously and leaned over to press a sweet, wet kiss on his mouth. He held her tighter.

''Can I ask you something?'' she asked.

''Anything.'' Knowing the way Kate's mind worked, she was probably about to ask him something sexual and intense, getting them both hot and ready to go again. His mouth went dry in anticipation, knowing they could play sensual games here all night long. He definitely wanted to try some different positions in front of the mirrors.

''Do you know how to play Bunko?''

''I've never heard of it.'' He raised a hopeful brow. ''Is it some kind of sex game?''

She bit her lip as she giggled. ''I certainly hope not.'' He felt her shoulders shaking as her laughter increased. ''Good grief, a sex game. Can you imagine? The women of Pleasantville gathering every other week to play a sex game in someone's living room? Complete with prizes and bourbon?''

"I think you could stock the prizes from right here at Bare Essentials."

She giggled even more. "Oh, my, I can just imagine Eileen Saginaw trying to choose her prize from between the strap-on vibrator or the two-headed dildo."

He rolled onto his back, tugging her with him until she lay on his chest. Her hair blanketed his stomach, flowing all the way down to his groin. He ran his fingers through its silkiness as he caressed her back, hip and bottom.

"So why are you asking about it?"

"It's some kind of dice game. I've been invited to come over to play with some of the women tomorrow night. I don't know much about it. The friends I hang out with in Chicago are more into lunch dates, shopping trips and cocktail parties than Tupperware gatherings or Bunko nights."

Her mention of cocktail parties reminded him of something. Knowing it was a long shot, given Kate's dislike of the Lilac Hill set in town, he asked anyway. "Speaking of parties, I've been asked to attend one at city hall Saturday night. A welcome reception for the new mayor."

She stiffened in his arms.

"I'd like you to come with me, Kate."

He could have predicted her answer. "I don't think that's such a good idea."

"Come on, what's the big deal? You're obviously getting involved with some of the townspeople, anyway. With your big Bunko orgy and all."

She laughed, probably in spite of herself. "It's not the same thing. Those are not the same type of townspeople."

He narrowed his eyes. "Oh, so you're a snob? You choose to associate only with *your* kind of people?"

When fire flashed in her eyes, he knew he'd said just the right thing. He prodded further. "Come on, you know you're every bit as good as any other person here. You're probably worth more than anyone who lives on Lilac Hill. Don't let childhood hurts affect the decisions you make today.''

She sucked in a deep breath, staring at his face. He saw a variety of expressions rush across her face...hurt, confusion, then acceptance. ''You're right,'' she whispered.

''That's my girl. The party is at eight.''

''I'm sure I have something in my closet I could wear.''

''Crotchless tights?'' he asked hopefully.

She lightly bit the skin just above his nipple. ''It's a little hot for that.'' As he sighed in disappointment, she whispered, ''But probably perfect for crotchless panties.''

THE NEXT AFTERNOON, as she stood in front of her closet trying to figure out what one wore to a Bunko night, Kate's cell phone rang. When she heard Cassie's voice, she told her about her plans for the evening.

''Are you sure it's a game, and not some swinging women's party with male strippers and livestock?''

Kate snorted. ''Why, would you like to come?''

''Nah, can't do it. I'm on my way outta town.''

Pausing with a jean skirt and a red peasant blouse in her hand, Kate said, ''Where do you think you're going?''

When Cassie explained she was making a quick weekend trip to New York for her agent's birthday, Kate tried to talk her out of it. Cassie was not to be dissuaded. She was sick of hiding out like a victim. She was going. Period.

''All right, Cass, but please promise me you'll be careful. And call me when you're leaving Sunday afternoon so I can drive up to the airport to get you.''

Kate cut the connection before she remembered to tell Cassie about tomorrow night's cocktail party. Just as well. She still couldn't believe she'd agreed to go, and wasn't sure she could make Cassie understand why.

Hell, she barely understood why herself. She only knew something had changed within her. Somehow, from the time she'd seen Mrs. McIntyre outside the Tea Room the day before, Kate had been unable to stop thinking about everything that had happened.

She'd been angry for years because Mrs. McIntyre hated her without reason. Now she wondered—was she any different? Darren's mother hated the Tremaine family because her husband had taken up with Flo. Kate had hated the Winfields because John Winfield had strung her mother along for two decades.

Yes, she had reason to resent Angela because of Darren, and prom night. But, really, who the hell cared what had happened in high school, ten years ago? No, she and Angela would never be friends, but there wasn't any reason they should be enemies, either. John Winfield was dead. His family wasn't responsible for his sins…they didn't even know about them! So what kind of hypocrite would she be to keep blaming them?

The thought rankled.

"And Jack." She had no reason to dislike Jack. Yes, she'd been hurt when he hadn't called her, but she sensed he was being truthful when he'd said he thought he had good reason.

She didn't want to put herself at the same level as Mrs. McIntyre—an angry, bitter person who blamed the wrong people for hurting her. Had she become so focused on self-protection, on not letting herself be hurt or abused, that she'd also denied herself the chance to build genuine emotion with a man?

Maybe it was time to rethink a *lot* of things.

Kate was still mulling over the whole revenge plan when she arrived at Eileen Saginaw's house that night. The older woman, who'd raised five kids and now had ten grandkids, gave Kate a hug and immediately asked her a bunch of questions about Edie.

"Last time we talked, she was determined to learn how to play golf so she could join a club in the retirement village," Kate said, pleased at the fondness in the other woman's voice.

Every woman at the party sounded just as regretful that Edie had left. There were no whispers here. No one acted as though some deep, dark scandal had forced Edie out. Not one person made Kate feel—in the three hours she stayed— the way the biddies in the Tea Room had made her feel in three minutes during her first visit back to town.

These were the real women of Pleasantville. And she was shockingly grateful she'd found them.

"Kate, I'm telling you, stop shaking the dice so much. That's why you keep getting snake eyes," Diane informed her as Kate prepared to take another turn late in the evening.

Kate blew an impatient, frustrated breath as she reached for her drink. Not bourbon—she didn't do bourbon. But thankfully someone had brought beer. "How can it be called snake eyes when there are three dice?" she muttered as she lost yet again, with all ones. "Snakes have two eyes, not three."

"Well, don't forget, there *are* snakes with one," Josie said with a suggestive wagging of her eyebrows.

When Kate gave her a confused look, Josie explained, using a bad Australian crocodile hunter accent. "I'm face-to-face with the deadly, one-eyed trouser snake, known to lead men into dark, dangerous places, and to enslave women with its potent power."

After a five-second pause all twelve women seated at the three card tables in Eileen's living room whooped with laughter.

It was, of course, inevitable that with each roll of the dice, the conversation degenerated into some outrageous sex talk. Kate figured it was standard operating procedure, given how freely the women spoke to one another, though, she had a really hard time picturing her mother here as part of it.

"You know, it'd almost be worth it to test that Viagra stuff, just to see if it'd be noticeable if I put it in Hank's coffee every morning," one woman introduced as Viv said.

"You mean, slip it to him, like a mickey? But how would you know if you gave him enough?" another asked.

Eileen reached for the dice. "Just keep pouring until the kitchen table starts rising off the floor right over his lap."

Josie snickered. "Yeah, I can see you explaining it to the doctor when Hank has a heart attack 'cause all his blood's trapped in his winky."

"At least he'd die happy," Diane pointed out.

"Please don't tell me I have to wait till my husband's a corpse before I can see him with a decent hard-on again." Viv poured herself another drink.

When the laughter died down, Kate spoke up. "Have you tried seducing him? Letting him know you're interested?"

Viv grunted. "Sure. Unfortunately, after he drinks the six-pack of Bud I've bought him to warm him up, he doesn't notice I've shaved my legs and I'm not wearing my period underwear."

Kate chuckled. "I mean it. Sexy lingerie, candles, scented massage oils. Then you tell him you've rented a special movie."

"The only thing he likes is Arnold Schwarzenegger blowing up stuff. Which isn't exactly my idea of romance."

"I meant something a little more…titillating."

"Oh, sure," Viv said with a groan. "I'll drive over to Emmitsburg to the Triple-X video store, fight off all the winos hanging around near the nickel booths, and rent some big-boobed-lesbians-in-love flick. Sounds like a real romantic evening.''

"I didn't mean porn,'' Kate explained patiently. "There are erotic videos made for women and couples.''

Hot sellers at Bare Essentials.

"Yeah, but I bet they don't show penises, do they?'' This from Josie who sounded indignant. "I mean, every erotic movie for couples I've seen—back when I lived in a town that had heard of such things—is camera-shy below the waist on the guy.''

Kate shrugged. "Is that so surprising? Isn't the point to get your man worked up—not yourself? I don't think many men are into seeing the competition, and women don't need as much visual stimulation, which is why adult movies are geared toward men.''

The women all thought about it. Then Viv sighed again. "You may be right, Kate, and if this were Chicago, I'm sure I could stroll to the neighborhood store to stock up on erotic movies. But this sure ain't Chicago.''

Her disappointed sigh was echoed by every woman in the room. Right then and there, Kate started wondering if maybe Jack had been right. Maybe, just maybe, opening a Bare Essentials right here in Pleasantville wasn't such a crazy idea after all.

As the evening drew to a close, Kate found herself one of the last women there. She'd tried to leave earlier, but Eileen had put a quiet hand on her arm and asked her to stick around. Finally, after Diane and Josie exchanged hugs and one last round of man jokes, they said goodbye and left.

"Let me help you clean up,'' Kate said, though the room wasn't too bad. Part of the rules of Bunko night—hostess's house didn't get left in a shambles.

Kate helped Eileen take the tablecloths off the card tables and began to fold them. "I can't tell you how much I enjoyed tonight. I appreciate all of you making me feel so welcome.''

Eileen gave her a sweet smile, which made her gray eyes twinkle. ''Katey, I am so glad you're here, even if you don't plan to stay—and I guess you don't.''

She shook her head.

''Anyway, I wish you'da come back sooner. Not that I'm criticizing. Three of my kids left, too. This town can be awfully hard on its residents sometimes.''

''Yeah.'' She wondered if Eileen knew how hard. No, Eileen didn't live on Lilac Hill, but she was married to a nice, well-liked gas station owner, and her beauty parlor, down in the basement, was a hot spot for most local women. So she probably hadn't experienced the worst Pleasantville had to offer.

''I guess you know it was hard on your mom and that's why she left. I wish she hadn't, it wasn't but a few nasty people.''

Kate laid the folded tablecloth on Eileen's dining room table. ''I'm sure you're right.''

Eileen held her eye, gauging how much to say. Then, obviously seeing something in Kate's expression, she said, ''You know, don't you. You know about Edie and John.''

Kate's jaw dropped. ''I'm surprised you do.''

''Oh, darlin', your mom and I have been friends since eighth grade. I was there the first time she saw him, the first time he asked her out. Heck, we double-dated to our senior prom.''

''Wait…you mean Mom dated John Winfield in high school?''

''Well, sure. Didn't you know that? The two of them were quite the talk of the town in those days, what with your mom being a Tremaine and all. He didn't care a bit. The two of them were crazy about each other.''

Shocked, Kate leaned against the table. "What happened?"

Eileen sighed. "They had a fight about something stupid. John went and did something even *more* stupid with Pat Pickering. She told him she was pregnant the day after graduation."

Pregnant? With Jack? She quickly calculated—no, couldn't be right, that would make Jack close to forty.

Eileen ushered her into the kitchen, putting on the kettle to make tea. "Edie found out, broke it off with John and left town. John married Pat. When there was no baby several months later, he came to me asking where Edie was. I told him the truth. She was happy with her new life in Florida. He stayed married to Pat and they made a go of it, I guess."

"Years later, Dad died and Mom came back," Kate whispered.

Eileen poured some tea, then sat. "First loves never die. John was so sad, trapped by Pat, his job, the town." Eileen shrugged. "Edie made him happy...they made each other happy. But she would *never* have let him leave Pat and those children."

A half hour later, after one of the most shocking and revealing conversations she'd ever experienced, Kate hugged Eileen goodbye and headed home. She wanted more than anything to call her mother, just to hear her voice. Edie seemed so different to her now, not a victim anymore, but a woman in love who did the best she could with what she was dealt.

Kate didn't know whether to applaud her or to cry for her.

When she arrived home, she immediately looked toward Jack's side of the duplex, to see if any lights were on. He'd told her he'd wait up, saying he wanted the full scoop on the Bunko orgy. Judging by all the lights, he'd kept his word.

She pulled into the driveway, surprised when she saw a rental car parked there. Unsure who would be visiting at this late hour, she walked up to the porch and glanced in the window.

When she saw the dark-haired person sitting on the couch, and realized who it was, she hurried into the house and launched herself into his arms.

11

IF JACK HADN'T ALREADY figured out that Kate's business partner was gay, he might be feeling seriously concerned right now. The two of them hugged and chattered with the easy camaraderie of long-time companions. They acted as if they hadn't seen each other in months, rather than a week.

"Armand, what are you doing here? I can't believe you came all this way," Kate said.

"I missed you. I had a fabulous new design I wanted to show you, and since we seem to have a decent staff for a change, I figured we could both be gone for a day or two." Armand sat on the couch, pulling Kate down to sit beside him.

Jack, who'd taken a seat on the other side of the small living room, couldn't help smiling at Kate's obvious excitement.

He hadn't quite known what to think when he'd seen this tall, dark-haired man knocking on Kate's front door an hour ago. When Jack had stepped outside to see what he wanted, the other man had asked about Kate. Jack's first instinct had been to tell the guy she'd left town and had left no forwarding address. Then, when he'd recognized the stranger as the one who'd been hugging Kate at her Chicago shop all those weeks ago, he'd invited him into his place to wait for her.

The first rule in any battle—know your competition.

He'd figured out the man's sexual preference within five

minutes. Not that Armand had tried anything—if he had, he sure as hell wouldn't still be sitting in his living room, friend of Kate's or no friend. No, what had tipped Jack off was Armand's reaction upon learning his name.

He'd acted just like one of Kate's gal pals.

"Oh, so you're Jack." He'd looked at Jack's arms and hands, raised a falsely surprised brow and said, "Hmm, no broken arms or fingers, did your building simply lose phone service for a month? Is that why you never called her?"

Yep. Definitely gay.

Once they'd gotten past those first awkward minutes, with Armand trying to punish him for not calling Kate, and Jack trying to change the subject, they'd actually enjoyed an interesting hour of conversation. The guy had even brought a six-pack of beer, two-thirds of which they'd already killed off.

Armand was part of Kate's other life. Her Chicago life. The life Jack fully intended to share when they both finished up what they had to do in Pleasantville and closed this door behind them. He wanted to see her through Armand's eyes.

Most of what he learned did not surprise him.

She loved the theater and saw nearly every touring production that came through town. A given.

She hated snow. Unusual, considering her Chicago address. But she did like long walks on windy days.

She'd put herself through college at night while working any job she could get, not finishing up her bachelor's degree until a few years ago. That reinforced what he already suspected—everything she had, she'd worked damn hard for. Nothing had been handed to her; she relied on her talent and her perseverance to succeed.

Her cousin Cassie had financed their Chicago shop, but, mostly due to Kate's excellent management, Bare Essentials had already earned enough to pay off the loan.

One more intimate little detail Armand let drop—Kate hadn't dated any man more than twice in over two years, and he doubted she'd slept with any either. *Well, praise the Lord and pass the ammunition.*

"So, how was Bunko night?" Jack asked when he could finally get a word in edgewise.

Kate grinned. "Wonderful. I loved it. And, I tell you, there might **actually** be a client base in this town for Bare Essentials."

Armand raised a surprised brow. "Get *out!*"

She told them about her evening, then said, "I know a woman named Viv who would probably adore seeing your new designs."

"It sounds like Tortureville hasn't quite lived down to your expectations," Armand said.

She didn't answer for a moment, looking deep in thought. Something seemed different about Kate tonight. She looked less pensive, much more relaxed. Jack didn't think it was only because of her friend's visit. Nor did he think it was entirely because of what had happened between them last night.

And again this morning in her bedroom next door.

"I think we both had a few surprises from our returns to Pleasantville," Jack murmured.

She looked up and met his eyes, a soft smile curling her lips. Next to her, Armand looked back and forth between the two of them. "Okay, it looks like somebody has forgiven somebody for his telephone-itis."

"Not *entirely* forgiven," Kate said.

Jack raised a questioning brow.

"But he's getting closer."

Seeing warmth in her gaze, Jack gave her a slow, steady look, telling her without words that he'd keep doing whatever he had to earn her forgiveness.

"I'm suddenly feeling very third wheel here. Kate, I do hope you have room for me to crash at your place, because I didn't make a hotel reservation or anything."

"I think the hotel in Pleasantville only rents by the hour anyway," Kate said with a grin. "Of course you'll stay with me. I don't have an extra bed, or very much furniture at all. But I do have a sleeping bag."

"You can stay here." Jack's tone allowed for no argument. "There's an extra, fully furnished bedroom." Two, really, since Jack fully intended to sleep in Kate's bed, anyway.

"Wonderful, thank you." Armand turned to Kate. "And tomorrow you take me downtown to show me the new store. Plus all the horrible places you remember from your teenage years. Your high school, the predictable barber shop, movie theater and fire station where they host pancake breakfasts. And you must introduce me to Viv. Does she have poufed-up blond hair, tacky plastic shoes and like to crack bubble-gum?"

Shaking her head, Kate chuckled. "Nope. Sorry to disappoint you, she's a pretty, forty-something housewife with an uninspired husband. I think you've been watching too many movies about small-town life."

"I was raised in a town just like this, by my father the fire chief and my mother the former dairy princess."

"Interesting background, considering your name," Jack said.

"Arnold Dettinger didn't work for me in Chicago," Armand explained with a shrug. "And since I haven't been home in twelve years, I'll consider this my trial run. Who knows? If no one starts dragging out the tar and feathers, I might follow your lead and plan a trip back to Milltown for Christmas."

Jack saw Kate squeeze her friend's hand. "I'm sure your parents would like that."

Armand gave a resigned shrug. "My mother, maybe. My father would be too busy ordering me not to embarrass him in front of the guys at the fire house to have time to be pleased."

Jack cleared his throat. "He might surprise you." Seeing Armand's doubting expression, Jack continued. "I have to believe that deep down fathers always want their sons to come home. Just don't wait until it's too late to find out."

LATER, with Armand settled into Kate's mother's old room, Jack followed Kate into the other duplex and up to her bedroom.

"So, you going to tell me the truth about the Bunko orgy?" he asked as she reached for the bottom of his shirt.

"You really want to hear?"

"Uh-huh."

"Well," she said, her voice a sultry whisper. "All the women were blondes except me, and they all had *really* big breasts. When we got there, we all took off our shirts and compared."

He snorted with laughter.

"Then, we squirted each other up with scented oils and gave each other massages, until we were just rolling around on the floor, one big mass of naked, squirming female bodies."

"You're evil."

"Isn't that every guy's fantasy orgy?"

"Well, no, actually he'd need to be there. Preferably on the bottom of the pile of naked, squirming female bodies."

"Men are so weird." She rolled her eyes. "What is the attraction of more than one woman at a time?"

"I have no idea," he explained, trying hard to retain a

serious expression. "I personally find that type of thing shocking and sordid."

She punched him lightly in the stomach.

"Oh, come on, you're buying into the male stereotype. It's at most a fantasy—the old 'me Tarzan, you Jane, you Janet' thing. Caveman-must-propagate-the-species genes rearing their persistent heads." When she crossed her arms impatiently, he continued. "Most men don't know what the hell to do with one woman and certainly couldn't handle two and they know it."

"True."

"Besides," he continued, "don't women fantasize about being with two men, too?"

"Not this woman. I would never want to be in bed with a naked guy who didn't mind being in bed with another naked guy."

Jack's shoulders shook as he laughed.

"Besides," she continued, "if a man likes other men enough to be naked with them, then there's one or two things I'm lacking that he's bound to notice."

"I'd rather notice the one or two very nice, feminine things you have," he said with a definite leer.

As he reached out his hand and traced the tip of his fingers along the top hem of her loose blouse, she gave him a languid smile.

"One is more than enough for me," she murmured. "Though, two yous might be nice."

He paused, giving her a mock frown. "Did you say two Hughs?"

She rolled her eyes and shoved him onto the mattress, falling on top of him. They rolled across it, wrapped in each other's arms exchanging laughter and hot kisses.

"I said two *yous*. Two Jacks. Two sets of these amazing hands." She brought his hand to her lips, kissing the tips of his fingers and sliding her mouth over his pinky. "Two perfect mouths on my body." She leaned up to press her lips against his. "Two tongues to taste me."

He tasted her, nibbling, kissing and licking his way down her neck, across her collarbone, to the hem of her shirt. She lifted up so he could tug it out, and Jack tossed it over his shoulder to the floor. "No bra at all this time," he murmured, his voice thick with appreciation as he saw her beautiful breasts and pert nipples. When he moved his mouth over one, flicking his tongue across the puckered tip, she jerked against him and groaned.

"Two mouths would be useful here," he murmured as he went back and forth, from one breast to the other, sucking, nibbling and stroking her into a frenzy beneath him.

Sitting up long enough to yank off his clothes, he helped her unfasten her jean skirt, then pulled it off her. Her flimsy panties followed, then he had to pause, to look at her naked body, bathed in the soft glow of the hallway light. She looked at him, as well, her eyelids heavy, her lips parted as she took in deep, ragged breaths.

"Would you prefer two of anything else, Kate?" he asked, as he bent to kiss her again, letting her feel his hard-on against her thigh. She instinctively arched toward it in an age-old signal of welcome from female to male.

"Hmm, no, I think I can stay quite busy playing with this one," she whispered as she reached for him.

She proceeded to play. Stroking him, cupping him, running her hands up and down his dick as they exchanged lazy, wet kisses and he fondled her breasts. He didn't think he'd be able to stand it when she bent to take him into her mouth. He had to lift his arms over his head and press his fists against the wall to try to hold on to his sanity. The way her long, thick hair spread across his body, draping between his thighs to caress his balls, felt almost as good as her hot, wet mouth wrapped around him. Almost.

After a few moments she kissed her way up his body to his lips, then slid one leg across his hips. She rubbed against him, letting her juices spread over his erection, and it felt so good, so damn good to be close to her, without the barrier of a condom, that he nearly came right then. He would like for there to be no barriers between them, of any kind. Ever.

"You amaze me," he admitted as he stared up at her.

"Even though there's only one of me?"

"One's all I want, Kate," he murmured. "One you."

She leaned down to kiss him, their tongues swirling languorously. Her breasts brushed his chest and her warm mound remained tantalizingly close to his penis.

"Not yet," he told her when she retrieved a condom from her purse on the floor next to the mattress.

Raising a curious brow, she stared at him. He smiled as he cupped her hips. Tugging her forward, he slid down to meet her. She watched him, her eyes wide and excited as she understood what he wanted. What he had to have.

"Are you sure you…"

"Oh, yeah," he replied as he positioned her bottom on his chest and her beautiful, sweet, wet opening right in front of his hungry mouth. Then he tasted her, holding her hips as she bucked in delight at the intimate contact.

The position gave him the perfect access to pleasure her, and himself. He licked, stroked and suckled her until she came right in his mouth, her body trembling and hot as she leaned against the wall above his head for support. And that wasn't enough. He kept tasting her, sliding his tongue into her, demanding that she give him more until she cried out as a second orgasm ratcheted through her body.

Only then did he let her go, rolling her onto her back and reaching for the condom she'd dropped.

"I guess two *is* better than one sometimes, isn't it? Twice the pleasure?" he said with a chuckle, referring to her orgasms. Sheathing himself, he plunged into her even before she'd stopped panting from her orgasms.

"Oh, yes," she cried.

He didn't move at first, just savored the wet heat in which he was enveloped. Looking at her face, he saw her parted lips, the flush in her cheeks, the long lashes on her lowered eyelids.

She began to move beneath him, her body telling him what she wanted. He gladly gave it to her. Slowly, with deep, steady, sure strokes, he moved in and out of her until she began to moan and roll her head back and forth on the pillow.

"More, Jack, please," she whispered, bending her legs even higher and tilting her hips up, inviting him deeper inside.

He knew what she wanted and how she wanted it. Faster. Harder. Mind-numbing and scream-inducing.

Kate didn't want sweet. Kate wanted hot.

He complied with a groan, tugging one of her legs over his shoulder and plunging harder than before. Her eyes flew open.

"Good?"

"God, yes," she muttered through choppy indrawn breaths. "I want you so deep inside me that I don't know if I'm feeling your body or my own."

"Oh, I think I can guarantee you're going to know it's mine," he said with a chuckle as he ground against her.

She hissed and met his every move, smiling as he gave her what she wanted.

He watched as she moved her hands up her legs, reaching for her own breasts. She plucked at her nipples with her fingertips, sexy little pants still coming from between her lips. "Four hands might be good right now," she said.

Remembering her incredible sensitivity right there, and wanting to give her everything she desired, Jack slid out of her.

"What are you..."

"Shh," he whispered, giving her a smile that said *Trust me*. She watched, wide-eyed as he reached for her hip and gently rolled her onto her belly. He heard her moan into the pillow, obviously realizing how he wanted to take her.

"Oh, yes, absolutely," she said as she lifted her curvy bottom and hips, offering herself. The most tempting offer he'd ever had.

"Up, baby," he whispered, pulling her to her knees.

She complied, rising to all fours, moving back to meet him as he slid into her from behind, then leaned forward until his chest touched her back.

Perfect. The position left his hands free to pleasure her, to tweak her sensitive nipples, to stroke the curves of her breasts and the soft flesh of her belly. Then lower, to play with her sweet little clit as he rocked into her until she came close. Damn close, judging by her cries.

"Now," she ordered. *"Now."*

He knew what she wanted—she wanted him to come with her. Straightening, Jack took her hips in his hands and drove into her with a few powerful, body-draining thrusts.

"Now," he agreed.

The moment she screamed in climax, his own overtook him and they both collapsed to the mattress. He instantly rolled onto his side, tugging her close to nestle against his chest. He pressed a kiss to her brow, then to her cheek. Then to her mouth, still open and panting.

"That was amazing," she finally managed to whisper between deep, shuddery breaths.

He nodded.

"But, you know, Jack, now you've got me spoiled."

He lifted a brow.

"I suddenly want two of everything."

Smiling, knowing by the way his body began to react to her all over again, he whispered, "Let's not set any limits, okay? Why stop at two?"

He caught her mouth in a deep, slow kiss as they began all over again.

ON SATURDAY, Armand took Pleasantville by storm, chatting easily with each person he met and seeming to really enjoy the small-town atmosphere.

He raved over the shop, and gave Kate some good suggestions on layout. He also helped her straighten up the dressing room area, asking once why there were crotchless tights strewn all over the floor. Thankfully, he hadn't questioned her blush.

Nor did he tease her too unmercifully about the thinness of the walls at the duplex, other than to say he'd heard some wild animals howling in the middle of the night, and wondered if there were coyotes in Pleasantville.

Later, during lunch at the Downtown Deli, he'd met Diane and Josie, charming them both completely. Josie had enough innate street sense to recognize his preferences in spite of his sexy charm. She seemed to like him all the more for it.

But the real highlight of the afternoon came when they walked out of the deli and straight into a couple, who stood exchanging heated words on the sidewalk.

"Angela and Darren," Kate whispered, instantly recognizing Jack's sister. "The banes of my teenage existence."

Surprised she hadn't run into Jack's sister before now,

she forced herself to take a deep breath and to remember that she was completely over any childhood hurts.

"High school tormentors, hmm?" Armand whispered as they walked within a few feet of the two.

"Hi, Kate," Darren said. He looked at Armand, then stood a little straighter. Armand, with his height and elegant sophistication, had that effect on men.

Angela's face turned red as she stared at Kate, her mouth opening but no sound coming out. She looked not only flustered by Kate's appearance, but also annoyed at the interruption of her conversation with Darren.

"Hello, Darren. Angela," Kate replied, her voice sounding much calmer than she'd have expected.

Darren gave her a big, friendly smile. "I'm sorry I didn't get to talk to you much the other day. It's great to have you back, Kate. I'm really glad things have gone so well for you."

Surprisingly, he sounded sincere.

Angela didn't speak to her; she was too busy glaring at Darren as he talked to Kate. Then, when the other woman finally noticed Armand, an appreciative expression lit up her face.

Funny, when she actually smiled, Angela didn't look quite so much like a cast-iron bitch.

"Introduce us to your friend," she murmured.

After the introductions Armand stepped into his role as if it had been created for him. He flirted with Angela until the woman was practically melting into a puddle on the sidewalk. Once or twice Kate tried to tug him away, knowing he was trying to get a little payback on her behalf by stringing the other woman along. He'd probably be dashing off some scathing rejection at any moment now. The second time Kate tried to hurry him away Angela shot her a dagger-sharp glare. *Well, to hell with helping you, lady!* She stopped trying to lead Armand away.

"So, you're here visiting your *friend* Kate?" Angela asked.

Armand shrugged. "We're business partners. We own a store together on the Miracle Mile in Chicago."

Angela's eyes widened. "Really?" She glanced at Kate.

"Is it the same kind of store you're opening here?" Darren said, stepping not-so-casually between Angela and Armand. Kate noticed and wondered if things were heating up again between the ex-spouses. It would explain why Darren looked anything but pleased about Angela's interest in Kate's partner.

"Yes, but now, we really have to go. I have things to do before tonight's party."

Angela frowned. "The party at city hall? You're coming?"

"Yes." Kate couldn't resist adding, "As Jack's date."

The other woman's face paled. "How…nice." Turning toward Armand, she said, "And you must come, too."

"Will you be there?"

Angela nodded.

"Then I wouldn't miss it for the world," he said, looking at her with a sexy, promising grin.

Kate kicked his ankle.

"Okay, I guess it's time for us to go," he said with a grimace. If he bent to kiss Angela's hand or anything, Kate swore she'd shove him in front of the next oncoming car.

As soon as they were out of earshot of the other two, Kate said, "That was really bad of you."

"Oh, come on, I know something about high school tormenters, babe. You're telling me you never fantasized about getting a little payback?"

If only you knew!

"Just don't, okay? Angela is Jack's sister!"

Armand whistled. "Whoops."

When they got back to the duplex, Armand insisted on helping pick out something for Kate to wear. She'd brought a few nicer dresses and was now glad she had.

"Red," Armand said as he pulled out a tight spaghetti-strapped cocktail dress with a band of glittering sequins right above the breasts. "Perfect. And it'll match. Wait here."

When he returned, he was carrying a bundle of tissue paper. "My latest design. Here you go."

Kate opened the packet, seeing a tiny pair of red, lacy panties. She dropped the paper and held them up, looking for the trick. No zipper. No slit. Not a thong. And they had a crotch.

The only thing unique about them was their weight. They felt heavier than they should, given the minute amount of fabric.

"Very pretty, and you're right, they will match."

He rolled his eyes at her lack of enthusiasm. "Go into the bathroom and try them on," he said, shooing her out.

Following his orders, she went into the bathroom and took her shorts and underwear off. As she pulled the new underpants up, she noticed the extra weight seemed centered in the crotch area. When she pulled them into place, she realized why.

"Oh, my God," she whispered with a shocked laugh.

The panties were padded with a spongy, soft middle, covered with a feathery fabric that cupped her private area quite deliciously. A firmer, ridged section toward the front pressed against her clitoris. "You've got to be kidding me," she yelled.

"Walk in them," Armand ordered through the door.

The bathroom was too small, so she wrapped a towel

around her waist and walked out into the hallway. Armand stood there, waiting for her reaction. As she walked, she had to admit it, the little ridge felt pretty damn good. Not to mention the soft middle, which made it feel like wispy, downy kisses were being pressed all over her opening.

"Nice?" When she nodded weakly, he practically bounced on his toes. "Try the stairs."

She did. "Oh, very nice," she admitted, almost purring at the pleasure of it.

"Good. You're wearing them tonight. And every time some pissy small-town matriarch wrinkles up her nose in your direction, you stroll right by her with a secretive, delighted smile on your face."

Sounded like a pretty good plan to her.

12

As he pulled Kate's SUV into the parking lot outside city hall, Jack could tell by the look on her face she was still uncertain about this evening's party. She wasn't frowning, but she looked deep in concentration, as if thinking of something else. Every once in a while, she even wriggled in her seat. "You okay? You're awfully fidgety."

From the back seat, he heard Armand snort a laugh.

She gave Jack a quick guilty look. "Uh, fine. I'm fine. Why do you ask?"

He shrugged. "You just seem distracted." Taking her hand, he squeezed it and said, "But you also look amazing."

She did. Her body turned the red fabric of her dress into pure solid sin. Though petite, Kate had curves men dreamed about. Curves *he'd* dreamed about many nights since they'd met.

Not to mention the fullness of her lips, the sparkle in her deep brown eyes. Her confidence, intelligence and attitude appealed to him even more now than the day they'd met. Especially since they'd become so intimate.

He got the shakes just thinking about the things they'd done together the night before in her bed.

He simply couldn't get enough of her. Kate was the woman he'd been casually seeking and had never really thought he'd find ever since he'd left home fifteen years ago. How funny that he found her right here in Pleasantville, the very place he'd been trying so hard to escape.

She'd pulled her hair back, letting cascades of curls drop over her bare shoulders. The dress was not too short, ending a few inches above the knee, but below it her legs were bare. Her strappy, red high-heeled sandals had caught his eye several times during the short drive from the house.

"I'm fine. Now, who is going to be at this thing? Should I have worn body armor?"

He shook his head. "My mother's not coming. She wasn't feeling well. Frankly, I think it's driving her insane to give up the title of First Lady of Pleasantville. She doesn't want to see her replacement holding court."

Kate chuckled. "But your sister will be here."

"Yeah."

"Ah, your sister, such a charming little thing," Armand murmured from the back seat.

Jack saw Kate shoot her friend a warning glare, but didn't have time to question it.

They made their way into city hall, blending into the crowd of people in the atrium. In a far corner a band played jazzy music and an area had been cleared for dancing. A bar had been set up on what was usually an information desk. Armand immediately beelined for it, offering to get a round of drinks, leaving Kate and Jack to circulate.

He felt her tension, the stiffness of her body. Her hands were like ice, though she maintained an expression of complete calm. Jack wondered again what it must have been like for her growing up here, if it could still make her so anxious all these years later. But she never flinched, never let anyone see a single sign of nervousness, not even when one of his mother's cronies glanced at her, sniffed rudely, and turned away.

He saw Kate's face grow pale. Leaning close, he brushed

a kiss against her temple and whispered, "Ignore the old bat. Did you know she wears a wig?"

At Kate's surprised expression, he continued. "My mother told me years ago. Seems she's got a nervous habit and pulls her own hair, so she thought it would be easier— and less painful—to just buzz-cut it and wear wigs."

Kate giggled. "That's her story and she's sticking to it, huh? I think she was rude to the wrong person and someone just snatched her bald."

"That's my girl." Right there in the middle of the crowd, he pressed a soft kiss to her mouth. Her tension seemed to ease as he took her arm and continued to lead her through the crowd.

Finally they came face-to-face with the new mayor and his wife. Kate's eyes widened in shock. "Mr. Otis?"

The elderly mayor, who, Jack remembered, used to teach drama at the high school, squinted and looked at her more closely. "Why, Kate Jones, how you've grown up!"

The mayor then proceeded to sweep Jack's date in his arms and give her a tight hug. "You've gone off to the big city and done quite well for yourself, haven't you?"

"Yes, I have. I had no idea you were mayor. I figured you'd retired from teaching and were off fishing somewhere."

"Fishing for trouble at city hall," he said with a wink.

While Kate and Mr. Otis chatted, Armand returned, carefully balancing three drinks. Jack took his beer, and Kate's wine, holding one glass in each hand.

"By the way," Armand said, speaking in a near whisper, "I meant to give you something before we left the house."

"What?"

Instead of answering, Armand removed what looked like a small black box from his jacket pocket. "You don't have the hands, I'll drop it in your pocket." He did so, then said, "Just something fun to ease Kate's tension."

Since Jack's hands were still full with the drinks, he couldn't reach in to see what Armand had put there. "You going to explain this?"

Armand shook his head then grinned. "Remember, roll the dial slowly and never take your eyes off her."

Then he strolled away, leaving Jack very curious.

Kate had never actually conceived of enjoying this evening, but as she chatted happily with her favorite high school teacher—now interim mayor of Pleasantville—she realized that she might. When she spied Diane walking around with a tall, red-haired guy who tugged at the collar of his suit as if it was itching him, she felt more certain of it.

"Well, I suppose I have to mingle," Mr. Otis finally said as someone tried to lead him away for a photo op. "It's so nice to have you back here, Kate. I hope you'll visit more often."

"Wow," she said to Jack when they were once again alone in the crowd of elegantly dressed people. "I never imagined Mr. Otis would be the new mayor."

Diane and her husband joined them. "He's been on the city council for a few years," she explained. "So's Will." She introduced her husband. Kate instantly liked the man, who looked as though he'd rather be anywhere but here, dressed in anything but his plain brown suit.

Jack, on the other hand, looked delicious in his dark blue one. Elegant, expertly tailored, it showed off his hard, lean form to perfection. With his thick, blond hair, vivid green eyes and sexy grin, he had the attention of every woman in the place.

He fit in with this crowd easily. But he was just as at

ease with Will and Diane, who obviously lived far from Lilac Hill.

Throughout the next hour Diane introduced them to several other newer members of the town's business community, all of whom went out of their way to tell Kate how happy they were about her opening a new store in the downtown area. Kate began to feel torn. Yes, she'd decided to open the store as revenge. But if that were the case, she'd be punishing these nicer people she was meeting, too.

Or maybe not. Ever since last night at Eileen's house, she'd had to wonder if maybe her store wasn't exactly what this town needed. New, fresh, daring—like a lot of these younger people circulating amid the old highbrow set.

The highbrow set increased by one when Mrs. McIntyre walked into the room. Kate, standing close to the door, had turned to throw away her cup, and nearly ran into her.

The woman's face went rigid enough to crack. She made a sound that was a cross between a groan and a harrumph before she turned her back on Kate and walked away.

Taking a deep breath, Kate glanced around to see if anyone had noticed the snub. Jack stood several feet away, pretending to listen to an older woman chatting his ear off, but his attention was focused directly on Kate. His sexy smile was conspicuously absent, his eyes tender and concerned. She felt his silent support as though he'd put his arm around her.

She gave him a little nod, trying to assure him that she was okay, knowing he'd never believe it. He murmured something to the woman, who walked away, then gave Kate a slow smile. His green eyes shone with interest as he reached into his suit pocket.

Before she could step closer to see what he was up to, Kate's panties came alive. "Oh," she said with a sharp gasp.

She froze, her mouth falling open as she focused on the sudden, completely unexpected sensations in her private area.

"Good Lord," she said with a breathy sigh.

Armand had outdone himself.

The spongy middle slowly undulated against her rapidly swelling and quickly aroused mound, while the harder nubbins began to flicker against her clitoris with incredible friction.

She closed her eyes, taking deep breaths, quite unable to move. Around her, the crowd chattered. Someone asked her a question, and she nodded dumbly. Someone else handed her a drink. She lifted it to her lips and gulped without even looking at it, only realizing it was champagne when she felt a tickling sensation in her nose and throat. Of course, that couldn't match the tickling sensation between her legs.

The slow vibration picked up its pace, increasing in speed. She even swore she could hear a tiny hum and almost gasped as she wondered if anyone else heard it. As she cast a quick glance around to see, she met Jack's eyes. His pleased, boyish grin told her he was responsible for what was happening. "More?" he asked, though she couldn't hear him. She read the word on his lips.

She shook her head and gave him a scolding look, unable to believe he was doing this to her in a huge crowd of people.

The look in his eyes as he reached into his suit pocket could only be called wickedly anticipatory. She shook her head again, not able to take any more, but not able to stop it. His hand kept moving, slowly, as he dragged out the tension. And, if she were to be honest, the anticipation.

Kate shot a quick look around the lobby where the party was being held, gauging the distance to the ladies' room. Too far. No way could she make it when her legs were already weak, her breaths choppy and her heart racing out of control.

Jack's hand had finally reached his pocket and as it slipped inside, she sent him one more pleading glance. At this point, she really couldn't have said what she was pleading for.

If the vibrations got much stronger, she'd go right over the edge and have a shattering orgasm in the middle of this crowd of elegantly dressed people.

If they stopped, she'd die.

The heat in Jack's stare as he cranked up the pressure was almost enough to make her come anyway. She shuddered as the intensity of vibration rose yet another notch. Reaching blindly for support, she found herself grabbing the corner of an information desk and her fingers sunk into some creamy substance. A quick glance down told her it was a slice of cheesecake topped with strawberries, but she couldn't bring herself to care.

The waves of pleasure began to roll through her, signaling her climax, and she leaned her hip against the desk. She heard someone say her name, but couldn't even turn her head. Her eyes were glued to Jack's and he nodded with encouragement, knowing even from several feet away that she was close.

"Yes," she whispered, closing her eyes as an intense bolt of pleasure shot through her. Her hands clenched, oozing strawberries and cheesecake between her fingers. Dropping her head back, she gasped for breath as the orgasm sent electric pleasure racing through her body.

Finally the vibrations between her legs slowed, then stopped. When she opened her eyes, she saw Jack watching her, looking hot and ready, as if watching her reach her climax had pushed him close to the edge, too. She was about to walk over to him when she heard Diane's voice.

"Good God, I've eaten cheesecake I'd consider orgasmic, but I never got off just from *touching* one."

"THAT WAS REALLY BAD of you," Kate whispered as Jack curled her tighter in his arms in the back of her SUV an hour later.

They'd escaped the party as quickly as they could, after ensuring Armand could get a ride home with Diane and her husband. By silent consent, they'd avoided going back to the duplex, instead driving up to a popular lake on the outskirts of town. Their clothes had come off a minute after Jack had engaged the parking brake and they'd barely made it over the back seat into the cargo area before he was inside her.

They'd been frenzied and ravenous. Now they lay quietly, exchanging slow, lazy kisses and caresses that were going to lead to sweet, long lovemaking. Jack didn't know how he could want her again, already, but he did.

"I thought it was your fantasy," he finally answered.

"My fantasy?"

"Being made helpless. Having to accept pleasure because you are powerless to stop it."

She laughed. "Yeah, but I meant something more along the lines of being tied to the headboard, not being brought to a shattering orgasm in a room filled with a hundred people. I can't imagine what Diane must have thought."

"I think she went to look for the chef to ask for the recipe for that cheesecake."

She giggled. "Maybe we should sell it at Bare Essentials."

He stretched to work a kink out of his neck. "I haven't had sex in the back of a car in years."

"This is my first back seat experience ever."

"Uncomfortable, isn't it?"

She nodded. "But exciting. I keep picturing a cop knocking on the window and telling us to get our clothes on." She arched closer, sliding her arm around his waist. "Or an ax-maniac with a hook. You know, the kind who always slaughters the teenagers when they run out of gas on lover's lane?"

"I'm fairly certain the parents of a teenage girl made up that story the night before her first date."

"So, was this your make-out spot when you were a teenager?"

He shook his head. "No way. Everyone in town knew my father and I never dared to bring a date out here."

He felt her tense in his arms at the mention of his father.

"I know what it's like to have everyone in town know your family," she admitted.

Leaning down, he pressed kisses on her temple, her cheekbone, then her lips. He kissed her lazily, gently coaxing her mouth to open. When it ended, he whispered, "I'm sorry I didn't know you then. I'm sorry I wasn't around to stop it when you were being treated so badly. By my sister or anyone else."

He wished he had been. He hated like hell to think of anyone hurting her. Ever.

"It was a long time ago, Jack. And you know, being back here has made me remember some of the better times, too. I guess I should be thankful for that. I'd been angry for a long time and let that anger color my memories. It's good to have some of those nicer moments back."

He believed she meant it. Hopefully, no matter what else happened, Kate wouldn't regret this time spent in Pleasantville. Seeing the town through adult eyes had evened out her feelings, much as it had his. "So you think you might come back someday? For a visit?"

She shrugged. "Anything's possible."

Before he could reply, they heard the sound of crunching gravel. The bright sheen of headlights washed through the windows of the SUV.

"Oh, my God, someone else is here," she cried.

They scrambled for their clothes like a couple of kids caught making out by their parents. He tossed her the magical little red underwear she'd worn at the party, watching as she shimmied into her dress. She was giggling hysterically. "Please be the cops and not a guy with an ax and a hook."

"You got your wish. It's the cops," he replied.

Jack was having as hard a time containing his laughter as Kate appeared to be. His first time going parking in more than a decade and they get caught by the town sheriff. Thank heaven it hadn't been ten minutes before or he doubted they'd have even noticed the approach of the other car.

He'd just zipped his pants when he heard a knock on the driver's side window, Thankfully, it was tinted. Recognizing Sean Taggart, with whom he'd gone to high school, he slid into the back seat, then opened the door. "Hi, Tag," he said as he jumped out. He shut the door behind him, giving Kate more time.

"Jack," the other man said with a nod. Tag pushed his sheriff's hat up on his head with the tip of one finger, trying unsuccessfully to hide a grin. "You out for a late-night drive?"

"Yep. Enjoying the view over the lake."

"Well, I can see why you felt the need to take off your shirt. Musta been awful hot with all that steam on the windows." He glanced at the lake. "But wasn't it hard to see the view considering you're parked facing the road, instead of the water?"

Before Jack could reply, Kate stepped out. "Hi, Sheriff," she said, her face awash with color.

Tag's eyes widened as he obviously noticed her crooked dress, bare feet and wildly tangled hair. "Kate, isn't it? Cassie's cousin?" When Kate nodded, Tag said, "Where is she? I heard a rumor she left town for a few days, which I couldn't believe since that'd be so incredibly stupid."

Sensing Tag knew about whatever trouble Cassie was in, Jack waited for her answer, as well. When Kate admitted her cousin had gone to New York for the weekend, and would fly home the next day, Tag swore under his breath. "When does her plane get in?"

"She's supposed to call me and let me know when she's leaving New York so I can go pick her up at the airport."

"Tell you what," Tag said, his calm tone not hiding his obvious anger. "You call me in the morning and tell me what flight she's on so I can go pick her up, and I won't arrest you both for public indecency."

"We weren't exactly in public," Jack said.

"Maybe not. Then again, I've just heard an interesting rumor about some mighty strange behavior by the two of you at the mayor's party, which was *very* public. Now, do we have a deal?"

Kate nibbled on her lip, then finally nodded. "Cassie's gonna kill me."

"Not if I kill her first," Tag muttered as he turned on his heel and strode away. He got into his car, but before leaving, he rolled down his window. "Next time, cut your lights before you pass by old lady Millner's place. She's a quarter mile up the road and calls every time a car comes down here late at night."

Then he drove away, leaving them standing alone.

"Sounds like he's speaking from experience," Kate said with a chuckle.

"Tag never had much problem with the girls back in high school."

"With those looks and that body? I can definitely see why he'd cause a sigh or two." She gave him a look out of the corner of her eye that screamed mischief.

Okay, Kate wanted him jealous. No problem. He grabbed her arm and tugged her close. Lowering his voice, he whispered, "I'm surprised you can sigh, or even talk at all, considering the way you were screaming ten minutes ago. Your throat must be sore."

Then he caught her mouth in a hot, wet kiss designed to drive the thought of any other person on the planet out of her mind. Her gentle moans and pliant body told him he'd succeeded.

When they parted, she sucked in a few deep breaths. "You're definitely scream-worthy, Jack," she said. "And you certainly know how to show a girl a good time." She started to giggle, then to laugh out loud. "Oh, my gosh, if Tag tells Cassie about this, she'll never let me live it down. We made a pact to never go parking with guys when we were in high school. We pinky swore and everything."

"You mean I was good enough to break a pinky swear for?" he said with a pleased grin. "Wow. I don't know if anyone's ever broken a pinky swear just for me."

She lightly elbowed him in the ribs. "Don't go getting a swelled head." She leaned back against the car, crossing her arms and letting out an audible sigh. "I'm going to be dead meat when I'm not the one who shows up tomorrow to pick Cassie up at the airport."

"Something's going on between your cousin and the sheriff?"

"I think so."

"Tag's a nice guy. And a patient one, which is good,

since I suspect your cousin could try the patience of a saint.''

"Good thing that doesn't run in the family," she said, giving him a deceptively innocent look. When he raised one skeptical brow, she rolled her eyes. "Okay, okay, I guess I can be a pain in the butt, too."

"Nah," he said with a deliberate shrug. "In spite of a deplorable lack of sweetness, you're not so bad."

Her grin widened. "Do you know how nice it is to be with someone who doesn't expect me to be sweet?" She straightened, stepped away from the SUV, and put her arms out to her sides. Spinning around, she almost yelled, "God, tonight was *fun*. Outrageous and naughty, and definitely not sweet!"

"Yeah, it was," he admitted, remembering how aroused he'd been by her at the party. He loved watching her again now as she almost danced in the moonlight, her hair swinging wildly around her face. "But I hate to break it to you, babe. I suspect you really are kinda sweet, deep down."

She stopped. "Keep that up and you'll be walking home."

He jiggled his pants' pocket. "I've got your keys."

She stepped closer, laying her hand flat on his bare chest and giving him a limpid look. "Wanna place a bet on how fast I can get into your pants and get them back?"

He shook his head. "I think we've already proved you hold the world's record on getting into my pants, Kate."

"Ditto," she admitted, trailing her hand across his bare chest to his stomach. "So does that make us both cheap and easy?"

"Only with each other." He swallowed a groan as her hand moved lower, brushing across the front of his pants.

"Fair enough."

Jack liked the humor on her face and the sparkle in her

eyes. He liked seeing Kate happy. He'd seen her that way much more often lately. The angry, mistrustful woman who'd come back to Pleasantville for revenge had been erased.

He hoped he'd had something to do with that. Because there was no question in his mind Kate had changed him. For the better. He doubted she'd believe it, he had trouble believing it himself, but he was falling in love with her. Falling hard and fast.

He'd started the slide the first time he'd laid eyes on her across Magnolia Avenue. Making love to her that same day had strengthened the feeling. Every day they'd spent together since then had been better than the one before.

"Come on," he said, tugging her by the hand. "Let's go down to the lake."

Though she wore an obviously expensive dress, Kate didn't hesitate. They walked hand in hand down to the edge of the lake, moving across the cool sand until they reached the shore. The warm water, lit by the bright, star-filled sky, lapped at their bare feet in a gentle rhythm. Not caring about his pants, he pulled her in deeper, until they stood almost knee deep. He tugged her close, sliding his arms around her waist. She came into them easily, curling against his chest, tucking her head beneath his chin.

"I used to come up here to swim late at night," he said as he gently slid his fingers into her hair.

"It's warm enough," she replied. "But I don't really want to swim."

"Me neither. I'd rather stay just like this."

With Kate wrapped securely in his arms.

That seemed to be exactly what she wanted, too.

THE NEXT DAY, before Armand left to go back to Chicago, Kate asked him if he'd had a good time at the party after they'd left. He'd simply smiled and said, "It was a night that won't be forgotten for a long time."

Thanking him for the panties, she'd admitted she felt the same way.

The night before had been magic. Not only the party, not just the frantic sex in the back of her car. But standing there, wrapped in Jack's arms as they stood in the moonlight, simply enjoying each other's closeness. They'd exchanged long, languorous kisses, sweet, delicate touches. They hadn't talked much, nor had they made love again. Somehow, though, the night felt like the most intimate one they'd shared.

At some point Kate had even been able to admit the truth to herself. Not only did she no longer distrust Jack, she was falling in love with him.

Not intentionally, probably not wisely, but there it was. She loved the son of the man who'd broken her mother's heart.

"Maybe it's fate," she told herself. "Maybe we can have the happy ending in this generation."

She told herself not to hope too much. After all, she'd gone through most of her adult life not believing she could ever trust someone enough to experience real love. Somehow, though, he'd worked past her defenses and captured her heart. She was simply unable to help it.

Cassie called Monday morning, and, to Kate's complete surprise, didn't even scold her for not picking her up from the airport. She did act very strange, though. Something had obviously happened between her and the sheriff after he'd picked her up, but Kate wasn't about to pry. After all, Cassie didn't question her about being caught having sex up at the lake with Jack. Kate had to figure it was because Tag hadn't told her. Cassie would never have let something that juicy go without comment if she knew. She'd instead been much more interested in hearing all about the Bunko party and the mayor's reception, seeming surprised to hear about the friendliness of so many of the women Kate had met.

When her cousin called again at noon, Kate instantly knew Cassie was in one of her wild moods. She sounded ready for something to happen. From experience, she figured that meant Cassie wanted something *dangerous* to happen.

Still, she had to admit, Cassie's idea was a good one. "You're saying we should have a pre-opening, private party for women only in the store tomorrow night?"

"Think of it as a very naughty Tupperware party."

It sounded ridiculous, outrageous and impossible.

And Kate loved the idea.

Their store would open in exactly one week. How better to test the waters than to invite some of the women Kate had met recently for a test run? They'd seemed modern and open about sex and relationships, and also starved for the type of products the store would carry. Deep down, she suspected they'd welcome Bare Essentials. The party would be the perfect time to find out.

That didn't mean she wasn't a nervous wreck. She liked these women, she really did, and she hated to imagine how she'd feel if they couldn't look past the titillation factor and see the potential for the store.

She wanted them to like Bare Essentials.

More importantly, she didn't want them to *dislike* her.

Kate did not pause to wonder when her goals had changed—she only knew they had. She no longer wanted only to cause controversy. Damn it, she wanted to succeed. She wanted the women of Pleasantville to be glad the Tremaine cousins had come back.

Thirty-six hours later, standing in the middle of a crowd of laughing women, she realized she needn't have worried.

"Oh, my God, Kate, no wonder you know so much about seduction!" Viv said as she greedily dug through the racks of erotic movies in the store.

"I never thought I'd say this, but these might be even better than Dr. Martens." This from Josie as she stood in front of a mirror, holding a jade-green silk teddy up against her body.

Diane went for the sex toys. "Anyone know which end is up?"

Crossing her arms and nodding in satisfaction, Kate met Cassie's eye from across the room. They exchanged a long, knowing look, each realizing that in spite of the way they'd started out, they were witnessing the birth of a bona fide success.

Who'd have ever believed it?

Soon the store was overflowing with chattering women. All the Bunko players came, and they brought friends. Cassie had also invited one woman, Stacie, who was a relative newcomer to town herself and seemed thrilled to meet all the others. Cassie and Kate could barely keep up with the sales, chatter and laughter. They passed around wine and hors d'oeuvres, and as the evening wore on, the sales added up.

"Well, all I know is, I want to buy whatever it was Kate had on under her dress at the party Saturday night," Diane said, fisting her hands and putting them on her hips. "Come on, show me. No cheesecake in the world is that good."

"Sorry," Kate said with a rueful shrug. "It's still in the testing phase. Armand is working on it, though, and I'm sure the store will be carrying them before too long."

"Armand," Diane said with a snicker. "He cracked me and Will up the other night. I don't know what he said to Darren and Angela, but I thought they were going to shit bricks."

Not knowing what she was talking about, Kate raised a brow.

"Oh, gosh, you and Jack had already left, hadn't you?"

"I know where they went," Annie the dispatcher said with a grin. "We got a call about a silver SUV at the lake."

Cassie jerked her head around to listen, giving Kate a curious stare. Feeling a blush stain her cheeks, she ignored the question in her cousin's eyes. "Get back to Darren and Angela."

"I don't really know what happened, just that Angela was dancing with Armand, getting all grabby and touchy-feely. Darren came up, Armand said something to them both, and they took off like bats outta hell in two different directions."

Kate winced. She had a feeling she knew what Armand had said. Probably something along the lines of, *Sorry, Angela babe, Darren's much prettier than you and he's the one I want. Kiss me, big boy.* Armand specialized in cutting down homophobics.

Suddenly very glad they'd left the party early, she made a mental note to strangle Armand when she got back to Chicago.

Well, maybe she'd kiss him first. Then, for sure, she'd strangle him.

13

"So THE PARTY WAS A BIG success and the rumors are already spreading throughout town about how fabulous your store is. Tomorrow's grand opening will be a hit, I guarantee it. What'd I tell you? You're going to fail to fail." Jack couldn't keep the smug tone out of his voice as he and Kate brushed another coat of varnish remover on the old concession counter at the Rialto on Sunday afternoon.

She stuck her tongue out at him. "Anyone ever told you it's not nice to say I told you so?"

"Anyone ever told you it's not nice to stick your tongue out at people? Unless, of course, you're issuing an invitation." He caught her mouth in a quick, hot kiss that left them both breathless.

When they reluctantly parted, she looked down at the plastic drop cloth beneath their feet, which was splattered with liquid. "Paint washes off. I think varnish remover would sting, though."

"There's no work going on down on the stage," he whispered. "And our table's still there."

"Miss Rose will be back from the hardware store any minute now." She sounded disappointed. Just like he felt.

They couldn't seem to get enough of each other. No matter how many times he made love to Kate, it was always exciting, always amazing. Like that first time had been, right here in the theater all those weeks ago.

Jack had a hard time believing how much things had

changed since then. In the past several days he and Kate
had spent hours and hours in each other's company. He'd
told her about his plans to open his own firm, she'd talked
about her desire to expand her store. They'd gone through
the past relationship comparisons, each trying to one-up the
other with stories about some really bad first dates.

They'd even talked about their families a little. She'd told
him what it was like growing up without a father. He'd told
her of his regrets at leaving Angela alone in a house with
his very unhappily married parents.

She'd grown uncomfortable when he mentioned his parents. "I think we ought to change the subject."

Though he knew she was right, he wished he could tell
her what he'd discovered Friday. He could hardly believe it
himself and had no one with whom to discuss it.

Dealing with his father's bank records had been nearly
impossible from the beginning. But suddenly, the other day,
he began to make sense of things. For the first time in
weeks, Jack started to realize that his father had, in his own
way, tried to do right by Edie.

For each and every month when there had been an un-
cashed paycheck made out to Edith Jones, Jack had found
a subsequent payment to a mysterious account at a state
bank. Some digging had revealed the truth. His father had
made several sizable payments against Edie's mortgage. He
doubted she'd even realized it was happening.

No, his father hadn't wiped the slate clean by any means,
but it was nice to know he had not completely taken advantage of Kate's mother. He'd obviously cared about her,
enough to help her even when she refused to take his help.

It didn't make things right. But at least it made them
better. It also made Jack wonder if he would ever really
understand the truth about their relationship. It seemed now
it had been more about emotion than just sex. Sex wouldn't

have taken the older couple through nearly two decades. There had to have been love.

Somehow that made it a little easier to deal with.

"So, what are you going to do now that your store's on the road to success? You can't just shut it down," he asked.

She shook her head. "I've been thinking a lot about that. Cassie and I have worked there a lot lately and we've been discussing some options. At least she'll be here until the end of the summer. And who knows what she'll want to do then."

He laid his brush down and stared. "No way would Cassie stay here long-term."

She shrugged. "I don't know if she actually would, but I don't think it's a bad idea. I kind of suggested it to her."

He raised a brow. "I can only imagine how she reacted."

"After she stops laughing, maybe she'll really think about it. She's got a great house. And she seems to have found some things she likes about Pleasantville." She snickered, obviously thinking about Tag.

"So you really think she'd stay?"

"I honestly can't say. But it's a possibility. We'll see how tomorrow's grand opening goes."

"Then in a week or two you'll go back to Chicago."

"Right. And you will, too."

He nodded.

"I'm going to miss having you right next door," she admitted. "Who'll nearly kill me when he bursts in to tackle me in the middle of the night?"

"I only hurt you the *first* time I tackled you in the middle of the night. Admit it, every other tackle since then has been painless." He gave her a suggestive look, telling her he meant their more amorous tackles. "Don't forget, I did kiss it better that first time."

"Oh, yeah, you definitely did."

Though he hadn't planned to bring it up, figuring Kate might not have realized yet that she was falling in love with him, he couldn't help himself. "Besides, we don't have to give up on having each other around once we get home. I have a big apartment. And if it's not big enough, I can design us something better. Closer to your store."

Her eyes widened. "What are you saying? You mean, you want us to…"

"Move in together," he said. "I know it's kinda fast, but we're practically living together now. Why don't we just make it official when we get home?"

She lowered her eyes, looking away. Jack called himself ten kinds of fool for bringing it up. *It's too soon.* Hell, he knew they hadn't been together long enough to start talking about cohabitation. But he was already picturing little dark-haired Jacks and blond-haired Kates! Marriage, happily-ever-after, all the stuff he'd once sworn wasn't for him.

Now he understood. He simply hadn't found the right woman yet. Until Kate. His future. The woman he wanted to spend the rest of his life with.

The one who'd gone silent and white as a sheet at just the mention of them moving in together. If he told her he wanted to marry her someday, she'd probably faint face-first into the bucket of varnish remover.

Kate was an unusual woman and she wouldn't approach things—including her love life—in the usual way. A complicated mix of modern vixen and smart businesswoman, she'd wanted the sex first, then the relationship. He couldn't forget that, because she might never have even thought about the future or long-term plans. Talk of those things might scare her off.

It killed him to wonder if she'd figured their involvement would end once they left Pleasantville behind. Because it wouldn't. It *couldn't.* He was never letting her go. Though she might not be ready to admit it, he knew damn well she felt the same way.

She couldn't hide the way she looked at him, particularly when he held her in his arms. There was love in her eyes.

"Let's talk about it later, okay?" he said, quickly backtracking. "We still have some time here, and I know you need to focus on the grand opening tomorrow morning."

She looked troubled; her eyes were bright, as if she had tears in them. He silently cursed himself again for putting her on the spot, pressuring her too soon.

Before he could say anything, or even think of what to say, a woman's voice intruded. "Speaking of the grand opening, Kate, I need you to set something aside for me tomorrow morning."

They both looked up as Rose joined them, her arms loaded with bags of supplies from the hardware store.

"I want one of them Kama Sutra sheet sets, so I can honestly say my bed has had every sexual position known to man performed on it."

Kate's worried expression faded as she ruefully grinned. "You got it, Rose."

KATE FIGURED the grand opening of Bare Essentials in Pleasantville would be discussed by its residents for years to come. Old-timers would reminisce about it the way they did the big snowstorm of '73, the high school girls' state championship team of the early eighties. Even Flo Tremaine's striptease and skinny-dipping session in the town square fountain thirty years back would take a back seat to this day.

The newest generation of Tremaine women were definitely giving them something to talk about.

The line to get into the store Monday morning wound down the cobbled sidewalk, blocking the entrance to the Tea

Room. That obviously ticked Mrs. McIntyre off royally, because she'd posted a snippy little sign saying Do Not Block
Stairs on her porch railing.

Kate heard later that a few of the Tea Room biddies had
made rude comments about the store. They'd been overruled
by the people in line, including Mayor Otis who declared
Kate and Cassie worthy of a civic award for their efforts to
revitalize Pleasantville's downtown shopping district.

A neighboring city had even sent in a news truck. Sure,
it was a teeny cable station, with a viewership of about
eight, but it was exciting, nonetheless. The reporter con-
ducted interviews with the customers, many of whom were
the Bunko women who'd come to the pre-opening party last
week. Their husbands were even more enthusiastic in their
support of the new shop.

Singles, couples, young and old, the populace of Pleasantville chatted and laughed, lauding the store as an asset
to the town while they shopped their hearts out.

Armand's lingerie was a huge hit, with sexy books and
fun-and-naughty gifts doing well, too. Kate suspected the
hotter items—dildoes, vibrators and the like—would sell
better when there were no throngs of townspeople present.
Or TV cameras.

If Kate hadn't already changed her mind about wanting
this store to fail, she might be feeling pretty upset about its
obvious success. Now, since she wanted it to succeed, she
should be feeling at least triumph, if not downright jubila-
tion.

Depressed better described her mood.

Stupid. It was stupid, juvenile and girlish, but she was
depressed about Jack asking her to move in with him yesterday.

The modern woman who carried a vibrator around in her

purse should have been thrilled, recognizing Jack had really been offering a sort of commitment in today's day and age.

A deeper, more vulnerable part of her had been very hurt.

Did he want her to serve the same function as her mother had? The woman who was good enough to mess around with, but not the one you married, not the one you had children with?

Men from Lilac Hill didn't marry trashy Tremaine women. They had sex with them in secret and left them stuff in their wills, but they certainly didn't introduce them to their mothers or give them wedding rings.

She knew her reaction was unfair. She'd seen motives and desires he might never have intended. And it wasn't as if Jack knew about his father's relationship with her mother, so he couldn't possibly have realized how she might take it.

Kate was intelligent enough to know her own deep-down insecurity had made her tense up when he'd asked. That didn't lessen the feeling, though.

At the end of the day, a few minutes before closing time, Kate found herself alone behind the cash register. Cassie had run an errand, most of the shoppers had left. There were one or two people in the dressing rooms, she believed. She was ready for them to get out so she could go take a long, hot bath. When the bell jingled over the door, she glanced up and saw, to her surprise, Darren McIntyre.

"Still open for business?"

She glanced at the clock. "You've got two minutes. Tell me what you're looking for. I'll point you in the right direction."

He shrugged. "How about the apology area?"

Kate dropped her pencil. "Huh?"

Darren walked over to the counter, not able to disguise his interest as he studied the various items on the shelves.

He chuckled. "Bet my father never pictured this display case being used for *those* when he had it installed." When Kate didn't reply, he said, "Look, Kate, I came to apologize. I know it was years ago, and I'm sure you've forgotten, but I was a jerk to you in high school and I'm sorry."

Well, indeed, a day of surprises. "That's nice of you, Darren. I appreciate it. I know it's probably not easy for you to walk in here, remembering your dad and all."

He shrugged. "My father had every right to do with this building whatever he wanted to. I'm sure he'd rather see it open as a ladies' shop than sitting here moldering away. My mother on the other hand..."

Kate snorted. "Yeah, I can imagine."

"Divorce can be tough." He glanced away. "On everyone. You marry someone you think you know, think you love, then you find out you don't really know them at all."

She figured he was referring to his marriage but didn't ask. After a minute of small talk Darren said, "I'd better go. I just wanted to wish you luck and to say I'm sorry. Your, uh, *friend* Armand reminded me the other night that you might have a score to settle."

Kate shook her head, putting aside not only Darren's doubts, but any of her own. "No, Darren, I don't." *Not anymore.*

Darren had no sooner left, shutting the door behind them, when Kate heard someone emerge from the dressing room area. She sensed her long, hot bath was going to be further delayed when she recognized Angela. "I didn't know you were here."

"Stay away from Darren," the woman said. "You got your revenge. Your friend made a big fool out of the both of us the other night, so leave him alone."

Seeing tears in the other woman's eyes, Kate had to wonder whether Angela had ever given up on her first marriage.

Any sympathy she felt for Angela evaporated when she saw the book she held. Her diary. The last time she'd seen it, it had been in a drawer in a desk in the storage room. "Snooping?"

Angela didn't even have the grace to flush. "Stay away from my brother, too. I won't let you hurt him in some nasty plot."

"You don't know what you're talking about." Suddenly so tired, Kate rubbed her eyes. She didn't want to have this conversation. Ever.

Angela slammed the diary on the counter, open to the page with Kate's revenge list. "Yes, I do. Didn't you write this? 'For Mom's sake, get even with the Winfield family,'" she read. "'Particularly John Winfield.' My father isn't around to hurt anymore, so you've decided to focus on my brother. A different man, but who cares, the name's the same, right?"

Kate took a deep breath, trying to remain calm enough to deal with Jack's sister, trying to have sympathy for her, given the way Jack had described her childhood. "Angela, that was years ago. I don't have any intention of hurting Jack."

The other woman crossed her arms. "Just like you didn't want revenge on me and Darren, by setting us up to look like fools at the mayor's reception the other night? Like you didn't want to hurt the town by opening up this shop? Don't give me that. You want to hurt my family the way your mother did."

Then it hit her. Angela didn't seem the least bit surprised her diary had spoken of Edie and John. She tilted her head and stared at the woman. "You knew. About their affair."

Angela nodded. "Of course I knew. I've known for years. Everyone knows, even my mother."

Everyone? Including Jack?

"The point is, Kate, your secret's out. I'm going to tell Jack all about this little revenge list of yours, which you've been crossing off since the day you hit town."

Kate shook her head. "You're wrong. I care about Jack."

She smirked. "Won't matter. Jack doesn't care about you. You've been about one thing to him from the very beginning. He doesn't love you. Winfields don't marry trashy Tremaine women who own sex shops or work as maids. He won't marry you any more than my father married your mother."

Kate's anger made her reply so quickly her mind barely registered the ringing of the bell over the front door. "Thanks to *your* mother." At Angela's puzzled look, Kate said, "She made sure of it. Trapping him into marriage with a fake pregnancy just to get him away from *my* mother, who was his girlfriend throughout high school! That's probably just what you did to Darren, only he didn't stick around like your father did after he found out. So don't talk to me about families being hurt. If anyone deserves some payback, it's the Winfields."

Angela had grown pale and looked utterly shocked. Kate regretted the words as soon as she said them, angry with herself for letting the woman goad her so. Kate regretted them even more when she realized who had walked into the store.

Seeing the late-afternoon sunlight shining through the front windows onto a familiar—and very dear—blond head, she felt the blood drain from her face. "Jack."

"Do I even want to know what's going on here?" Jack forced a note of calmness in his voice as he walked across the store to the counter, where Kate and his sister both stood. They looked equally as disturbed by his appearance.

"This is a misunderstanding…"

"She came here for one reason. To get revenge," Angela

said at the same time. His sister thrust a small book in his hand, obviously a diary. "She's been plotting it for years. Against me and Darren—we were both totally humiliated by her gay friend the other night. But she's not satisfied yet, she's out to get the whole town, including *you*."

He didn't look at his sister, focusing all his attention on Kate. "Angela, would you please leave?"

He thought she'd argue, but she didn't. Looking confused and upset, more than angry, Angela grabbed her purse and hurried out of the store. As soon as they were alone, Jack put the diary back on the counter.

"It's not like she said…"

"I know about your revenge list, remember?" he interrupted softly. "You don't have to explain it to me."

She looked relieved. For a moment, anyway.

He continued. "I once asked you if it would be bad for me to see the list. When you said yes, I figured it mentioned Angela. Was she right? Was there more to it than that?"

Kate took a slow, deep breath, then nodded.

"You knew about my father and Edie."

She crossed her arms tightly. "I found out on prom night."

He absorbed her words and said a silent curse. Both Kate and his sister had learned as teenagers of their parents' affair. He again kicked himself for leaving town, for not being around when he might have been needed.

"When did you find out?" she asked softly.

"The night I met you," he admitted. "*After* I left you at the theater. I had absolutely no idea who you were until then. I didn't even know your last name, remember?"

She glanced away, her face growing even paler.

As a heavy, uncomfortable silence fell between them, Jack mentally replayed what he'd heard of the conversation. He still had trouble believing it. Not that Kate had written a revenge list, he'd known about it before, after all. He just hadn't known his entire family was part of the plot. Somehow, it had been easy to imagine she'd gotten over any high school hurts, so he'd accepted her assurances that she really wasn't opening her store for revenge. Now, however, he had to wonder.

"I have to know," he finally said, "was your list on your mind when you came back here? When we got involved?"

She stared at him, not answering.

"Tell me, Kate. When you decided to come back to Pleasantville, did you think about a little payback? Getting involved with me, then breaking my heart, like you thought my dad did to your mom?"

She countered with a question of her own. "You tell me something, Jack. The night we met, when you found out who I was, that Edie *Tremaine* was my mother…is that the reason you never called? The reason you decided we couldn't get involved?"

He answered easily. "Of course."

She stiffened, as if offended by his honesty, though he didn't know why. He opened his mouth to elaborate, to tell her how hurt he'd been for Edie, how he'd wanted to make it up to her and not take advantage of Kate.

Before he could say a word, however, she picked up her purse and keys. "Thanks for being honest. Now, you want the truth? Here it is. I came back here with every intention of seducing J. J. Winfield." Stepping around the counter, she met his stare steadily with her own. "I planned to get him to go crazy over me, then stomp his heart into the dust with the heels of my six-inch-tall slut-puppy boots."

Without another word, she turned and walked out of her own store.

14

WHEN NURSING A BROKEN heart, it really sucked to live next door to the person who'd done the breaking. Kate found that out late Monday night when she lay on her mattress bed in Aunt Flo's duplex, listening to Jack arrive home next door.

As soon as she heard his truck outside, she bit her lip to stop her tears. She definitely didn't want him to hear her through the wall.

She'd been crying for hours. Whimpering like a sissified baby. Wishing she had someone to talk to, but knowing there was no one. Cassie would be too pissed on her behalf to be of any help. Plus, the last thing she wanted to do on the day of the triumph at the store was to tell Cassie someone she thought she loved still looked at her as unworthy.

When Jack had admitted he'd decided to end their involvement because of who she was—a Tremaine—Kate had wanted to die. All she'd heard were his sister's angry words, the echo of taunts of her childhood, the deeply-buried-but-not-erased voice of her subconscious that had told her she would always be just a trashy Tremaine. Never good enough for decent people. Worthy of sex but not love, fun but not commitment.

Living together, but not marriage.

Even though her heart was breaking, she'd still almost gone back to apologize, to tell him she might have first intended to get involved with him for revenge, but knew she could never go through with it. Because like a colossal fool, she'd fallen in love with him. And it had hurt her to see the pain on his face at her confession.

Pride had kept her walking out the door the same way it had sustained her on prom night when she'd walked home in the rain.

She didn't sleep more than one straight hour all night long. Kate knew she looked and sounded like hell, so when she called Cassie the next morning, told her she wasn't feeling well and would be late coming in to help in the store, her cousin hadn't protested. She felt like a heel leaving Cassie holding the bag at Bare Essentials. Still, she doubted their day would be anywhere near as busy as yesterday had been.

Jack left the house early—before eight. She watched him from the upstairs window, careful not to let him see her. She needn't have bothered. He never spared a glance at her half of the duplex as he got in his truck and drove away.

Once he'd gone, she cried some more. Ate some donuts. Took a shower. Finally, sick of feeling sorry for herself, she pulled her cell phone out of her purse and called the one person she knew would understand.

Her mom.

JACK DIDN'T WANT to see anybody Tuesday. He had no interest in being anywhere near his mother or sister. Nor could he stay at the duplex, knowing Kate was right next door.

Sleeping there the night before had been sheer torture. He had lain awake most of the night, thinking about what had happened, replaying the scene at the store. He'd tried to find some explanation, but couldn't deny the truth. She'd said the words herself. She'd fully intended to get involved with him for the express purpose of hurting him as some kind of whacked-out revenge on his father.

Mission accomplished.

Damn, it was almost easier when he thought he'd never fall in love.

After driving around for a while, he went downtown and parked outside the Rose Café. Across the street, Bare Essentials remained dark, not yet open for the morning. When he went inside the café for breakfast, he took a seat away from the front windows. He really didn't want to see Kate arriving for work.

After he ordered, he tried to figure out just how much more he had to do for his family. There were one or two more legal issues, but the real estate situation was taken care of, as were the banking problems. At this point, all he wanted to do was to wrap things up and go home to Chicago. He frankly didn't care if he never saw Pleasantville again.

Just as the gum-chewing waitress deposited a plate full of artery-hardening breakfast on the table in front of him, the café door opened. As Darren entered, Jack looked away. He did not want to talk to anyone, particularly his ex-brother-in-law.

Unfortunately, Darren had other ideas. "Can I sit down?"

"Do I have any other choice?"

Darren took the seat opposite him in the booth. "I need to talk to you. About Angela. She came to see me last night and told me what happened with Kate."

Jack raised a brow, practically daring Darren to make one slimy comment about Kate. "And?"

"Apparently Kate said something to Angela that made her do some serious thinking. About us."

"You and Angela?"

"Yeah. She asked me if I'd left her because I thought she faked being pregnant to get me to marry her."

Jack calmly took a sip of coffee. "Did you?"

Darren answered with a slow nod. "I was convinced she'd made it up, that there had never been any baby. Because I'd overheard your parents arguing about it one night. Your father accused Angela of being like your mother, who'd done the same thing to him."

Jack could only shake his head. Kate had been right about that much of the story, it seemed.

Before Darren said anything else, the door to the café opened again and Angela came in. Her face was lit up by a huge smile, and her eyes sparkled as she looked around the room. She spotted Darren and walked toward them. Her steps slowed when she realized he was sitting with Jack. Squaring her shoulders, she sat opposite him, sliding easily under Darren's outstretched arm. The two of them might as well have started cooing like doves.

Jack raised a brow. "I see you've worked things out."

Darren nodded. "Angela made me realize how wrong I'd been."

Angela had the grace to admit, "I had no idea, Jack, about Mother and Dad. It never occurred to me what Darren thought until Kate accused me of it last night. I had to make sure he knew the truth. I wanted to be sure Darren understood how much I grieved for our very real baby." She swallowed hard. "I guess I owe Kate one."

Well, let's give a round of applause for Kate, matchmaker and revenge seeker extraordinaire.

"You should probably know," Angela continued, "Darren confirmed what Kate told me. About Dad and Edie being together before he married Mother. I guess...well, it doesn't make it right, what they did, but I think I can see Kate's side a little better now." Angela cast a quick, nervous glance at Darren. He smiled and nudged her, obviously trying to give her courage. "I also, uh, should tell you, I know you only heard part of our conversation. Kate wasn't the only one who said nasty things, Jack. I was pretty mean to her first.''

Angela expressing regret? He could hardly believe it. "If it's any consolation," Jack said, "whatever happened with Armand, whatever revenge you think he got on you? I don't think Kate was involved. He's just very loyal to her."

Angela stared at him. "You're in love with her."

He gave her a rueful look. "Crazy, huh?"

"Wow." His sister bit her lip, looking more nervous. "Jack, one of the mean things I said to her was that you, uh…"

Starting to feel very anxious, Jack leaned closer. "What?"

Darren took her hand, squeezing it to give her courage. "Come on, Ang. New leaf, remember?"

Angela spoke in a rush. "I told her you could never love her. And that you'd never marry a trashy Tremaine woman any more than our father ever would have."

Jack sat silently for a minute, beginning to understand, to make sense out of what had happened yesterday.

Probably without even realizing it, Angela had pushed exactly the right button to hurt Kate the most. Because in spite of how put-together, confident and successful a woman she was today, there was still that vulnerable, defensive, wrong-side-of-the-tracks kid lurking underneath Kate's beautiful exterior.

Kate's childhood had molded her into the striking mix of sweet and tough, gentle and outrageous, smart and self-doubting.

Jack had fallen in love with all of her.

But she didn't believe that.

"I've got to go," he said. Dropping cash on the table for his uneaten breakfast, he barely spared a glance at his sister.

"I'm sorry, Jack," she called as he walked away. "I'm sorry I hurt her."

Not as sorry as he was.

RIGHT AFTER Kate's long telephone call with Edie, she hung up, hearing her mother's words again and again in her mind.

"Oh, honey, don't you think for a minute I regret loving the man I loved. And don't think I didn't know how much he loved *me*. Heavens, John asked me to marry him more than a dozen times over the years, starting all the way back in tenth grade." She'd laughed softly, as if remembering something warm and tender. "After Angela grew up and got married, I started to think we could really be together. Then her marriage failed. As did her second. And her third. Pat blamed John for his bad example and guilt made him stay. But we still loved each other. Why do you think I had to leave Ohio when he died? Do you think some narrow-minded people could have forced a Tremaine out?" Her voice had broken and Kate had somehow heard the silent tears she knew were rolling down her cheeks. "It was too painful to stay, Katey. Knowing he was gone."

After she hung up, Kate shed more tears. This time not for herself. But for Edie.

A short time later she grabbed her purse and keys and went to find Jack. One thing her mother had said rang true…if she loved the man, pride had no place in the equation. Any chance for happiness was one worth grabbing.

She took a deep breath as she slowly drove by the Winfield house on Lilac Hill. No truck in the driveway. Thank God. She needed to see him, but she wasn't ready to face his family.

She tried the downtown area next, cruising along Magnolia, looking for his golden hair shining in the bright morning sun. She still didn't see him. Finally, thinking hard about where he might have gone in this town, she turned down a side street toward the Rialto.

Bingo.

Parking her SUV behind his truck, she walked to the front doors and entered the lobby. The overhead fixtures were off out here, but she saw a sliver of light from the main auditorium area. Pushing through the swinging doors, she paused in the back of the theater, looking around in the murky shadows of the cavernous, dimly lit room.

Jack sat in one of the old plushly covered seats in the back row. She saw him there at the same instant he saw her.

"What are you doing here?" she asked.

"I was looking for you. I went to the house, and the store. I finally figured you'd show up here. So I sat down to wait."

He was right. Eventually, even if she hadn't gone looking for him, she would have shown up here.

He remained seated, while Kate stood. She didn't know what to say, now that she had finally found him. There didn't seem to be an easy way to apologize for admitting what had once been the truth. She really had thought she could set out to hurt this man. This amazing man who'd captured her heart and soul.

It now seemed almost inconceivable.

Finally, as if realizing she couldn't find the words to begin, Jack stood and extended his hand. She stepped closer, taking it, letting him pull her into the seat next to his own.

Finally she heard him say, "I'm not J. J. Winfield, Kate."

She bit her lip.

"Maybe J. J. Winfield was someone you once wanted to get even with. But that's not me."

"I know," she admitted. "Jack, as soon as I saw you, as soon as I realized who you were, I dropped any idea of revenge. I knew I was too vulnerable to you." She lowered her voice. "I already liked you too much. I knew from the beginning I could care for you."

"I knew it, too," he said. "I never would have believed it if it hadn't happened to me, but I knew from the first time I saw you something amazing was going to happen between us. I started to fall in love with you before I even heard your voice or knew your name."

Her name. Yes, back to the issue at hand. Kate thrust away the thrill of pleasure that had raced through her body at hearing the word love on Jack's lips. "My name. Who I am. That's the issue, right? The reason you didn't call."

She felt his level stare as he carefully answered. "Kate, finding out your name, learning you were a member of the *infamous* Tremaine family, had absolutely nothing to do with me staying away from you." He sighed, shaking his head. "You want the truth? Here it is. I couldn't handle the guilt. I really thought my father had used and abused your mother, and I wasn't about to follow in his footsteps. In case you didn't know it, I don't have a great reputation as a stick-around kind of guy."

There was no question of doubting him, the sincerity in his voice was matched by the look in his eyes.

"So, when you asked me to live with you…"

He cocked his head. "You were upset about that?"

She glanced at her fingers. "I just figured it was history repeating itself. Tremaines are good enough to live with…"

She almost expected him to react in anger, but instead he laughed, long and loud. "God, have we ever been at cross purposes." Turning in his seat, he grabbed her around the waist and lifted her over the armrest, pulling her onto his lap. "I'm crazy about you, Kate. I want the whole nine yards. Marriage, kids, P.T.A. meetings."

Marriage? Kids? She choked on a mouthful of air and

had to hack into her fist. When she could breathe again, she said, "P.T.A. meetings?"

"We'll go together, unless, of course, you're busy peddling sex toys at your store."

She couldn't even laugh, still too amazed to see what she wanted was truly within her grasp. "You're serious? You want all that?"

He brought her hands to his lips, kissing her palm. "I absolutely want all that." He pulled her closer, until her head rested on his shoulder. "I figured you'd laugh in my face if I started talking about that kind of stuff, though. You, Miss Lusty Vibrating Fingertip, seemed to not only enjoy doing things backward, but you seem to want to make them as outrageous as possible. I kinda figured love and marriage stuff would turn you off…make you think I thought you were sweet or something."

She sat up and punched his shoulder. "I am sweet, damn it."

He gave her a hopeful smile. "Hopefully not too sweet for those slut-puppy boots."

She lowered her lashes, giving him a coy look. "If you're good. But in the meantime, get back to the L word you mentioned."

"Lusty?"

Their laughter faded as Kate stared intently into his fine green eyes. "Love. Did you mean to use that particular word?"

He reached up and slipped his hand into her hair, caressing her gently as he tugged her mouth toward his. "Yeah. I meant to use that particular word. I love you like crazy, Kate."

Just before her lips touched his, she whispered, "I love you, too, Jack."

Epilogue

LYING IN THE UNFAMILIAR king-size bed in their hotel suite, Jack listened to Kate get up and go into the bathroom. He'd thought she was asleep. Heaven knew, she should be after their strenuous evening. But maybe she was still too keyed up to sleep, too happy, excited and relieved that they'd actually made it. As he was.

Jack waited for her to come back, then smiled in the darkness as he heard the sound of the faucet turning and the gush of water in the tub.

A late-night shower.

What a way to start off married life.

He didn't get up to join her right away, content instead to listen to her from the bed. He waited for the pulling of the plastic curtain, the clink of the rings on the metal rod. The gurgle turning to a hiss as the shower jets came on. Kate's light, off-key humming.

Remembering lying in bed at the house in Pleasantville, listening to her all those months ago, he had to laugh. They'd come a long way. Physically and emotionally.

Unable to hold out any longer, he got out of bed, almost tripping on Kate's white sundress and shoes, which he'd tossed to the floor earlier that evening in his rush to make her his wife in every sense of the word.

Her wedding dress. And the flip-flops she'd worn for the small beachside ceremony.

They'd had a perfect sunset wedding with two bartenders at the couples-only resort serving as official witnesses. A beach vendor had made Kate her bouquet and a housemaid had caught it. A steel drum player had riffed in the background, competing with the sound of the surf and the low, lyrical voice of the island minister who'd married them.

Considering their two mothers couldn't stand one another, they'd thought it best to fly to the Caribbean for the ceremony. Maybe someday they'd all have to be together— probably when he and Kate started having kids. But for now, long-distance family relationships seemed the wisest solution.

Their families certainly wished them well, for which they were both grateful. Edie and her new boyfriend had thrown them a big engagement party at the retirement community in Florida at Thanksgiving. And his own mother—who had decided to give Mayor Otis a run for his money and seek her late husband's seat—had done the same on New Year's Day a few weeks ago in Pleasantville.

Jack still cracked up remembering the expression on Kate's face when his sister Angela had hugged her, telling her how sorry she was her pregnancy would prevent her from being maid of honor. He'd had to cover his mouth so Darren wouldn't see him snort with laughter.

The best party of them all, however, had been the bridal shower at Bare Essentials, hosted by Armand and Cassie. He hoped to God Kate had packed some of the gifts they got *that* night.

Unable to wait any longer, Jack walked into the bathroom. Seeing several conveniently placed candles and matches, he lit a few, then turned out the light. Kate's silhouette shimmered through the shower curtain in the soft glow of candlelight.

She said nothing, obviously waiting for him in the semi-darkness. When he stepped inside the tub, pulling the curtain closed behind him, she leaned back against his body and turned her head to look up at him. ''I thought you were asleep. I didn't mean to wake you.''

''I wouldn't have missed this. Our first married shower.''

She was hot and wet, slippery and lithe. Jack wanted to touch her everywhere. Pulling her closer, he knew she felt his hard-on slipping between her thighs. He groaned as she rocked back on it, rubbing her curvy backside against his groin. Sliding his arms around her waist, he held her tight as he bent to press his mouth to hers for one long wet kiss after another.

''Hope they paid the hot water bill,'' she said when their lips finally parted.

Remembering some of the other showers they'd shared over the past few months, he hoped so, too.

''I love you, Kate,'' he said as he pushed a long, dark strand of wet hair off her brow.

She rubbed her cheek against his palm, whispering, ''And I love you.''

He kissed her again, sweetly, cherishing her tonight as his wife as much as he already cherished her as his mate. Finally, spying a bottle of body wash on the edge of the tub, he reached for it. ''Want me to wash your back?''

She nodded, giving him a look of sultry heat. ''And my front.''

Oh, without question.

''It's a deal.'' He grinned. ''Just remember the rule…''

She rolled her eyes and gave him a disgruntled look. ''Okay, I know. No singing in the shower.'' Then she raised a brow. "Just don't you forget your rule, either, *angel*."

Remembering their first time together back on the stage at the Rialto, he chuckled. "No wings until I ring your bell."

Their laughter, their loving...and their shower...lasted long into the night.

* * * * *

Don't miss
Cassie Tremaine Montgomery's story,
NAUGHTY BUT NICE,
Blaze 63, by Jill Shalvis.
In stores NOW.

Turn the page for a preview.

1

"WHAT ARE WE DOING HERE?" Cassie asked Tag as the car pulled up to the lake.

Without a word, he got out, came around to her side and opened her door.

"Please?" He held out a hand.

She stared at that large, work-roughened hand. If he'd said anything else, if he'd been a jerk and hauled her out himself, she would have been able to tell him to go to hell in a handbasket.

But he'd said please, in that low husky voice that could charm a nun. "I suppose it's hot enough that I could dip my feet in the lake for a few minutes."

"Good. Bring that deck of cards."

"Why?"

His lips curved slightly but he said nothing as she got out without accepting his help and walked to the empty beach, making sure to walk the walk.

Tag caught the walk. His gaze was pretty much glued to her hips as she swung them all the way down to the water. He knew she had no plans on letting him get any closer than it took to drive him wild with desire.

Yeah, he wanted her. Badly. But something had happened to him that night she'd accused him of being like every other guy. Oh, he wanted the sex. He wanted the sex with her. And yet, he wanted more.

And he wanted her to know that. He wanted her to face

it, accept it, because he had the feeling no one had ever given her that more. Ever.

In front of him, she kicked off her shoes and sat on the rocks. She'd pulled up her skirt to her knees and leaned back, appearing relaxed and at ease.

Coming up next to her, he took in the gentle rise and fall of her bare stomach as she breathed. He sat beside her, then picked up the cards, shuffled and dealt them each five cards. "Want to play?"

"I'm good," she warned.

"So am I. Poker?"

Her eyes lit with pure trouble. "*Strip* poker?"

"If you'd like."

"You're going to lose. You'll be buck naked in no time flat, big man."

"If I lose, I'll strip." He lifted his gaze. "And if you lose…"

"I won't lose."

"If you lose," he repeated. "You have to answer my questions."

"Questions?"

All of which had been met with resistance so far, but he was a patient man. He had this wild, incredible woman alone on the beach with nothing but the water for company, and he was just smart enough to take advantage of it. "You're not afraid of a few questions, are you, Cassie?"

"What about the strip part of the strip poker? Don't you want to see me strip?"

"If it suits you."

"It's going to suit you." She gestured to her cards. "I'll take two."

She accepted the cards then flashed him a straight. Keeping his gaze locked on hers, he tossed his cards away and peeled off his shirt.

Her eyes flared as his bare chest came into view, and she made no attempt to hide the way she looked him over. "You're in pretty good shape," she murmured. Again her eyes went on a little tour and he wondered if she'd noticed he was hard as a rock. "Now, deal the cards."

Oh, he'd deal. "Holding?" he asked sweetly. He had a full house.

She laughed and slapped down one card. "Hit me once, but don't hold on to your pants, cowboy. It's nearly over for you."

"All talk, Cassie," he said softly, letting out a husky laugh when she shot him a saucy look.

"We already proved I'm not all talk," she reminded him, her voice just as soft. "Or do you need another lesson?"

He dealt her another card and waited while she lifted a sly eyebrow, cocky as hell, so damned beautiful it almost hurt to look at her.

"Don't look now, Sheriff," she said, fanning out her cards for him to see. "Time for you to get naked."

HARLEQUIN® *Blaze*™

Bare Essentials

Bare Essentials—Revenge has never been *this* good!

Kate Jones and Cassie Montgomery have a few scores to
settle with their hometown. When they turn their attentions
to the town's tempting first son and the sexy sheriff,
temperatures rise and things start getting interesting....

#62 NATURALLY NAUGHTY
by Leslie Kelly

#63 NAUGHTY, BUT NICE
by Jill Shalvis

**Don't miss these red-hot, linked stories from
Leslie Kelly and Jill Shalvis!**

*Both books available November 2002
at your favorite retail outlet.*

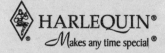

HARLEQUIN®
Makes any time special ®

Blaze

◆ HARLEQUIN® Blaze™

From: Erin Thatcher

To: Samantha Tyler; Tess Norton

Subject: Men To Do

Ladies, I'm talking about a hot fling with the type of man no girl in her right mind would settle down with. You know, a man to *do* before we say "I do." What do you think? Couldn't we use an uncomplicated sexfest? Why let men corner the market on fun when we girls have the same urges and needs? I've already picked mine out....

Don't miss the steamy new Men To Do miniseries from bestselling Blaze authors!

THE SWEETEST TABOO by Alison Kent
December 2002

A DASH OF TEMPTATION by Jo Leigh
January 2003

A TASTE OF FANTASY by Isabel Sharpe
February 2003

Available wherever Harlequin books are sold.

◆ HARLEQUIN®
Makes any time special ®